DOWN AND DIRTY

RHYS FORD

Dreamspinner Press

Published by
DREAMSPINNER PRESS

5032 Capital Circle SW, Suite 2, PMB# 279, Tallahassee, FL 32305-7886 USA
http://www.dreamspinnerpress.com/

Down and Dirty
© 2014 Rhys Ford.

Cover Art
© 2022 Reece Notley.
reece@vitaenoir.com
Cover content is for illustrative purposes only and any person depicted on the cover is a model.

ISBN: 978-1-63216-614-2
Digital ISBN: 978-1-63216-615-9
Library of Congress Control Number: 2014951380
First Edition January 2015

Printed in the United States of America
∞
This paper meets the requirements of
ANSI/NISO Z39.48-1992 (Permanence of Paper).

Readers love RHYS FORD

Dirty Kiss

"This is a great romantic suspense novel with a gritty film noir atmosphere and a sexy, heartfelt romance."

—The Book Vixen

"I don't know how Rhys Ford was able to drag me into this story so quickly and easily. I fell in love with the characters, the writing, the scenarios."

—Mrs. Condit & Friends Read Books

Dirty Secret

"Another outstanding book by Rhys Ford."

—On Top Down Under Reviews

Dirty Laundry

"This is such an absolutely fantastic addition to a wonderful series… During the last few pages I.Did.Not.Breathe."

—Live Your Life, Buy the Book

"From the first page until the last *Dirty Laundry* held my attention… Fans who love mysteries must really give this book, as well as the other two a try."

—Top 2 Bottom Reviews

Dirty Deeds

"Rhys Ford is a master of story telling, and I enjoy how the overall story arc in this series builds around the mystery arc in each book."

—3 Chicks After Dark

By Rhys Ford

RAMEN ASSASSIN
Ramen Assassin

415 INK
Rebel
Savior
Hellion

MURDER AND MAYHEM
Murder and Mayhem
Tramps and Thieves
Cops and Comix

SINNERS SERIES
Sinner's Gin
Whiskey and Wry
The Devil's Brew
Tequila Mockingbird
Sloe Ride
Absinthe of Malice
Sin and Tonic
'Nother Sip of Gin

COLE MCGINNIS MYSTERIES
Dirty Kiss
Dirty Secret
Dirty Laundry
Dirty Deeds
Down and Dirty
Dirty Heart
Dirty Bites

MCGINNIS INVESTIGATIONS
Back in Black

HALF MOON BAY
Fish Stick Fridays
Hanging the Stars
Tutus and Tinsel

HELLSINGER
Fish and Ghosts
Duck Duck Ghost

WAYWARD WOLVES
Once Upon a Wolf

There's This Guy
Dim Sum Asylum
Clockwork Tangerine
Wonderland City
Detroit Kiss

Bad, Dad, and Dangerous Anthology

Published by DSP PUBLICATIONS

INK AND SHADOWS
Ink and Shadows

KAI GRACEN
Black Dog Blues
Mad Lizard Mambo
Jacked Cat Jive
Silk Dragon Salsa

Published by DREAMSPINNER PRESS
www.dreamspinnerpress.com

For everyone who read the Dirty Series and said, "God, I want Bobby to get what's coming to him."

This book, dear reader, is for you.

ACKNOWLEDGMENTS

If you've read any of these, you know I am always going to mention The Five (Jenn, Tamm, Penn and Lea), Ree, Ren and Lisa. Because raaawwwr.

A huge thank you and dearest affection to Grace, Brian, and the rest of my editing team at Dreamspinner. Poor things. I am so sorry. So much thanks to everyone else at Dreamspinner, especially Elizabeth, for polishing my coals into diamonds.

More thanks to the Guinea Pigs, my First Betas (including the San Diego Crewe) who deal with my gnashing of teeth, and the second Betas who deal with my flailing. Wow, you guys put up with a lot.

Lastly, hugs and thanks to the inkers down at Flying Panther Tattoos. You might inflict a lot of pain on me, but damn, you leave some nice ink behind. Thank you for your artistry and professionalism. Best studio ever.

CHAPTER ONE

BOBBY DIDN'T know why he'd let himself get conned into fighting LAX traffic and then back up to Hollywood, but Cole asked for a favor, so when a guy's best friend coughs up gas money and a Starbucks gift card for a trip to Air Cargo, he'd have to be an ass to say no.

He wanted to say no. God knows he wanted to. Because transporting the heavy leather massage table to Hollywood meant getting up close and personal with Ichiro Tokugawa, Cole's hot and definitely off-limits little brother.

There were rules.

Lines a guy did not cross with regards to friends.

A guy didn't drink the last beer. He didn't throw up on anything without cleaning it up, and a good friend paid his friends with beer and pizza when they sacrificed a Saturday to help him move. A guy got drunk with his friend at funerals and wrote embarrassing speeches about them when they married the love of their life. A guy did not date an ex—an ex defined as someone who once was considered an actual boy/girlfriend and not a trick. Same thing went for siblings and possibly cousins.

Especially where *good* friends were concerned.

Doubly so when the other guy was the best friend Bobby'd ever had in his entire life.

But that all meant shit, because deep down—and not so deep down—Bobby was keenly aware of one glaring claxon of trouble.

He badly wanted to fuck Cole McGinnis's younger brother.

Hollywood Boulevard at noon was a game of Frogger and Dodge-the-Ped. Oblivious tourists didn't seem to understand the black stripe going down the middle was filled with cars, and the various freaks working the strip in superhero costumes or their own version of weird were more than willing to risk dying under American steel as streams of buses disgorged fat-walleted victims. Every inch of space along the street's main stretch was filled with people, sound, and a riot of color.

Old-school glamour and faded glitz fought valiantly against the encroachment of the shiny-bright, neon-rich flash of buildings marching up from the coffers of a newer Hollywood. Only bits and pieces remained of the days when a woman asked a man if he knew how to whistle, and those remaining shreds were being quickly swallowed up by glass and steel monuments to capitalism.

"Jesus, Dawson," Bobby muttered under his breath. "When the fuck did you get so old?"

He didn't *feel* old.

He could still beat Cole down in the ring and hit a mile mark in six minutes. Hell, the night before he'd kept up with the three twinks trolling the Down and Dirty looking for a good time. He'd shown them a hell of a good time, even going so far as to dip more than his wick into the blondest of the trio, but fifteen minutes into wringing cries for more out of the man, Bobby's mind drifted off. Instead of concentrating on the blond he'd impaled on his dick, Bobby found himself thinking about Ichiro, a snarky Japanese man who was more off-limits to him than a radioactive vibrator.

"Like the goddamn apple in the Garden of Eden." Stopping long enough to let a gaggle of visor-wearing tourists cross the road, he stared out the window at a sea of bobbing Hawaiian shirts and zinc-slathered skin. "You know you want a bite, Dawson. One big fucking bite, and if you do it, your world's going to go to shit. And no guy is worth that kind of trouble."

But damned if Ichiro didn't look like he'd give it his best shot.

The man was just swinging off of a Harley Fat Boy Lo when Bobby pulled up in front of Ichiro's new shop. Snug leather chaps framed Ichiro's ass and ran down his powerful legs, the leather nearly blending in with his black jeans. After taking off his helmet,

Ichi shook out his razor-edged mane, running his fingers through the bright red-streaked strands to work out any knots, his leather jacket wrinkling as his shoulders moved. Mirrored sunglasses shielded Ichi's cinnamon brown eyes from view, but nothing could hide the man's lush mouth. Its plump lower lip promised sin and wickedness with every moue and nibble from Ichiro's white teeth.

"Fuck, get your shit together." Bobby took advantage of the truck's higher profile and tugged at his crotch to loosen the denim around his growing bulge. "It's just another piece of ass. Just like the thousands you've looked at before."

Then Ichiro bent over his Harley's seat to lock it down, and Bobby's mouth crackled with the sudden lack of moisture on his tongue.

"Goddamned cock tease."

Getting out of his truck, Bobby nodded a hello to Ichiro, who was digging something out of his pocket. The worn-in chaps didn't seem willing to give up their prize, but the leather finally gave in, and Ichi tugged out a loop of jingling metal keys.

"Hey, thanks for going to get the table, Bobby." Ichiro's roiling purr was huskier than his older brother's, and he caught each word carefully before speaking, as if testing out its flavor before letting it go. His English was flawless, a tinge of softness to his consonants, but his voice was firmly masculine, a rough velvet Bobby liked listening to.

Damned if he didn't like hearing the man say his name.

Even better if he could hear Ichiro scream it.

"Not a problem." That was a bald-faced lie.

The Air Cargo guy had given Bobby a ration of shit about picking the table up, and even when he'd been promised someone from the back would help him wrestle the thing up into the truck, no one seemed willing or able to pitch in. A passing security guard finally took pity on him, and after unboxing the damned thing, they'd gotten Ichiro's table loaded onto the truck bed.

He'd left the packing materials strewn about Air Cargo in a passive-aggressive fuck you to the man smirking from behind the dubious safety of the receiving counter, driving off without a shred of regret when the attendant barreled out to scream at him.

"Really, thanks. I wasn't expecting them to send a full sample, and not like I could go get it on my bike." Ichi fumbled a bit with the keys as he walked up to a shop with painted-over windows. "We probably can get it in through the double doors here. The back entrance's got a tight hall for some damned reason. The construction crew's going to take it down tomorrow."

It wasn't much to look at, and from what little remained of its former life, he'd gathered its last incarnation was a hair salon. Sandwiched between an antique car showroom and a costume shop, it was a sad, tired place with fallen plaster painted up with bright neon symbols marking where work needed to be done. Old duct tape crisscrossed the front windows, the sun dulling the silver adhesive strips holding together a few thick cracks in the glass. The shop stood out like a sore thumb among the other businesses. Hell, even the trashy lingerie store selling scraps of lace for fifty bucks a pop looked better than Ichiro's new place.

"You on schedule?" Bobby eyed the shop's exterior, wondering if it wouldn't have just been easier to demo the place out and start over. "You're planning to open when? A couple of months?"

"No, not for about six months. Maybe more." Ichiro got a key into the lock and squeaked it open. "I don't need to rush things, and I'm guesting over at a couple of local places. Between inking, looking for artists to work here, and fighting to get permits, I'll be lucky if I get the place open before the end of the year."

"So you're going to give it a go, then?" Bobby flipped down the truck's tailgate. "Staying here, I mean."

"Yeah," Ichiro replied as he locked the double doors open. "Family—the guys are—I want to get to know them better."

"You and Cole seem to be doing pretty good." If the conversation got any more inane, Bobby would have sworn he was back in high school chatting up the quarterback just to get a whiff of his sweat. In about five minutes, he'd start asking Ichi if it was hot enough for him. "Mike can be a bitch sometimes, though."

"Cole's easy to get along with. Mike's harder. He likes to boss people around." Ichiro's grin was a flash of sardonic white against the shop's black shroud. "He sees me as a younger brother and tries to treat me like he does Cole. Thing is, I don't like being told what to do."

"Yeah, neither does Cole, but Mike hasn't caught on to that yet." Bobby chuckled. "You'd think after all these years, he'd figure that out by now."

"Mike is... tenacious." Ichiro laughed at Bobby's smirk. "Maddy I love. And Jae—ah, he's like a best friend I found after being gone too long. I also think he likes someone who sides with him when Cole's being stubborn. No one can do pigheaded like my older brothers. You'd think they were the Ox instead of me."

"Ain't that the truth," Bobby replied. "Okay, you grab that end, and we'll pull it out. Doesn't weigh a shit ton, but the thing's bulky as hell."

"Just let me take my leathers off first," Ichiro murmured as he reached down to undo the laces of his chaps' waistband. "I'll be sweating like a pig otherwise."

He should *not* have been watching Ichi slide the black leather off his ass. At the very least, Bobby knew he should have found something else to stare at besides the wiggle of Ichiro's hips and then the man's back bowing up as if taking a cock while he tugged the chaps down his legs.

There'd been a momentary glance at the sidewalk, long enough to spot the stars for Perry Como and Eartha Kitt. His attention even caught on one set into the walk for Burton Holmes, and Bobby spent about half a second wondering who the hell Holmes had been before his eyes once more wandered up Ichiro's long, muscular body and snapped to the tightness of his ass clenching under his soft jeans.

Sadly, that's where Bobby's eyes were fixed and not where they needed to be—mainly on the fire-engine red Ford Focus barreling out of the cross street directly across the boulevard.

The first sign of trouble should have been the opening blare of what sounded like graduation music bouncing through the streets. French spooled out alongside the music, a rumbling baritone competing with a full-bodied bass as they oompahed words over a ceremonial jangle. It wasn't until Bobby spotted the flaming-red car screaming through the intersection and as the speakers' fuzziness cleared up it dawned on him he was hearing the Canadian national anthem.

In Southern California. Without a damned Mountie in sight.

Unsure about where the out-of-control Focus was going, he somehow crossed over the sidewalk before the car threaded through a frightened scatter of pedestrians and flung Ichiro up against the truck, covering the man protectively as the car whizzed by them onto the sidewalk. The inker rolled under him, a flash of muscle and bone beneath Bobby's legs and chest. An elbow caught Bobby's chin, but they were too tangled up to do anything more than hope for the best.

Metal keened as the small Ford tore through the space between two trees, its side mirrors peeling off and shattering upon impact. For a second, Bobby thought the car would lodge itself between the massive trunks, but either God had a sense of humor about suicidal tiny specks on wheels, or the driver was going too fast for mere mortal wood to stop her from reaching her goal. The Focus emerged through its Death Star run with long scrapes on its sides, its red paint gouged down to bare metal, and if anything, it picked up speed as its driver gunned the engine one final time before plowing into the showroom's window.

Glass went everywhere, and a horrific crunching of smashed steel overwhelmed the blaring music for a brief moment, metal pinging like popcorn kernels on a hot plate. One of the trees gave in to its damage and toppled over, crashing to the sidewalk in a furious spit of dirt and bark shreds. Leaves scattered across the cement, one branch nearly burying Ichiro's motorcycle.

From inside the showroom, the Focus's driver-side door creaked open, and a small, slender woman crawled out, her arms raised in triumph as she took in the damage she'd caused to three classic muscle cars. Taking a deep breath, she joined in on a chorus of the anthem still endlessly blaring through the Ford's speakers, her fists pumping in the air as she danced around the carnage.

"You okay?" Bobby checked over Ichiro's legs and ribs, trying not to get hard at the press of the man against his crotch and belly.

"What the hell, just… what is wrong with her?" Ichi coughed, rubbing at his chest.

"Yeah, no words. Probably pissed off because she drives a piece of shit car that shakes when it gets close to blue-hair speed," he replied softly. He was about to say more—or at least help the younger man to his feet—but his cell phone rang out loudly. "Shit, that's your brother texting me. I recognize that foul ring anywhere."

Feeling like he'd been caught boldly fondling Ichiro in broad daylight by Cole, Bobby got up and checked his phone. What he read made his stomach clench, and the blood in his veins ran to ice. Ichiro's phone sang as well, and when Bobby looked up from his message, he saw Ichiro wobbling to stand up.

"What… why?" Ichi's pupils were blown out, dark and hungry with shock. "I…. Oh God, Jae. Who would… shoot…?"

He couldn't believe the words either. Not those words. Not the echo of a past rearing up to bite Cole McGinnis once again. The blood of another lover had been spilled over him, and for all Bobby knew, his best friend would be burying another piece of his heart in cold, hard dirt before the day was out.

"Yeah, I know, Sunshine." Bobby slammed the tailgate back into place, then gathered Ichiro up from the sidewalk. "Come on. Let's get you into the truck, and then we can head over to the hospital. Cole's going to need us right now—something fierce."

HIS TONGUE was sour with the taste of Jae's blood.

The world was sideways—so much pain, fear, and a deep, bone-chilling sorrow Ichiro would have given his soul never to feel again in his lifetime.

And amid the cries and burbling sounds of frightened people, he'd somehow gotten dried flakes of Jae's spilled blood on his mouth.

Someone at the cold, numb vacuum of an American hospital—he wasn't sure who—gave him Cole's jacket to hold onto. Where or how they'd gotten it, he had no idea, but Ichi clung to it, a macabre ill-formed teddy bear made of nightmares and comfort. They'd taken everything else, or so Mike'd told him, and somehow someone'd missed a small speck of Jae's blood on the leather. Ichi didn't know what happened to Jae's clothes. He supposed a police officer took them as evidence. Powder-burned and punctured through with hate-flown steel, Jae's shirt was being picked apart for whatever it was the police looked for—someplace in the warren of Los Angeles's grinding bureaucracy.

Another someone muttered forensics was a waste of time. Ichi couldn't track whose voice cut through the high-keen chatter around him, but it rankled something in his spine, and he stiffened, ready to snipe back, but the moment was gone before he could gather up the thin threads in his mind.

Everything was just so—damned cold.

He dealt with blood on a daily basis. It was a constant in his life. He knew the smell of it, especially laid over with the scent of chemicals and astringent. The feel of it sliding under his fingertips, even through black latex gloves, was familiar. Mingled with the slight grit of ink, it permeated his life nearly as deeply as the art he drove down under his clients' skin.

So why was the smell of Jae's blood so horrible?

Why couldn't he get it out of his nose?

And why was it so bitter on his tongue?

Some part of his mind flittered over a worry about getting sick—a constant sharp-fanged terror skulking in the shadows of his life and work. It flopped about, a broken butterfly searing its cracked body on the hot cement of Ichiro's pain and worry. He knew Jae was clean. Fuck, they'd talked about the risky things they'd done when they loathed who they were. Hatred made a man do foolish things, and when that man hated who he was, it was easy enough to kill off his greatest enemy—himself.

But they'd come out of that violent storm whole and hearty—only to have an echo of a dead friendship fold back over and try to extinguish Jae's life.

"Here. Drink this. You're as white as a fucking ghost." A hot cup of something was shoved under his nose, and Ichiro blinked, the flare of his dug-in fears suddenly doused by the tall, gruff-voiced older man Cole loved as a brother. Whatever was in the paper cup smelled as bitter as the taste of Jae's blood on Ichi's tongue, but he took it, numb from grief.

Even with the hot liquid scalding a path over his tongue and down his throat, Ichiro couldn't quite figure out if it was some kind of tea or the remains of a brown crayon left too long in a cup of bitter melon soup. Swallowing, he felt the caffeine hit his bloodstream, juicing up the nightmares grazing in his mind. Startled by the flare of alertness, they fled, leaving him alone with Bobby and the crackling clang of the hospital's waiting room.

"What is this?" Ichi gasped through the sour stew. It wasn't getting any better. If anything, the liquid's oily residue seemed to be spreading, coating his teeth and the insides of his cheeks. "It's horrible."

"Supposed to be a cappuccino." Bobby gave him a small smirk, but it was halfhearted, pulled down by the heavy weight of Jae's shooting. "Or at least that's what the machine said—cappuccino espresso something or other."

"I think you read it wrong." He grimaced, shakily setting the cup down on the table next to the bank of seats he'd claimed as his new home. "Because this is more capuchin piss than anything else."

"Drink it anyway. You need the sugar," Bobby insisted.

They sat there, cold rocks in the hot stream of blue uniforms and hospital personnel. Sometime in the past few hours, they'd lost Mike to the cops as well. Something about the American justice system was skewed, because in the wake of an ambulance arriving to whisk Jae to the hospital, a mob of policemen descended upon the couple, taking Cole down and arresting him when he insisted on going with Jae.

Cole got there after Ichiro'd arrived, his face bled white from a bone-shattering fear Ichiro hoped he'd never have to experience for himself. Blinking slowly, Ichi suddenly realized he'd gotten the jacket from Cole as he rushed by, shoving the leather into Ichiro's hands before disappearing into the depths of the hospital's surgical ward.

None of the blue-uniformed crowd gathered near the swinging doors stopped him. No one moved to tell Cole he couldn't go through the doors, and from the purpling swell under his right eye, it looked like he'd already won one battle to reach Jae's side. The determined look on Cole's face practically dared someone to start round two, because he seemed ready and willing to raze the city if someone so much as looked at him wrong.

No one even dared to meet his desperate, searching gaze, their eyes sliding away from his tense body as Cole stalked through them.

It was hard seeing his brother so torn apart. Ichi clutched the jacket tighter, wishing he'd done more—could have done more—to wipe away the anguish on Cole's face. The heartbreak and fear emanating from Cole as he rushed to Jae's side gouged deep furrows of pain into Ichiro's heart. It was bad enough to worry for Jae. Worrying for Cole felt like enormous stones pressing down on his already laden chest.

"I wish someone would tell us something," Ichiro muttered. His English was suffering. The pure accent-free tones he'd worked so hard to achieve were gone, leaving him with a stumbling thickness over certain words. It was a trivial thing to focus on, especially since they didn't know how Jae was doing. "Why would they arrest Cole? I don't understand it."

"Because cops deal with what they find. Cole had blood all over him and a weapon." It was a truth Ichi didn't want to hear, not from Bobby's mouth, and he forced himself to unclench his fists, or he'd punch Bobby in the face. Eyeing Ichiro, he continued, "I don't like it any more than you do, but they had to take him in. It's procedure, and the first person you look at in a shooting is the spouse. He wasn't arrested. Just taken in for questioning, and they probably did a gunshot residue test on him. They *have* to eliminate him as the shooter, Sunshine."

"It's fucking stupid," Ichi growled back. "A blind man could see Cole would never hurt Jae. Like he'd shoot someone."

"Look, we're lucky that one of the patrol guys found a witness. Someone at the cat-shit coffee shop actually saw the shooting. She went in to dial 911. Fuckers put her on hold." Bobby leaned forward, rocking a bit in the chair. "Took her a bit before she just chucked it in and went back outside, but by then, they'd already dragged Cole down to the station."

"I can't believe they thought he'd do that. Cole! You've met Cole. Anyone who's met Cole would know better. Even a stranger." The idea of his fierce-willed older brother shooting anyone was mind boggling, and Cole murdering Jae wasn't even something... it was impossible. "He should have been here. He *needed* to be here! Took too long to get him released and now—shit, suppose it'd been too late? Suppose—"

"They needed to exclude him, Ichi, but yeah, there was a better way of doing it. The asshole who fucked with him is probably going to be driving a desk for a few weeks. O'Byrne'll see to that."

Bobby took up more space than Ichiro felt comfortable with, and the heat from the man's body bled off the cold from his skin. Ichi breathed him in, pulling in Bobby's strength with each pull of his lungs. The older man made him feel safe or at least not alone. There was a coldness inside that didn't seem to get warm no matter how much hot coffee and tea Ichiro poured into himself.

"Hey, you look like you're about to pass out there, Sunshine. How about if we take a walk or something?" Bobby rumbled, his dark eyebrows pressed in over his knuckle-fractured nose. "You could probably use some air. Play your cards right, and I might even buy you another cup of shitty coffee."

There was a spicy flirtation in Bobby's words. Habit or... something else, Ichi didn't know, but Cole's best friend definitely rumbled with a rough sensuality every time he spoke.

The man was handsome in a rugged, woodsy way with strong features and a light scruff over his jaw. His hair ran to a color Ichiro thought of as mink, with a faint bit of silver dusting through the close crop. He'd have loved to see it a bit longer, enough to wrap his fingers in while he guided Bobby's hard, profane mouth down over his cock. There was something piratical about the former cop, a bad boy born to wear a badge and a gun, with only a thin, steel-strong ethical spine holding him to the straight and narrow.

Bobby Dawson was a scoundrel and a rogue, a bit of a rebel with a dangerous smile, and Ichiro found himself drawn to the man Cole called his best friend as if he were a moth and Bobby was the only light source left in the universe.

Dawson was *not* someone Ichi wanted to focus on at the moment, and he damned his dick for even straying in that direction.

"Air?" Ichi snorted. "God, I think I need something to drink more than I need air. Hell—"

A commotion erupted near the doors as a blood-speckled surgeon emerged through the sea of blue uniforms. There were so many people cluttering up the space, and Ichiro caught a glimpse of a traumatized Scarlet being held up by her Korean lover as the doctor waited for everyone to gather in. Maddy joined the fray from an adjoining hall, Mike trailing behind her with his cell phone plastered to his chest to drown the noise out of the call he'd been making.

The doctor looked worn, probably as tired as they all felt, but his gentle smile was enough to send a ripple of relief through the crowd. He spoke, but Ichiro couldn't precisely pinpoint anything the man said, other than Jae would be okay, and Cole was able to be with him in a private room as soon as they got everything settled.

A buzz rose up, too many voices starting up like a murmuring of starlings before a storm, and Ichiro sat down, falling heavily into the chair he'd been sitting on a few seconds earlier. Legs became a tide of motion around him, and he focused solely on breathing, then on keeping down the sour crawling up his throat with its sandpaper claws.

"God, I need to… throw up," he gasped, reaching out blindly to the man next to him.

"Yeah, I'm here, Sunshine," Bobby murmured, turning in so he blocked out most of the light. The warm darkness felt good, comfortable, and Ichi folded himself into it, pressing his shoulder against Bobby's to anchor himself against the man's solid form. "It'll be okay. He's all good. You heard the doc."

"I know," he confessed. "Now…. God, I don't know if I want to sleep, get drunk, or get fucked."

"Hey, I'm up for the fucking," the man teased. "The other two would be okay too."

Startled, he looked up, drowning in Bobby's glittering attention. It would be so damned easy to suck on the man's mouth. Even better, it would feel good, the rush of pleasure and aching release after the hours spent tied up in knots and worry.

Odd how the feeling of losing everything suddenly made a man feel alive, Ichiro thought as he stared up into Bobby's rakish face. With the tightness of his skin loosening, he needed a release, a primal drive to spread a part of himself over another person— preferably one who could take him hard and fast and give as good as he got.

Bobby Dawson looked like that kind of man, and for a moment—a brief, insane, fiery moment—Ichiro seriously considered finding a broom closet somewhere and spreading himself open for Bobby's dick and fingers.

One. Brief. Insane. Moment.

Just so he could feel safe… and maybe for a second, loved.

"You are my brother's best friend. And from what Cole's told me about you, not someone I'd wake up to the next morning," Ichiro murmured, scrubbing at his tired face. Peering out between his fingers, he barked a short laugh. "Fucking you would be a huge mistake, Bobby."

Bobby's laughter was nearly as bitter as the coffee he'd brought over for Ichiro to drink. "Well, if there's one thing I'm good at, Sunshine, it's making huge fucking mistakes."

CHAPTER TWO

IN THE early hours of a foggy Los Angeles morning, JoJo's gym was empty except for the lingering smell of leather, sweat, and pain. Bobby grew up breathing that soupy thickness, and as he taped his right hand up, he sucked in the gym's rank musk, wondering what was so broken in him that the stink of men made his cock harder than a newly minted steel bar.

In the six months since Sheila shot Jae, Ichiro Tokugawa haunted Bobby's every step and breath. Being Cole's best friend was never easy. It was a job fraught with danger and sometimes immense stupidity. He could live with the occasional gunshot and maybe even a knifing or two, but what Bobby found he couldn't deal with was the slightly sarcastic and temperamental artist seemingly stitched to Cole's shadow.

He was growing sick with the wanting, and to make matters worse, the damned man seemed oblivious to the reaction he got when he brushed up against Bobby's body. The inside of Bobby's cheek was chewed up from his teeth closing in on the tender meat in an effort to control his response to Ichiro's casual touches.

It'd gotten to the point where he had to verbally antagonize Ichiro just to keep the man away, then promise Cole he'd work on being Ichi's friend. He'd thought being a cop and in the closet was a bitch. Nothing said caught between a rock and a hard place like lusting for a best friend's hot and very untouchable younger brother.

"You're a sick fuck, Dawson, if sweat and men turn you on. Okay, maybe not sick, just off in the head." He wrapped up his wrist and took a small jab at the heavy, long bag dangling from a chain coming off an overhead beam. "And shit, Ichi's the same age as your kid. Anything that young is fuck-and-drop only... not something Cole wants for his little brother."

A familiar prickling formed at the base of his spine. He could put a name to it if he wanted to. Shame. Disgust. And sometimes even—fear. He smacked the bag again, hard enough to make it sway back, but its tremendous weight kept it stable and ready for Bobby's fists.

The bag held faces, or at least some shadowy remnants of people in his past. More importantly, the gym seemed to whisper as he struck the long bag, grunting when the shock of his fist hitting its solid form traveled up his shoulder and down his spine. Bobby kept going, laying out his punches against the bag's length as if in a street fight. Minutes later, his tank clung to his skin, soaked through with sweat, but the buzzing in his head remained, tiny doubting whispers he couldn't seem to exorcise.

He didn't hear the front door open, but the steady thump of JoJo's stiff leg striking the floor was loud enough to break through Bobby's strikes. The old man would either come sniff out why Bobby was up before the roosters crowed or not. Some small part of him didn't care one way or another.

Or at least that's what he told himself.

JoJo thundered over, a grumbling stick of bones and wrinkled pitch black skin. The years hung heavy on his face and shoulders, his back rolling from side to side as he lumbered toward Bobby's spot in the gym. A vicious beatdown when he was younger left his legs weak and wobbly, and he'd lost his right eye, but JoJo'd fared better than the white referee who'd been caught sucking JoJo's cock. *His* body was found crab-eaten and bludgeoned under the Santa Monica Pier, long strands of kelp wrapped around his bloated, crumpled corpse.

It was something JoJo never spoke about, and Bobby never felt like he had to ask. He didn't need to. The older man screamed his pain and anguish with every stoic drag of his foot across a floor.

"So whatcha doing in here so early, boy?" JoJo dragged over a tall wooden stool and set it down a few feet from Bobby's area. Settling down, he stretched his legs out and groaned. "Damn, it gets harder every day to get old. When are you going to learn that? Or you still think you can beat the old out of your body?"

Bobby caught the bag in his arms, hugging it to still its sway. Leaning felt damned good, and his legs cried out for some respite from the shuffle, crouch, and lunge repetitions he'd been using. Setting his shoulder into the bag, he rested his weight on it, taking some of the pressure off his knees.

"I don't want to beat the old out." Bobby chuckled. "I've just got to be fit enough to keep up with the younger guys. Cruising's kind of like being out in the woods. I don't have to run faster than the bear, I've just got to run faster than the next guy."

"Huh," JoJo grunted, working his palm over his knuckles to warm his joints. He'd brought the smell of sour coffee and liniment with him, and Bobby's eyes began to water when the air grew thick with menthol. Catching Bobby's assessing look, he shrugged. "Getting old myself. Joints ache like a son of a bitch today. Ain't going to be running faster than a damned dead dog, much less a twink. You can have them all."

"Yeah, I'll do my best." He winked playfully. "Seriously, if you're not up—"

"Don't you be telling me to shuffle off and climb into my coffin just yet." JoJo shook a fist at him. "Just because I'm not sticking my dick into any guy who'll let me doesn't mean I can't knock some of your teeth in. I'm old. Not sick."

After letting go of the bag, Bobby balled his hands up again and smacked the leather lightly. His legs were beginning to stiffen. He'd been standing too long without cooling down, and his muscles were quivering for release. Stretching his limbs out, he caught JoJo studying him.

"What?" He shuffled to the side, dropping his shoulder down to round another soft punch into the bag.

"You're getting too old for that shit, you know?"

"Now what the fuck are you talking about, JoJo?" He needed a cooldown, but JoJo's offhand comment threw him for a loop. "Guys a fuck of a lot older than me work the bag and ring. Hell, you still get in there when you're up to it."

"I'm not talking about the ring, boy. I'm talking about fucking every piece of ass you see. About time you grew up. Be an adult."

"I did the adult thing, remember?" Bobby left off jabbing and began to stretch his legs out. "Got married, had a kid, fucked guys on the side and screwed up my life. Hell, how many of us did that? At least Marsha and I ended it so she could find someone to make her happy. I think I'm doing pretty good right now."

"Your kid know? That you stick your dick in guys' asses?" JoJo's verbal scores were as sharp as his punches. "Or you still keeping that on the down low?"

"My kid doesn't need to know. Jamie's... we're good as we are." He shrugged. "Life is what it is. I don't have any complaints."

"But your life's still fucked up, isn't it?" JoJo pointed out. "Why else are you here at six in the morning beating the shit out of a bag and talking to a half-blind black man who can't get it up anymore?"

"Because I own half of this place?" Bobby shot back, annoyance peppering his tone. "And I've got a key?"

"Boy, you come here because you're frustrated. You don't even know what you want. When was the last time you slept with someone you liked waking up to?"

"I like every guy I fuck. For as long as I fuck them. Sometimes even a little bit afterwards too. And I don't really *sleep* with them. Not my style."

"This the kind of life you want, Dawson? Like me? Sitting in the fucking cold mornings counting your aches and wondering why there isn't some warm body keeping the aches away when you wake up?"

"Seems to me there was a time when any of us was just glad to wake up." Bobby twisted about, then shook his arms out, working the feeling back into his fingers. "Wasn't too long ago when we were all running scared because fucking guys was a death sentence—and not just because some asshole caught us sucking each other off."

"Boy—"

It was a low blow, but Bobby jabbed anyway, searching for a weakness in JoJo's words.

"I'm not talking about guys getting worked over or killed because they're gay. That shit still goes on. You and I both know it. It wasn't that long ago when even a hint of being sick meant people shunning you. People were afraid to hug anyone who even flounced a bit. Fucking disease ate through us, and if we weren't pariahs before then we sure as fuck became one afterwards. You ever think about what that did to us?"

"Yeah, people died. Guys died. I don't forget those days. Shit, I still wake up wondering if my next test is going to show something I can't handle," JoJo shot back. "Don't you think your kid has the right to know it weighs on you?"

"I'm saying that it changed us all—defined how we look and how we act. We have to look healthy. Shit, buff is good. Toned at the least. We're more worried about how we look than a fricking trophy wife from Brentwood, and it's all because of a disease people wished we would die from.

"You don't think I worried about bringing it home every time I went out? Fuck my health. I was worried about giving it to Jamie. I was worried about touching my own kid because I'm gay." Bobby stopped, inhaling sharply. "Damn it, JoJo. I just want to live my goddamn life outside of the fucking closet. I don't need a husband and a white picket fence. And why the fuck are you bringing this up now?"

"Because I saw the way you looked at Cole when his lover came by the other day." JoJo's rough voice gentled, as if Bobby was a skittish horse in need of soothing. "I saw how much you want what he has—"

"I do not want Jae—"

"I'm not saying you want his boyfriend. You don't poach. You're a fucking whore, but you ain't got time for someone who cheats... well, once you got the cheating out of your system," JoJo continued. "I'm talking about how they are. You want that, Bobby Dawson. I could see it in your face like a dog craving a steak. Tell me I'm wrong about that."

"You're wrong, JoJo." Suddenly another few rounds with the bag didn't look too bad, and Bobby started up an off-rhythmic set of jabs. "Because who the fuck's going to want someone like me? Too old to be pretty and too much of a slut to be faithful. Even Cole the Boy Scout will tell you that."

"COLE'S GOING to kill me," Ichi grumbled under his breath at Jae's back as the Korean scaled the crumbling interior of the abandoned theater. "You're already going to be dead, because you're going to fall and break your damned neck!"

"I'm fine," Jae-Min shouted down at him. "Just make sure you're out of the way when I start shooting, and watch out for security. Let me know if anyone's coming."

Cupping his hands around his mouth, Ichiro yelled across the theater's cavernous interior. "What do you think you're going to do if someone *does* come? Fly down?"

"I'll think of something! Just… oops." A piece of plaster broke off under Jae's foot, and Ichiro's heart came to a stuttering halt at the dusty trickle starting beneath his friend's sneaker. "I'm okay. It was already cracked."

"Like your fucking head." Ichi knew he was talking to himself. Jae had other things on his mind besides his own mortality. Listening to his best friend's cautionary tale of plummeting to death during an ill-advised wall scaling wasn't at the top of his list.

Of course, in his own way, Kim Jae-Min was a perfect fit for Ichi's older brother, Cole.

They both seemed to have a death wish, and they possibly could have scraped up half an ounce of common sense between them.

Which was why Ichiro insisted on accompanying Jae on his latest death-defying adventure of breaking into the old theater down the street from Ichi's tattoo shop. Tagged as a historical building, the theater was a white elephant, too beautiful and cherished to tear down but woefully expensive to restore. It languished with a soft, decaying air, a once vibrant and gorgeous grand dame now faded and worn down.

The interior was mostly faux-Italian, full of sweeping plaster embellishments, lush velvets, and trompe l'oeil vistas meant to whisk theatergoers to a lush Vienna celebration. The balconies were reminiscent of gondolas, toothy woodwork and black with swirling gold curlicues amid a sea of spangled stars and dusky skies. A pair of balconies wide enough to hold two or three people sat near the top of the stage opening, once meant for an operatic chorus to stand in during performances, and it was one of these outcroppings Jae was struggling to get to, using a slender shelf nearly a story up off the theater floor as a bridge.

Someone in the theater's past bricked off the platforms and removed the access stairs, most likely during its revival as a cinema. If Ichiro could go back in time, he'd punch that someone in the face, because watching Jae inch his way to one was going to give him ulcers.

"Should you be doing that anyway?" Ichiro couldn't stand it any longer, and he paced down the side of the theater floor, walking down the steeply angled aisle until he was directly below his friend. "You were shot."

"I was shot months ago, and the doctor said I could resume normal activity—within reason."

"This is so not within reason." Ichi's heart leaped up into his throat as Jae reached the balcony and threw one leg over the balustrade. "I don't think he'd agree being Batman was normal activity—or even close to reasonable."

"This is nothing. You should see—oof—what Cole and I—"

"I don't want to hear that. Not about my brother. Or you. I don't need that in my head." He took a few more steps, hovering beneath his friend. Jae's camera swung from a strap around his neck, and the lens nearly caught against the railing when Jae slid over into the balcony. "I'm not sure I'm going to survive this."

"Aren't you supposed to be watching for security?"

"I'd rather we get arrested. Who is going to catch you if you fall? Me? I need my hands. I'm an artist. I swear I'm going to let you drop."

"I'm not going to fall," Jae promised, dusting his shirt off. He rotated his arm, unable to stop a slight grimace from showing on his face as he stretched.

"I saw that. How the hell are you going to get down from there without killing yourself?"

"I'll grow wings. Now shut up and get underneath me so you're not in any of the shots," Jae scolded. "I'm losing light. The sun won't be coming through those windows for long."

Ichiro glanced up at the windows, the long panes once covered by blackout curtains now hanging in tatters from wrought-iron rods. Chains dangled down from metal rings set between the fabric, their ends heavy with elaborately carved wooden pulls. It'd been a risk to pull the curtains open. There were too many what-ifs involved—mostly whether or not the fabric would even hold together as it was gathered up to the end of the rods, but other than a heavy spray of dust and a few dead insects, the curtains parted easily.

He certainly wasn't looking forward to pulling them closed—any more than he was excited about watching Jae extract himself from the tiny balcony above him to get back down to the theater floor.

"Just don't kill yourself. I don't want to have to explain to Cole why I'm bringing you back in a plastic baggie."

"Please stop saying that. Besides, he wouldn't blame you. I can hear him now—oh, *agi*, what have you done now? Like he can talk for all the stupid things he does."

"Why do you let him call you that? It's like calling you a baby. Like a *baby* baby. It's kind of… strange."

"Because it's silly. He called me baby the first time, and I told him if he was going to call me that, it should at least be in Korean. It took me a while to figure out he meant it in a good way. I thought he was telling me I was a kid." Jae sighed loud enough for Ichiro to hear. "So now it's a word between us. I like it. It's… warm. Hard to explain. Now shut up so I can work."

"I can hear myself now. Sorry, but Jae's a pancake, Cole. A Jae-Min pancake," Ichi grumbled under his breath when Jae hissed at him from above. "Work fast. I've got a bad feeling about this."

Snugged up against the wall, Ichi sniffed at the cloud of mold and dust surrounding him. The dankness of wet wood and soaked-through plaster clung to his nose, and he stifled a sneeze, rubbing at his face to make it go away.

He could appreciate the beauty of the theater. Even in its disgrace, the interior was gorgeous. Despite the flaking paint, black damp splotches, and disintegrating fabrics, the place had good bones, and the stonework was incredible.

Now if only Jae would hurry up so they could get the hell out of there before someone caught them.

A whirring click-snap song cheerfully went on above him, Jae's camera furiously working to capture the theater before the golden light streaming through the dirt-splattered panes faded. He was about to check his phone to see if any of his prospective artists had gotten around to answering him back when Jae called out to him.

"Do you want to come over tonight? Cole wants to do a barbeque thing. He's asked Bobby, and he was going to call you, but since you're here with me—"

"Stupidly here with you, you mean."

"Do you want to be fed or not?" Jae's camera kept up its merry little mariachi tune. "Just a small thing. He got a new grill and wants to burn steaks on it or something. He said five, but you know him, he won't start cooking anything until six."

"Bobby, huh?" Ichi tried ignoring the tingling want in his crotch at the mention of the man's name. "It's like they're Siamese twins or something."

"Sometimes. Usually when they can get into the most trouble."

There was something about the older man that gutted him. He wasn't sure what. He'd never been drawn to the world-weary, sarcastic athlete before, but the grittiness of the man's rugged features and rough voice grabbed Ichi's balls and squeezed until he admitted he'd thought hard about Bobby taking him over the back of a couch or even on the inking table he'd brought out for Ichi the day Jae'd been shot. Ichi was fond of the man's breadth, his shoulders and legs tight with muscle, and Bobby's calloused fingers were long, thick enough to promise a good working of Ichi's hole.

It was probably wanting what was bad for him, he'd thought the last time he'd checked out Bobby's ass when the man walked by him in old 501s and a tight black shirt. He'd never been one for happily ever after—not like Jae and Cole seemed to have built up—but Ichi was damned and determined to at least be friends with whomever he shared his bed with.

No, Bobby Dawson looked like a good fuck—hell, even a great one, judging by the heft Ichi'd seen one day when the man came by in sweatpants—but he wasn't a friend. Not by a long shot. And fucking Bobby—or being fucked by him—was bad news all around.

He knew that even before Cole warned him off, and if his brother said his best friend was no good, then Ichi probably should pay attention and stay as far away from Bobby Dawson as he could.

Probably.

"Anyone else or just the four of us?" Ichi called out. A crowd would be good to give him a buffer against Bobby's proximity. Hell, he wasn't sure if inviting all of Koreatown would be enough of a crowd to drown Bobby out of Ichi's awareness. "Kinda small, no?"

"Maybe? I never know. Cole always ends up inviting a hundred when I think two are coming over." The whirring stopped, and Jae's voice dropped to a hushed panic. "Was that the front door?"

The creak was loud, as was the pair of male voices breaking through the dust-mote-heavy air. A crackle of a walkie-talkie battled with a querulous, authoritative demand to know who was in the theater. Another voice answered, distant and echoing from a speaker, informing those on site the police had been called and to avoid engaging if suspects appeared to be armed.

"Fuck that, Ralph." The speaker's thick Latino accent carried a hot anger through his voice. "I say we go in and show these kids they can't break in here no more. This place deserves some fucking respect."

"Sam, dispatch said to wait for the cops. I think we should—"

Whatever Ralph's objections were, Sam clearly had no intention of listening to them, because a second later the curtains partially blocking the view to the entrance came tumbling down, and a plumped-up harbinger of doom in a button-strained security officer uniform walked in, then stood stock still, his gaze sweeping over the space. With his feet set and his legs spread apart, Sam put his hands on his hips, a blue Atlas straddling the remains of a carpet river, his eyes fixed on Jae standing above Ichiro. He raised the walkie-talkie to his mouth and began to inform whoever was on the other end of the radio that they'd caught the intruders and were moving in to apprehend.

"Fuck, get down!" Ichi pushed off the wall in time to see Jae swinging his leg over the balcony railing. Before he could blink, Jae's camera tumbled down toward his head, and Ichiro had to stretch to grab it before it hit the ground. "Jae, what are you—oh shit!"

"Don't drop me," Jae warned as he slid down the side of the balcony to grip at the slight edge bulging at its base. Dangling above Ichi, he craned his head over his shoulder, watching the now steaming Sam barreling down the theater's debris-covered aisles toward them. "Grab my legs and—"

"I'm not that tall! *No one* is that tall. Shit." Ichi looped the camera over his head, then stretched up to snag Jae's feet. He could barely reach his friend's toes, and the rubber of Jae's Converses stung his fingertips. "Fuck—wait, shit."

Jae let go.

Ichi grabbed anything he could, tightening his arms around Jae's body as the man dropped. Something caught on the camera, probably Jae's ass, and his neck jerked down with the added weight. Choking slightly, Ichi held on, the skin on his cheek roughed up from Jae's torn jeans. With Ichi unable to do more than slow Jae's descent, they tumbled to the floor, then rolled down the incline a few feet until they slammed into the stage's front drop.

The wind left Ichiro's lungs, and his head swam with tiny prickles of stars and hammers. Shaking off the hit, he tried getting to his feet but couldn't find which way was up. A tug on his hands helped. Then the weight of the camera was off his neck while a torrent of pissed-off Spanish peppered the air.

Wood chips clung to his hair, digging through the strands to reach his neck, but Ichiro didn't stop to brush them out. Not when he spotted Sam digging through the mounds of trash in a desperate attempt to reach them and Ralph, a thin, scraggly beanpole of a man, climbing over the auditorium's back row to get to the clear aisle on the side they'd been standing on.

"Ichi, hurry." Jae's English was gone beneath a torrent of Korean, and Ichi stumbled to his feet, feeling every ounce of Jae's weight along his bruised body. "Back door."

"Back—" There was no time to talk about anything, not with Ralph clearing the rubble and rapidly moving toward them. Ichiro allowed himself to be dragged up the short flight of stairs to the stage and then into the cool confines behind a sea of backdrops and rolled-up canvases. A projection screen hung askew from its bar above their heads, and it swayed dangerously when Jae brushed against it. Ichiro didn't like the creaking noises the enormous cracked sheet made, and when he tried to slip past its worn edge, he liked the rumbling shriek of its fabric tearing even less.

The wall of fabric tumbled down, striking Ichi in the shoulder as he went by. A wave of dust vomited up into the air, clogging Ichi's nose and watering his eyes. Barely able to see through the stinging makeshift dust storm, he pulled back in alarm when he felt someone's fingers on his wrist.

"Ichi, come on!" Jae exhorted, shouting through the noise of falling chains, ropes, and frightened security guards. "The door's right there."

They hit the back exit coughing up mud and gasping for air. The day's heat struck hard, searing Ichiro's eyes, and he blinked, trying to see through grit and tears. Jae spat out a mouthful of saliva and grime, smearing a trail of gray-speckled saliva across his cheek when he rubbed at his lips with the back of his hand.

"Jeep. Get in the Jeep," Ichi ordered, already digging the keys out of his pocket. His chest hurt from where Jae'd hit him, and the back of his neck stung as if rubbed raw where the camera strap caught on his skin. Resigned to take inventory of his wounds later, he came up with the ring of keys just as the back door began to creak open behind them.

"Walk, don't run," Jae hissed in English, tucking his camera under his arm to hide it as much as he could. "If the cops see us—"

"They'll see us less if we run. Go!" Shoving Jae forward, Ichiro headed to his Jeep, hoping his friend could keep up.

His legs ached a bit, and from the twinge in his knee, he knew he'd be icing the strained joint as soon as he collapsed someplace safe. Getting up to a full trot, Ichi limped around the corner and spied his waiting vehicle. A chirp of the alarm key opened the Jeep's locks, and he slid in, hitting the ignition before Jae could get to the passenger-side door.

A siren cut into their heavy breathing, and Ichiro slowly pulled into traffic, losing himself in the steady stream of cars and delivery trucks filling up the boulevard. Chancing their safety, he turned toward the theater, driving by its street entrance as police cars began to pull up in front with their sirens and lights going full blast.

Breathing a sigh of relief, Jae collapsed into the Jeep's cushioned seat and grinned mischievously over at Ichiro. "See? Told you we wouldn't get caught."

"You're going to get me killed one day, Kim Jae-Min." Ichiro's breath was still coming hard and fast, and he wondered if his heart would ever slow down its skipping beat. "Fuck, my knee hurts like a son of a bitch. I can't believe you jumped on me."

"I wouldn't have had to do that if you'd been watching the front."

"We wouldn't have gotten out of there if I *hadn't* been there to catch you. How were you going to get from the balcony to the floor? They were through the door like rabbits."

"True," Jae agreed, his eyes bright with energy. "But it was fun. Does your knee really hurt?"

"Badly," he murmured, bending it slightly to test its flexibility, then wincing as the joint protested loudly. "Yeah, okay it hurts a little bit. I probably just strained it."

"Come to the house, then. We can put ice on it and get something for inflammation. My car's safe at your place. I can get it later." Jae settled back, extracting his camera from under his arm. "Besides, Cole wanted you to have dinner with us."

"And Bobby," Ichi grumbled. "Maybe I should have let the cops catch me."

"Bobby isn't bad." Jae shrugged off Ichi's muttering dissent. "When I needed him to check on Cole, he was there. During—when things were going bad between us. He's a good friend to Cole. As long as you don't go to bed with him, everything is good."

"That bad in the sack?" Ichi teased. "And how would you know?"

"Don't know. Don't care," Jae sniped back. "He's bad for the heart. He goes through tons of... men... over the past few months. The longest I've seen him with someone was three weeks, and that's because I think he was actually twins—one good and one naughty. He's a good friend just bad for the heart, I think. Not for you."

"Not like I'm planning to go to bed with him, Jae." He eased the Jeep into another lane. "Yeah, nice to look at but—you don't need to warn me off. Look, don't touch."

"Just don't ever let it go beyond that, or things will get very messy. I don't need to know who Cole would choose, you or Bobby, and if things go as they always do with Bobby, Cole's going to end up having to make that choice."

CHAPTER THREE

NEVER IN the history of man had one barbeque been so torturous. There'd been other feasts that ranked up there in the crimes against civilization—any dinner invitation from Vlad Tepes came to mind—but sitting at a picnic table groaning with food while directly across of Ichiro Tokugawa sucking on a rib bone had to qualify for at least waterboarding, if not bamboo slivers under his fingernails.

With a possible chaser of hot sauce in his eyes and coarse jalapeno salt rubbed into his wounds.

"That's my brother you're staring at there, old man," Cole muttered into Bobby's ear as he sat down beside him. "No need to try to get him pregnant with your eyes."

"A guy can look, Princess," Bobby shot back, digging into his potato salad with a plastic fork. "Maybe you should tell your baby brother not to suck that thing off like he's trying to remove chrome from a tailpipe. Might give a man the wrong idea."

"He's not—"

One of the neighborhood flotsam invited to the casual dinner made a hungry noise despite the mound of food she'd just shoveled into her mouth, and Bobby grinned up at his friend. "Maybe even give a woman the wrong idea too."

Cole shook his head at Bobby's teasing, picking at the label on his beer bottle. As long as Bobby'd known the man, Cole's effervescent nature shone through even the darkest of moods. The man's skin vibrated with energy, his gold-green eyes sharp with intelligence. Long months of pain and stress left a faint hint of crow's feet at the edges of Cole's slightly turned-up eyes, but it did little to detract from his strong cheekbones and handsome face. His thick brown-black hair was almost shoulder length again, more from neglect than any attempt to grow it out, and a few strands tangled into his long lashes, falling across his nose.

It was easy to see a resemblance between the brothers, even though Cole's shoulders were wider, and his features bore the stamp of his Irish father. Both men had their mother's mouth, a full, rich shape made for kissing or biting.

Thing is, he'd never wanted to bite Cole, whereas Ichiro was beginning to look mighty tasty.

"Remember, Dawson," Bobby muttered through a mouthful of salad. "Vlad's got nothing on a pissed-off Cole."

"What?" Cole jostled into Bobby's side, their elbows doing a quick dance for space. "Going crazy? Talking to yourself now?"

"Yeah, well, if I want intelligent conversation with you around, talking to myself is my best bet." He made a show of looking around the yard, taking in the small clusters of brightly dressed people scattered about. "Who invited Greenpeace? You or the boyfriend?"

"We've come to an agreement. A détente. For the good of the neighborhood." Cole flashed a quick smile, brightening the shadows in his eyes. "Besides, they brought dessert. The cake's awesome."

"Never thought you'd show belly over a cake."

"It's chocolate," he shot back. "I'd show belly, dick, and the inside of my butt crack for a good chocolate cake. I'm thankful as hell Jae doesn't bake, or I'd be up shit creek."

"I think you're already there, Princess." He shot another quick look at Ichiro, who'd ambled over to where Jae was poking at what looked like tofu chunks on the new grill's griddle attachment. "Any word about Sheila?"

He'd dug far enough to strike molten rock, or maybe the anger in Cole's eyes was merely simmering on the surface, because a green fire lit in their depths. A piece of chicken on Cole's plate suffered from an intense plastic tine stabbing before Cole shook his head.

"Nothing yet." Cole's attention roamed over the yard as if he were searching through the shadows for his dead partner's wife. "I don't like that she's out there. And I really don't like that I can't find her."

"She'll show up." Bobby hoped he sounded encouraging, but the odds of them finding the woman were slim. Los Angeles had a way of hiding its deadly secrets, and most didn't surface until it was much too late to do anything about them.

"Yeah, so I keep saying, but so far, nothing." Cole must have grown tired of pushing his food around because he shoved his plate across the table. He turned sideways until he straddled the bench to face Bobby. "Talk to me about what you've been up to."

"Getting touchy-feely with me, Princess?"

"Look, life's good for me—well, except for waiting for Sheila to go all say-hello-to-my-little-friend on me. Talk to me about how horrible your life is skipping from boy to boy." Cole sipped his beer, rubbing his fingers through the condensation on the glass when he was done. "And how come you never bring anyone around for dinner? You can, you know."

"I barely get their names. I don't want to actually feed them. Twinks are like stray kittens. Feed them and they stick around, thinking they can move in. Look at what Jae's stuck with."

"Hey, I don't think food had anything to do with it," Cole protested softly. "It's... good between us, you know? Different. Kind of nice. Well, more than kind of. Really nice."

"Hell, what's the going price on a white picket fence?" Bobby snorted as he peeled off a piece of skin from a grilled chicken breast. "Want it?"

"Skin's the best part." Cole took the crispy curl and popped it into his mouth. "And white picket doesn't go with the house. I'd say we could go get a minivan and a dog, but I don't think Jae's a minivan kind of guy."

"I don't think Jae's a dog kind of guy," he remarked with a laugh. "Maybe you should get one anyway. Just to change things up."

"If I want to change things up, I just get different stuff for the bedroom. Or buy a new piece of furniture. Easier than taking care of a puppy." Cole shuddered. "Okay, sexy times and dog got way too close together in this conversation for my liking."

"How good is it?" It was like poking a sore tooth. Bobby didn't want to know what Cole and Jae were doing, but the happiness on the

Korean's face shone, and the wall Bobby'd always sensed in the man seemed to have crumbled down if not totally away. "He's okay with wearing the pink triangle out in public now?"

"Baby steps. Not like I'm a big PDA kind of guy." His friend cocked his head, a smile touching his mouth. "Okay, a little bit of PDA, but not too much. Jae's still… working on some things, but he's happy, Bobby. You know? It's like he can breathe finally. It's nice."

"He seems better. More open," Bobby admitted slowly. "It looks good on him."

"Feels fantastic, even if…." Cole trailed off, shaking his head. "I wish his mother didn't draw so hard a line, but his sisters seem okay. Tiff's come around, and he's got support from Mike, Ichi, and Maddy. Scarlet's great. Shit, without her—I don't know how we would have made it. I need to buy her a car or something."

"She doesn't drive." He had to think about whenever he'd seen the Filipino man Jae called his *nuna*, but for the life of him, he couldn't think of a single time he'd seen Scarlet behind the wheel of a car. "Does she even know how to drive?"

"She says she can, but Jae tells me she's bad at it."

"Hell, if Jae says someone's a bad driver, that scares me she even gets *into* a car." They laughed together, and Ichiro glanced over, catching Bobby's gaze. His chuckle died in his chest, and the lust springing up from his groin set his insides on fire. Breaking the contact, Bobby reached for his beer, hoping the cold brew would quench the burning in him.

"Really, dude, I'm serious, though. If there's someone you ever want to bring over, just let me know. Don't feel like you can't drag someone around, okay?"

"Trust me, Princess. There's no one I want to drag around," Bobby said through a gulp of his beer. "And there's never going to be."

"HOW IS your arm?" Ichiro slipped into Korean as he smiled at a frizzy-haired woman going on about lavender and organic lemonade. "You look stiff."

"I'm okay. Sore a bit, but I caught Cole in the shower, so I've got an excuse if I get bruises later." Jae rubbed at the back of his neck. "We also need a new hanging thing in there—the shampoo bottle thing. I think I dented the other one we had with my head."

Lacking the words in Korean, Ichi switched back to English. "Did you tell my brother you were almost arrested?"

"What Cole doesn't know, he doesn't worry about," Jae grumbled back.

"It's supposed to be what he doesn't know won't hurt him," he corrected.

"He banged his back against the hot-water knob because he didn't know about it. It still hurt him."

"Very American 1950s of you. Distracting my brother with sex." A flash of red caught his eye, and he turned to watch a young woman toss a Frisbee over to a bearded man wearing a porkpie hat. "Do you have two twin beds in the room too? Sleep with one foot on the floor? Isn't that how it was back then in old television shows?"

Angled toward the table, Ichiro found Bobby's attention wandering away from Cole and focusing on him. As the man's eyes narrowed they raked over Ichi's body, and something hot and wild burned in their brown depths. A part of him wanted to go over to the older man, shove him up against the picnic table, and use Jae's method of distraction to get rid of the hot itch growing between them.

A very vocal part.

There was something undeniably sexy about Bobby Dawson, a something-bad-to-tangle-with sexy that set warnings off in Ichiro's common sense each time the man was near, but with every brush of their hands or the rough scrape of Bobby's voice over his skin, Ichiro knew he was going to end up in deep trouble.

Bobby Dawson was built raw and handsome, definitely a man raised up among the stone and blood of a violent environment. He'd come out of it with a twist of sardonic humor and an iron will with a thread of unshakeable authority, which probably served him well when he wore a badge and a gun.

Yes, Bobby Dawson definitely looked like someone who was born to hold a piece of hot steel in his hand and to part a crowd with a single booming-bass shout.

And it certainly didn't hurt that the man was sculpted from stone, his broad hands scored with rough breaks of skin and blunt fingernails, and had a lived-in face with open promises of hard, fast sex dirtied by filthy words and sloppy kisses.

Ichiro'd definitely done stupider things. In fact, that very afternoon's run from the cops after breaking and entering into a historic building wasn't even at the top of his list of insane things he'd done in the past year alone.

Tangling with Bobby Dawson suddenly didn't seem as far-fetched as it was a few seconds ago.

"Don't." Jae leaned in close and whispered.

"You don't know what I'm—"

"I know that look. I *had* that look when I thought about getting together with Cole-ah in the beginning. Don't tell me I don't know."

"You and Cole didn't do too badly." He smirked at Jae, nodding toward the house. "Can't say the same for your bathroom accessories, but you two? Seem to be fine."

"Cole's… he goes into things with his full heart—full soul. I knew even then it wasn't—he wasn't looking for a few months of fun and games. Your brother doesn't chase after things—or people—he doesn't intend to catch." Jae looked away, his gaze finding his lover amid the small crowd of people behind the Craftsman he now called home. "I didn't want to get caught. It would change things—change my life. And it did."

"Do you regret any of it?" Ichi probed. "Okay, maybe not the gunshot, but the rest of it? Wasn't it worth the risk? You and Cole?"

"Me and Cole? Yes, he was worth the risk, but I was right. Your brother pursued me to the end until my entire world was empty without him. He made it worth even the loss of my family, but Bobby? He's not going to give you anything other than complications. You're too much like your brother, Ichiro. You're not someone who's happy with an empty bed in the morning."

"I don't mind casual. Hell, you're one of the few friends I have that I've *not* done casual with." He pushed at Jae's arm, lightly shoving the man away. "And I like my head, so while I'd do you, don't get offended if I don't chase after you. I don't want to test my brother's love for me."

"The difference between your past and now is that Bobby is not your friend."

"You're telling me you've never wanted to take a chance on something? Just to know what it was like?" Ichiro cocked his head at Jae. "Not once?"

"More than once," Jae replied softly. "That's how I got kicked out of my aunt's house and dancing at Dorthi Ki Seu. So yeah, Ichiah, maybe this isn't a chance you should take."

"AH, I can breathe." Ichiro sank down into a soft couch in Cole and Jae's living room. "How can there be too many people *outside*?"

The small function grew while he wasn't watching, until suddenly he was drowning in chatter and warm bodies. Between the smell of cooking meat and a sudden cloud of floral perfumes, Ichi needed a break—and since his car was blocked in by stacks of vehicles, the house seemed like a good place to go hide until his head stopped spinning.

Staring at Bobby Dawson hadn't helped his aching head one bit either.

His phone burbled a tune, something American and thumping. Not what he'd had programmed in. Sliding it out of his pocket, he answered it, thinking it was Cole to brag about changing the ringtone.

Instead of his brother's velvety baritone, he got a choppy bass iced over with disapproval.

And in Japanese.

"Hello, Father." It was petty, but Ichiro kept to English, digging yet another centipede bite into his father's conservative outrage. The older Tokugawa's sniff frosted the speaker, and a low-simmering grumble crackled across the phone, building an ice bridge between the lines.

"Is that any way to greet me?" Unlike his sniff, Tokugawa's spit of Japanese was hard, hot metal fragments meant to cut through Ichiro's soul with a rapid-fire accuracy. Ichi shook it off. He'd been dodging his father's shrapnel for years, and his reply was a short grunt, barely a sound to acknowledge the conversation.

"You're up early." He did the math quickly in his head, but the numbers jumbled together before he fixed on his father's schedule. "Before lunch anyway."

"I'm surprised you're conscious. Or are the drugs keeping you awake?" His father's rumbling censure echoed in Ichi's ear.

"The only drug I'm on is sex these days," Ichi responded quietly. "An occasional beer or whiskey. But then, I can still get it up, and I'm not that picky, no?"

"At least have the decency to die in a woman's bed. There's enough shame attached to you already. Have a care for the rest of the family if not for yourself."

It was an old dig, certainly not original, and Ichiro refused to let his father hear even a shred of exasperation in his voice. He wasn't going to deny anything. Engaging the old man in a give and take was best kept to a minimum, with each volley of spite kept shallow and on changing subjects.

There would be no denying any accusation. It was useless to convince the old man of anything other than the reality the senior Tokugawa constructed for his family. Ichiro'd given up trying to escape the maze his father made of smoke, lies, and mirrors.

Switching tactics, Ichi went on the offensive. "Any reason you called? Other than to tell me I'm worthless."

"I would think after all of this time you would not need me to tell you that."

Ichiro took a long, shuddering breath through his open mouth. Laughter and conversation bled in from outside, sliding through an open living room window. Someone he didn't know was teasing her girlfriend, talking about a disaster regarding cupcakes and salt. The taunt was gentle, as were the reproachful accusations of sabotage. A child squeed with glee while another counted down from ten, very loud young whispers calling dibs on hiding places.

The *normal* of his brother's life dug its own sharp fangs into Ichiro's psyche, leaving its bittersweet poison in his blood. Caught between the glittering stab of his father's constant barbs and Cole's very American life, Ichi wondered if he'd go mad before he was crushed between them. As much as he denied it, the loss of his father's approval *hurt*, and every second he spent with his brothers held a lingering anguish as Cole silently wondered why their mother abandoned her sons.

He hadn't had the heart to tell Cole their mother abandoned everything—everyone—including herself.

A tangle of ache erupted between his eyes, and Ichi rubbed at the spot, willing the headache away before it spread into his brain. The children's laughter ached, skipping aural stones across his pain, the sound rippling over his jangled nerves. He couldn't remember laughing like the kids outside were. The giggles were like water drops, washing away the dust he'd built up over the years to cloud his memories.

With his father's voice ringing scorn through his calm, Ichiro blinked, and the world spun back—to a time when he stood barely thigh high to the man who ruled his life with a sharp word and disgust. Nothing he did or achieved reached Tokugawa's exacting standards, and he'd spent his waking moments in misery, wondering why his father'd been given such a weak son.

His tattoos were less a rebellion and more of a birth, the wash of ink marking his break from his familial placenta, and he'd thrust himself gasping into a world where he'd wear who he was on his skin. Turning away from the family was like cutting off a cancerous chunk of his flesh, and although he keenly felt its absence—like a missing arm—he'd known living as Tokugawa Masahiro's son would eventually have killed him.

He could live with the metaphorical missing arm.

Ichiro tried to shove back the long days of classes, stiff uniforms, and civilly greeting businessmen as they came to beg forgiveness or mercy from the unyielding man he called father and others called sir.

He should have hung up. He should have done a lot of things—changed his phone number, removed his name from the registry, never expected anything but the hard edge of his father's words up against the soft skin of his belly.

"Why did you call, Father?" He fell into Japanese, taking comfort in the stilted formality of his mother tongue. Gods and *kami*—his mother. "What do you need from me?"

"I need nothing, but Megumi, she would like something," his father replied softly. "Your stepmother—"

"Megumi is *not* my stepmother. She is your wife but not my mother. Do not call her that. She and I are the same age. She will never be a mother to me. Especially not after...." This time the centipede's bite scored his skin, prickling through layers of thick denial. "She was my fiancée, and you married her, what... a month after I left for school? Even in your twisted mind, you have to know I will never think of her as anything *but* your wife."

"She will also be the mother of your sister."

If talking to his father was a minefield of heartache, discovering the woman he'd once loved—thought he'd loved—was carrying his sibling had to count as a nuclear storm. Ichiro closed his eyes as if the hot wind made of complicated emotions couldn't burn him if he couldn't see the world.

It was a foolish thing to do, like a child hiding under a blanket so the *oni* wouldn't chew him up at night.

He did it anyway.

But the monster still found him, dragging Ichi out from under the blanket to devour him in a bitter soup of unshed tears and painful betrayal.

"Should I say congratulations? Or are you looking for condolences because she is carrying a girl?"

"A daughter is just as useful. Her husband can carry the Tokugawa name. I just have to find someone I like for her. Someone strong."

"Because who wouldn't want to erase his own family when he can be placed on the Tokugawa *koseki*? Is that what you want to do? Steal someone else's son because you're not happy with the one you have? Your daughter isn't even born yet, and you are already bargaining with her as if she's your property." Any hope of keeping his temper was gone, and Ichi's searing anger ate up his calm. "When will you ever learn—"

"When will you ever realize you are Japanese?" His father cut through, slicing past Ichi's arguments. "The Tokugawa—*our clan*—have a dynastic responsibility to the people who work for us. Not just the corporation but everything else. The farms. The homes. We are—"

"We are responsible for ensuring their lives are enriched and they have the means to be successful. It doesn't mean my sister—my goddamned unborn sister—should be whored out so you can live out some feudal wet dream," Ichiro spat back.

"It is funny how you did not feel that way about Megumi," Tokugawa growled back. "You were set to marry *her* until you turned your back on your family."

"I didn't turn my—you stick your knives into me as if you have no blame in what happened between me and Megumi. After I went to school, how long did you wait to convince her to marry you? Or were you already sniffing at Megumi before I even left Tokyo?"

"The family has obligations. My *children* have obligations."

"Including Megumi's daughter? Are you going to use her like you used me? Is she going to be bound to someone before the doctor cuts the cord to her mother? Like you did me?"

"I did what is best for you. The Tokugawas remain strong through good ties with other families. You would have benefitted from your marriage—a marriage you chose to walk away from. Now you blame me for taking up that debt? We *owed* Megumi's family. *You* owed her family."

"I owed them nothing. I owed you nothing," Ichiro snorted when his father hissed through the phone. "That is all family is to you, old man. Coin you create out of thin air to pay off blood debts. The Tokugawa line is so tied up in familial debt we cannot turn around without cutting off our own skin."

"You speak of the family *koseki* as if you haven't already tarnished our name. If Megumi carried a son, your own name would be but a memory on our registry. I would erase you as quickly as I erased your mother. There—"

Ichi hung up.

Then for good measure, he threw his phone against the fireplace, reveling in the crackling splinter of plastic and metal on stone. A black puff of fur exploded out from under a side table, hissing and complaining while scrambling across Ichiro's leg. Neko gave one final indignant mewl and launched off Ichi's shoulder, rocketing upstairs, where she'd be safe from flying pieces of technology and angry tattoo artists.

"Fuck, that was stupid." Juvenile even. And Ichi felt a hell of a lot better for it. "Son of a bitch. Fucking son of a—"

"Whoa there, Sunshine. What the hell did that phone do to you?" A shadow loomed over Ichi, blocking out the waning sun coming through the windows. Sighing, Ichi looked up at Bobby, too pissed off to enjoy the view even as he mumbled a regretful apology at his outburst. Bobby studied him intently, then lifted his foot, nudging Ichiro's leg. His cockiness was gone, instead Bobby sounded... sincerely concerned. "You doing okay? You look like you're about ready to skin someone alive."

"Don't tempt me." As if an alarmingly rotten and unobtainable temptation of Bobby's crotch in his face weren't enough to seal Ichiro's bad mood, spotting his oldest brother's shock of black hair bobbing past the house's windows was enough to make him go over. "Fuck. Family. I just—don't want to fucking deal with them anymore."

Mike would take one look at Ichiro and work to excavate what was wrong. Ichi's oldest brother existed to run other people's lives—

mostly Cole's, but Ichiro was now a close second and a ready substitute in Mike's eyes. Bobby glanced out the window, and Ichi could have sworn he winced painfully when he saw Mike ambling by.

"I was going to ask if he'd been the one to piss you off, but I'm guessing no," Bobby said, jerking his thumb toward the back of the property. "Usually that's how Cole is after he's tangled with Mike a bit."

"Good to know my brother and I have so much in common." He experienced a small pang of regret for his phone's shattered corpse. "My father drives me fucking crazy. Mike has a long way to go before I do something as childish as throw my phone against the wall. God, I'm stupid. I'm more together than this. I don't *lose* my temper."

"Fathers can do that to you. Mothers too." Bobby's wince rippled over his whole face. "Uh… sorry. About the mother crack. Shit. I just came in here to pee."

"I just came in here for some breathing room. Can't leave. My Jeep's blocked in. Just—too many people, and I needed…." Ichi debated what he'd thought he wanted when he fled the laughter and conversations. "Guess I needed to sulk. Maybe pity myself for a bit."

"Yeah, I throw that party all the time. Only send out one invite so everyone I want there shows up." Another nudge, this time hard enough to dislodge Ichiro's attention from the phone and back onto the man standing next to him. "Want to blow this Popsicle stand? Get some space from the hordes?"

"And do what?" Ichiro eyed him warily. Mischief quirked Bobby's expressive mouth, and for all his mistrust, Ichi was tempted. Family was suddenly complicated, but Bobby Dawson— was a different sort of trouble all together.

"Dunno. Get drunk? Go dancing?" He shrugged. "Does it matter? You won't be here, and I've got a bottle of whiskey we can break in. Call it a favor to the kid brother of my best friend. You look like you could really use it, and you nearly took out the television, Sunshine. Cole loves that TV. Think of the technology."

He was beyond tempted. Drunk sounded good. Drunk and stupid sounded even better.

Because going with Bobby would be the height of stupidity. Even for him.

"Sure, why not," Ichiro murmured, standing up from the couch. "What's the worst that can happen? I puke all over your floor?"

"Wouldn't be the first time it's been horfed on." Bobby grinned at him. "Just let me go pee first, and I'll take you out of here. Then you can tell me what your dad said that ticked you off so much you had to go and kill your poor phone."

"Yeah, that's the thing," Ichiro admitted softly. "I never found out why he called. Well, except that I'm going to be an older brother. Guess he finally got around to knocking up my ex-girlfriend."

CHAPTER FOUR

ICHIRO TOKUGAWA was gorgeous. Hands-down gorgeous. With liquid-chocolate brown eyes and a kissable mouth, his face was a blend of innocent and wicked topped off with a shag of red-streaked black hair soft enough to feel like mink through Bobby's fingers. The body beneath the jeans and T-shirt was tight with lean muscle and soft, sleek skin. A man anyone would look twice or three times at, then declare him gorgeous when he walked by.

But a drunk-off-his-ass Ichiro was simply adorable.

Adorably cute even. If Bobby had any opinion on the matter.

Not that his opinion was being solicited, because at that moment, Ichi was busy ranting about the flaws in a classic television show, gesturing with his shot of tequila as he rambled on.

"See, I've *been* to Hawai'i. That damned island they're on… no fucking way is it three hours away from anything. Fuck, you can *walk* across a sandbar during low tide to get to the damned thing. And where the hell did the volcano come from? It's like *dorayaki*! But without the black beans. The island… it's flat. *Dori*—what is he doing?" Ichi cocked his head, studying the flickering screen. "How the hell can that one make a battery out of salt water and coconuts, but they can't fix the fricking boat? Explain *that* to me."

"It's a TV show. You telling me they don't have fictional shows in Japan?" He kept his voice light, but it was difficult, especially with Ichiro's long, warm body snuggled up against his.

"There are! They're just not like… this. This is… I'm pretty sure the one with the batteries is gay. He doesn't even *look* at the women." A bit of tequila sloshed out of Ichi's glass as he waved it around, making his point to a fairly empty room. "I didn't watch a lot of television in Japan. There was never any time. No time for anything."

"Isn't that what kids are supposed to do when they come home from school? Grab something to eat that's bad for them and watch stupid television. Those fake monster shows came from over there. Someone had to be watching them." Bobby took the glass from Ichiro before he could spill any more alcohol on the couch. Not that his couch was pristine by any means, but Bobby was pretty certain it was about three drops of alcohol away from being incendiary if someone had so much as a brilliant idea near it. "Color-coordinated suits, bendy ninja moves—"

"Nope, not for the heir to the Tokugawa family. I went from school to more school. Then I woke up for more school. Like my father before me and his father before him," Ichiro mumbled. He touched his lips, skimming them with his fingertips. "I'm numb. I mean, I was numb before, but this… wow. I can't feel my lips."

"Too much tequila. How about some coffee, and then you tell me why you went to school twenty-four seven?" Bobby was about to get up off the couch when Ichiro put a hand out across his chest, stopping him from moving.

"No, no coffee. Not yet. Numb is good." Ichi's eyes lost focus and grew wet. "Fucker. God, I hate him. Spent all my fucking life trying to be good enough for him, you know? And all he did was push-push-push. He would say to me all the time, 'Be your own man, *heppiri*.' Total lie. He didn't want that."

"What does that mean? *Heppiri*?"

"His nickname for me. It means useless person. Said calling me that would make me rise to challenge him. He lives to fight—to dominate. It is his… I think he masturbates to that emotion. Causing others pain for no reason other than his own pleasure."

Bobby frowned, not liking the picture Ichiro was painting. "What about your mom? Did she say anything to him?"

"Ah, Bobby, my mother—she was a piece of rice soaked too long in hot water. People tell you she's nourishing, but there is no taste, nothing to fortify you. I hear Cole's pain in his voice when he talks about missing her in his life, and I want to tell him, she was not strong." Shifting on the couch, he gave Bobby a mournful look. "He would have spent his entire life trying to get her attention, but she was—she would look past you, even if you were her son. She was a ghost the moment she was born. And I loved her, but... she was not someone to reach for. Your hands would go right through her."

"Well, the one he got in return wasn't a picnic. I think he'd rather have had your mom—and you—instead of Barbara. *That* is one cold bitch. She and Cole's dad take asshole to a new level." Bobby rubbed at Ichiro's arm. "Your dad doesn't sound any better."

"You know he used to blame my mother because I'm stupid—well, I sucked at some parts of school, but stupid?" Ichi snorted. "He used to blame my mother. Said she was a bad influence."

"Was she?" Bobby traced the vibrant inked lines on Ichiro's bared forearm. "You had to have gotten this kick from someone."

"Hah. She was like plaster on the wall in my life. A firm substance of my house but added nothing to function. I don't even know why she married him." He belched, his tequila-scented breath strong enough to curl Bobby's nostril hairs. "This is a nice townhouse... loft... whatever it is. Did it come decorated in early *Animal House*? That was such a weird movie. Why would someone pretend to be a zit?"

Bobby looked around at his living room, slightly disgruntled at the description. It wasn't the Craftsman mansion like Cole owned, but the divided-up paper-mill warehouse had its charms, especially since the one wall he shared with his crazy cat lady neighbor was a brick one, and being on the second floor, he had the advantage of the building's old enormous window banks.

Scavenged from a defunct law library, eight-foot-tall solid-backed wood bookcases made great walls, partially to carve himself a bedroom out of the loft space but also so he didn't have to make his damned bed if he had company. The kitchen was mostly stainless steel and big enough for him to cook in, and other than an enormous television, good sound system, and comfortable couches, Bobby didn't think he needed much else.

"Okay, let's get some coffee in you, Sunshine. When you start insulting a man's house, it's time to de-drunk you."

"I wasn't insulting it. You have no dining room table. Where do you eat?"

"Mostly the bedroom if it's important. On the couch if it's a quickie," he snapped back with a smile to soften his teasing. "Coffee for you. And maybe some food. Did you eat at Cole's or what?"

Bobby reached for Ichiro to gently move him out of the way, but the man had other ideas. Slapping away Bobby's hands, Ichi slithered into Bobby's lap, straddling him.

The once cool loft suddenly got very hot, and for the life of him, Bobby didn't know where to put his hands.

"Not a good idea, Tokugawa," he warned.

Even through the layers of their jeans, Ichiro's round ass was hot against his crotch, and Bobby groaned when Ichi spread his legs apart to dig his knees into the couch cushions and leaned forward to grab at the couch back with his strong hands.

"Ichi—"

"You know what I want?" Ichiro bent his head down until their foreheads touched lightly. "Something really hot and juicy. Something like—"

"I am more than willing. Fuck, I could hammer nails right now, but Cole will kill the fuck out of us." He spread his hands over Ichiro's sides, cupping his rib cage. His cock was more than happy to dance its way into Ichiro's scalding hot body with its promise of velvety clenches and sweat-shiny skin.

Damned if Ichi didn't smell as fucking good as he looked, a hint of oranges mingled with tequila and masculine musk. Up close, Bobby saw amber flecks in the man's deep brown eyes, sparkling fireflies drowning in strong coffee. Much like he was drowning in them. Looking down didn't help. All it did was bring his focus to Ichi's full lower lip, now wet from a slide of his pink tongue.

"Yep, some kind of special hell. He promised me. Populated by people who talked at the movies or something. Your brother's a little cracked in the head, but he would definitely kill us—or at least me."

"Because I want a hamburger?" Ichiro cocked his head slightly, his eyebrows pulling into a confused frown. "Why?

Because I didn't eat anything there? I wasn't hungry then. Now I want a hamburger. A really thick one. Something big to bite into—"

"Okay, off of me, then." He slid his hands down to Ichi's hips and quickly maneuvered him off. Dumping the slender Japanese onto the couch, he stood, wincing when his jeans dug into his hardening dick. "Coffee and a hamburger. Stay the fuck right there."

"I'm going to have more tequila," Ichi muttered as he reached for the bottle Bobby left on the coffee table. "Where'd my glass go?"

"God, you're going to fucking kill me. No more drinking for you. Coffee." Taking a few steps back, he snagged the bottle out of Ichiro's hand. "Shit, I'd offer you a shower, but I don't think I could take the thought of you naked and wet in the other room while I'm making you food."

"Thought we weren't going to do that—sex thing. We agreed, didn't we?" Ichiro's eyes narrowed slightly. Then his focus went back to the television, catching on the opening screens of another episode of castaways and a maybe gay professor who was a master with bamboo and seawater. "How many of these fucking things did they make? Wow. This one's in black and white?"

"Yeah, you just focus your shit on that," Bobby grumbled. "Fucking cock tease. Maybe I'll be the one to take a cold shower."

He got as far as dragging preformed patties out of the freezer when he felt Ichiro peeking into the cold box behind him. His heart slammed into his ribs in shock, and Bobby nearly dropped the parchment-wrapped burgers on the floor.

"What the fuck?"

Ichiro seemed enraptured by the freezer's contents. "Do you have fries? I like fries."

"Do you see that barstool over there? By the kitchen counter?"

"Yeah." Ichi glanced over his shoulder, nodding.

"Go put that sweet ass of yours on it and let me get you a damned burger." Bobby gestured to the counter. "And don't get sick on my floor."

"I'm not drunk." Ichiro stepped back, stumbling against the counter. "I'm fine. Really."

"Sure you are." Bobby guided Ichi to the stool. "Need help getting up there?"

"I can get...." His foot missed the rung on his first try, but eventually Ichi climbed up. "See? I'm good."

"Don't fall off," Bobby warned. "I'm going to make you some of that instant Vietnamese shit your brother pushes on me. It's like he's a smack dealer."

"Okay." Ichiro folded his arms on the counter, arching his back so he could rest his chin on the back of his hand. Scrunched up and with his hair falling into his face, he looked much younger than Bobby felt comfortable with.

"Thought you'd be all badass and hold your liquor better," Bobby teased, getting steaming hot water from his in-line coffee maker. After dumping two of the instant coffee packets into a mug, he stirred the brew until it frothed, then put it down in front of Ichi. "Inked up and owning a hog—I'd have thought you could drink me under the table."

"Mike says I'm a sloppy drunk. Beer—is good. Anything stronger, pfah—he doesn't know what he's talking about. I'm fine." Ichiro hiccupped, cutting off his next sentence. "Except for that. I get *those*. Something else to piss my father off."

"Okay, you're going to have to explain that one." Bobby tapped the mug he'd place under Ichi's nose. "And drink that. I'll make you your damned hamburger."

"The Japanese—we drink. Usually after business. Or during business." Ichi shrugged, sniffing at the cream-swirled coffee. "He'd take me with him sometimes so I could meet the men he pushed around. I'd get hiccups after one round, and he'd get so pissed off. It was kind of funny, really. The more I drank, the louder they got. Then he'd get mad because I was too hungover to go to school the next day, because *he* could go to work."

"How the fuck old were you?" Bobby turned away from the stove to stare at Ichiro.

"First time? I was eleven. I was sick for a week," he mumbled, sipping his coffee. "*Aish*, this is hot. He stopped taking me when I was sixteen because he found one of his competitors groping me under the table. I was so drunk—I think I thought I was dreaming or something. He was more mad at me for conspiring with his rival. So mad. He had me taken home, and when he came in to yell at me, I threw up on him. *That* was awesome."

Leaving the hamburgers to cook on the grill top, Bobby leaned on the counter opposite Ichi. The man glanced up, his thick lashes nearly obscuring his eyes, but they were moist and fiery with a hint of anger. Despite his gut screaming to back off, Bobby reached over to brush Ichi's hair out of his face, stroking his knuckles over the man's cheekbone.

"I'm sorry, Sunshine. Really. You deserve better than what you got. You and Cole."

"Not Mike?" Ichi grinned, sniffing slightly.

"Nah, Mike probably crawled out of your mom with a business plan in one hand and a gun in the other," he teased. "Does your dad know about your... what you like to do in bed? Or who you like to do?"

"Sort of. Yes. Okay, very much yes." Another sniff, but this one came with a wicked grin. "I told him if he wanted my leftovers, he could have her—which wasn't fair to Megumi, but shit I was pissed off."

"Megumi is your... stepmother?"

"Ex-girlfriend. Well, fiancée really. Our parents had it all planned out before they even decided if they were going to cut the skin off the end of my dick. I veered from my dad's life plan and went to art school. So, my father decided; fuck my son. I'm going to marry her myself." A nod soon followed Bobby's disbelieving grunt. "No, really. Probably the most screwed up week of my life. Well, that and the time my dad said I was *kutabarizokonai* when I came home to tear him a new asshole. My grandmother—his mother—slapped me because I spoke up against him. The family— way too traditional. So I went out, got drunk, and committed the ultimate sin. I got a tattoo, thus sealing my fate in the family."

"Okay, back up. What does koo-tah mean... less Japanese than a box of Gansitos here, bud. You've got to throw me some clue."

"Somebody who wouldn't be missed if they died—because you know, *he'll* be mourned by everyone who even knows he exists."

Ichiro guffawed, nearly toppling his coffee. "Pretty sure when he goes, the company should give everyone a week's vacation to sleep off the hangover they're going to get from celebrating. He's... mean. Just mean. I don't know why Megumi married him. She says she loves him, but... who the hell can love *that*?"

"Your mother must have."

"Want to know what my mother's last words were? She grabbed my hand and told me to run and be free. Go find my brothers." Ichiro played with the rim of his cup. "That's what her dying wish was. She couldn't take care of the son she had with her, but she couldn't let go of the ones she abandoned. I promised myself I wouldn't be like her— wouldn't let my father erase me like he did her. So here I am. Inked and owning a motorcycle... but still not any better at holding my tequila. Shit, this coffee isn't working. I still can't feel my lips."

"Drink some more coffee. I'm going to turn the burgers over." The meat was sizzling, and Bobby scrabbled through his kitchen utensil drawer for a spatula. He grabbed the pan's handle, shaking the skillet slightly to help break the meat's sear from the cooking surface, then carefully slid a spatula under one of the plump, juicy patties. "You know the one thing I wished your mom had done? Take a picture with Cole, because for a long time, he thought she had, but then Mike opened his big fucking mouth and told him the baby she was holding was really him. I wanted to pound the shit out of your older brother— gotta tell you. Not like Cole—"

A light snoring stopped Bobby in midflip, and he let the burger fall where it landed in the skillet. He turned off the heat, then wiped his hands of any grease splatters, walking around the kitchen counter to reach Ichiro's side.

"Shit, kid—" He stared down at Ichiro, shaking his head. "Yeah, I know. Not a kid, but fuck, it's easier for me if I call you that. Because... well, fuck."

It was easier to think of Ichiro as a kid. Older than most of the twinks Bobby fell into bed with, calling Ichi a kid put him out of reach. A stupid mind game he played with himself, much like setting the clock in his truck ahead twenty minutes so he was never late.

But the body he gathered up to pour into bed definitely did not belong to any kid—not by a long shot. He gave a halfhearted hope Ichiro could walk on his own steam, but a few fumbling tries to get him up onto his feet only showed Bobby how Ichi's legs could double as overcooked noodles.

Giving up, Bobby leaned over and slid one arm under Ichiro's bended knees. Ichiro tumbled backward, and Bobby caught the brunt of his weight with his other arm, lifting him carefully off the ground. His burden muttered something that sounded more Korean than Japanese. Then his head flopped over, resting in the crook of Bobby's neck.

"Watch your teeth there, Sunshine," Bobby scolded when he felt Ichi's mouth moving against his throat. "Jae told your brother I took you home after you fucked up your phone. I don't want a hickey when we go into the ring tomorrow. I like my teeth."

"You smell good." A flick of Ichi's tongue on his skin shocked Bobby, and he nearly dropped the man. "God, I wanted to bite into you the first time I saw you, but then Cole—he says you're an asshole. And no… no touching Bobby. No licking Bobby. No everything Bobby."

"Don't talk like that, Ichi. Just… out of your head, okay? Probably the tequila—" His words were buried under a loud, burbling snore, and Ichiro went slack, becoming dead weight in Bobby's arms. "Shit, no—no. Don't do this right now. Christ, you're too skinny to weigh this much."

The bed was unmade, but he was pretty sure the sheets were at least clean. He dumped Ichi onto the mattress, then stared down at the unconscious man for a second, wondering if he should strip him so he could sleep more comfortably.

"Hungry." A slow, simmering murmur escaped Ichi's parted lips, making Bobby's decision for him.

"Okay, let's talk about what we don't say when we're drunk tomorrow, okay? Or better yet, let's just not do this again." He patted Cole's younger brother on the head, then grabbed a pillow. Taking one last look at Ichiro's sprawled body nestled into his sheets, Bobby sighed. "Fuck, I wonder how much tequila is left? Could use a damned drink."

CHAPTER FIVE

A WEEK after his disastrous encounter with a tequila bottle and his brother's muscular, older best friend, Ichiro found himself on a wild goose chase to find Bobby's loft. He didn't remember much about the neighborhood Bobby lived in other than brick warehouses, golden stone buildings, and the smell of old city clinging to the sidewalks when he'd stumbled out to the street and caught a cab back to Cole and Jae's home. Ichi hadn't taken the time to explore the long streets filled with street vendors and colorful streams of people. Instead, he'd woken up groggy, hungover, and horny—a sure sign he and Dawson hadn't done more than sleep during the night.

It kind of pissed him off—kind of.

The Fashion District in Los Angeles wasn't the glittering press it was in New York—at least certainly not with the Big Apple's reputation. Sprawled out in the shadow of Downtown's towering skyscrapers, the area gave up fighting off the harsh sun and sweltering grit and packed itself in tight, dedicating long stretches of alley and reclaimed buildings to selling cheaply made goods and wholesale flowers.

With the sun flirting with the horizon, the sidewalk buzzed with activity, and the air hung heavy with the scents of cooking meats and aging bouquets. A wave of powdery carnation slapped Ichiro when he made a U-turn onto a side street. A splash of lime and carnitas chased off the florals as he waited for a round Hispanic woman to hustle her brood across an alley entrance so he could turn back the way he'd come. He'd become an unwary victim of Los Angeles's tangled one-way and truncated streets, suddenly discovering a building in the middle of an up-till-then reasonable grid pattern.

The area resembled an enormous swap meet, cheap, glittering goods meant to entice passersby, much like a pitcher plant tickles flies' senses with the scent of honey and splashes of color.

And from what Ichiro could see, Downtown LA was just as deadly, especially while driving, and he wouldn't have been at all surprised if he came upon a minotaur in the city's labyrinth of streets.

A forced right turn, and Ichi stared in amazement at the brick edifice he'd been hunting for. Ignoring an irritated honk from a man in a listing delivery truck, he jammed past a line of traffic, then parked his Jeep in a pockmark of asphalt set aside for the converted paper mill Bobby lived in. Pulling a brown grocery bag out of the backseat, Ichi gathered up a stray zucchini that'd gone rogue during his drive, then locked the doors behind him, hoping he hadn't parked in someone's covered space, because the last thing he wanted to deal with was springing the Jeep from car jail.

"No, the last thing you want to face is Dawson." Juggling the bag and his keys, Ichiro pressed an intercom button at the building's entrance, hoping Bobby was home.

The buildings' half-underground parking level was tenant only, and while he could peek through the level's grated half-moon openings, it was too dark to see anything other than shapes and a spot of bright color where a neon green Volkswagen Bug waged its own battle with Los Angeles's fine buff grit.

"Yeah?" Bobby's gruff voice crackled across the intercom. Before Ichi could answer, the older man snapped out, "Ichi? That you? What the hell?"

The door buzzed, and Ichiro took it as a cue for him to go on up. He vaguely remembered passing through the glass-enclosed lobby with its sleek black floors and steel door elevators, but for the life of him, he couldn't recall the number of Bobby's loft. A glance at a bank of old-fashioned filigree mailboxes helped, especially since the residents of the building appeared to be in it for the long haul, because each box boasted an engraved plaque and loft number above its scrollwork front.

"Two-oh-six," he repeated after he got off the elevator and wandered into the hall. Curiously, the elevator appeared to have dumped him on a hallway nestled against the side of the building, with tall windows stretching nearly floor to ceiling to let in the Los Angeles evening's neon and orange light. With six doors to choose from, Ichi followed a trail of increasing numbers until he got to a thick steel door at the end of the hall. Looking around, he shook his head in amazement. "Don't remember jack about this place. Sheesh. How out of it was I?"

"Pretty jacked," Bobby answered gruffly through the partially open door. It swung open the rest of the way, and the man stepped into the threshold, taking up most of the space. "What are you doing here?"

He'd seen the riot video on the shop's television while he'd been unpacking ink, and in every single angle and frame, Bobby Dawson went down hard into the cement and then up against the side of a police car, his arms stretched up until his elbows nearly reached his skull. Ichi's spine ached every time one of the seemingly endless video clips played, as apparently every amateur moviemaker was shopping on that corner.

The rasp of cement burn on his cheek did not detract from Bobby's strong, handsome face. He'd not shaved, probably to avoid scraping at the speckled scatter of healing skin, and the silver-fleck scruff gave him a slightly piratical look—or at least added to his already roguish appearance. His short dark brown hair stood up a little bit, ruffled away from his face, probably from a rake of fingers through the thick strands before he answered the door. His mouth was hard, its edges tight over his firm jaw, and Bobby's odd light brown eyes were hooded, turned to shadow from his long lashes. Topping Ichiro's decent height by a few inches, he looked down at his unexpected visitor, then shrugged.

"Sunshine, I've got no patience for a back and forth with you right now. In or out. Your choice," Bobby muttered as he limped into the depths of the loft, leaving the door open behind him.

The couch Bobby eased himself onto was very familiar, and Ichiro's memory tickled with something about sliding over Bobby's hard body and pressing into the man's chest. Bad timing on the part of his brain, because his face flushed hot as he closed the door behind him.

From the line of empty beer bottles on the coffee table, Ichi guessed Bobby'd crawled home from the riot's aftermath and promptly begun to self-medicate himself and his pride.

"Why are you here, Tokugawa?" Bobby winced a bit when he stretched forward to grab one of the unopened bottles. A twist of his fingers, and the cap popped off in his hand. Then it joined a few others on the table with a tinny clatter. "Guessing you saw my takedown. Damned little uniformed shit kneed me in the crotch when he spread my legs. If that's what they're teaching rookies these days, I'm glad I'm the fuck out of there."

"Thought I'd bring you some food," Ichi replied, hefting the bag for Bobby to see. "Jae called to tell me Cole's bruised up, and I thought you'd be too. So—"

"And since I don't have my own personal Korean love toy, you'd thought I'd go for a—" He cut himself off, weariness digging lines into the corners of his eyes and mouth. "Sorry. That was… uncalled for. Fuck, I don't know where my head's at. Well, I *do* know, 'cause the damned thing is pounding like crazy. Thanks for the food, but I don't know if I want anything other than liquid oatmeal right now."

"Are you mad at me for leaving the other day?" Ichi grabbed the proverbial bull by its horns, damning himself to a fight. When he'd woken up in Bobby's bed, he'd done a quick body and smell check to see if he'd had sex and was left more embarrassed for getting passed-out drunk on the man who'd rescued him from a family interrogation. "I probably should have left a note or something. Not like we—shit—I should have said thanks. So," he continued, holding up the bag he still had in his hand, "this is my thank you, because everyone on God's green earth knows you've had a shitty day."

"They teach you American sayings in one of those fancy Japanese schools you went to? I don't think anyone under sixty says God's green earth anymore."

"Shows how much you know. A rodeo guy used to say that all the time." Ichiro padded over to a kitchen area he'd barely recalled and put the bag down on the counter. "But then I think he was from Kansas. Is it green there? I thought it was mostly gray."

"Some green. A few hills. Don't really remember. I think I drove through it once." Bobby bent forward to get up, but Ichiro shook his head.

"Nah, don't get up. I got some stuff to make *daeji bulgogi*, and I grabbed some rice, because chances of you having a rice cooker are about as good as me having one of those hamburger grill things in infomercials."

"Hey, I had one of those grill things. It was awesome. I think I lost it in the move." Bobby grunted in muted pain when he shifted on the couch. "You want to do me a favor and toss me that bottle of ibuprofen? Damned ribs hurt a bit, and I think I've got to beat your brother to shit tomorrow morning."

"Really? He's not moving too well either. You guys do that every day or just after buildings fall down on you or something? It's like you think you're Batman."

"Nah, that's—okay, Cole can't be Batman. He does some sick shit. He's more Captain America or Shazam. Is he still around?" He caught Ichi's soft lob of the pill bottle with his left hand, snatching it out of the air. "Don't give me that look. Shazam. You know? Captain Marvel? Big lightning bolt?"

"Nope. I don't know who that is. Only one I know with lightning bolts is Thor."

"Christ, make me feel old already. Bad enough I got taken down by some kid who can't even grow enough hair to shave." Bobby rubbed his temple with his fingertips.

"That beer isn't going to help you with that headache—"

"Seemed to help just fine before you showed up."

"Yeah, well not now." Ichiro mimicked Bobby's rolling grumble back at him. "Let me find something to grill the meat on, and I'll help you."

"The ibu should kick in soon. There's a grill thing that goes on top of the burners." Bobby pointed at one of the cabinets. "But nah, I'm good."

"Found it. How about if I put the meat on later? It'll cook faster than it'll take me to soften that hard head of yours."

"I'm not sure I can take your hands on me right now," Bobby grumbled. "This thing—you and I've got—"

"We've got a thing? I thought we both agreed we're assholes? Only civil to each other because you're Cole's best friend, and I'm his favorite younger brother."

"I don't let assholes come into my house, get drunk, and tell me stories about their shitty childhoods."

"Ah, then I'm good still being an asshole, because I don't think my childhood was shitty," Ichi replied dryly. "Just my father. We can make things even. You can tell me your dad was shitty."

"Can't. Didn't really know him. He caught a bullet before I was really old enough to know who I'd be missing. A guy can't really know his father until they're both men, I don't think." Bobby's face hardened again, and the tired stretched even further from his eyes, sinking into his expression. "My Uncle James—my dad's brother—kind of stepped in. He's a tough old goat but only if you're a thug. Old-school kind of cop. Up until last year, he was still out on his lawn screaming at kids to pull up their pants. Now he's at one of those senior apartment things, yelling at the staff because the rice pudding is too runny."

"Don't think I've ever had rice pudding." Ichi wrinkled his nose. "What's it like?"

"It's like tapioca pudding. Sweet, creamy. Some people make it with nutmeg or cinnamon. It's got… chewy stuff in it. You know, tapioca—but rice. You know rice, Sunshine."

"Yeah, but normally we pound the shit out of it until it's gooey and then make it sweet. So the tapioca? It's like *boba*?"

"Those little fish-eyeball things you guys get in your slushie drinks?"

"Yeah, those."

"No, those are disgusting. This is edible and tiny. Like they should be," Bobby retorted. "Now I've got to go to the store every week for rice pudding before I go see him, or there's hell to pay. I give him one of those fish-eye things, and he'd use it in his nine-mil to aerate my butt."

"Head massage or pain?" Ichi leaned on the counter, slightly lost in the conversation's traction. "It's a thing-free offer. No strings. No puke. Just a head massage because you look like shit."

Bobby studied him for a moment, then nodded slowly, as if moving his head too quickly would break him apart. "Yeah, okay. Because hell, anything to take the edge off would help."

It was a short distance to the couch set in the near middle of the loft. Bookcases and screens portioned off a bedroom from the space, taking up the west-facing side of the end unit. The lower bank of tall windows were covered with heavy burgundy drapes, but the upper rows of broad louvers were left undressed, some partially cranked open to let out any built-up heat. The ceiling was painted black, as was the ductwork running above them, with wooden beams tucked in between industrial air-conditioning vents to support hanging pendulum lights.

A bathroom was carved out of the space next to the kitchen, a high drywall enclosure that looked big enough to hold an orgy Caligula would have been proud of. Ichiro couldn't imagine what Bobby had installed in it—and since he'd fled the loft without even taking a piss, he'd probably lost his one chance to find out.

But then again, maybe he had used it, and it was drowned under the sea of tequila he'd tried to suck into his body.

"Thanks for... well, letting me get puking drunk the other night. I needed it." Ichi dragged a high-back chair over to the back of the couch, then handed Bobby a wet washcloth he'd rinsed in ice water. "Here, put that on your forehead. I'll sit behind you and massage your scalp."

"Dude—you sure you know what you're doing there?"

"Now you sound like Cole. Why the hell are you guys so suspicious?" he teased. "Trust me. I learned how to do this when I worked at the hair salon. Part of shampooing. Bonus points if you can get the client to fall asleep so the stylist can finish who they're working on without someone bitching."

"Really? A hairdresser? Was there a gay-boy checklist you were marking off?"

"Yep. Your asshole status is secure. And no, interning at a tattoo shop doesn't pay the bills, so I needed a job. If you want to learn how to ink, you pretty much volunteer to get abused." Ichi settled into the chair. "I'd cut ties with my father, and I didn't want to touch the money my grandfather left me in case I really needed it later. So sweeping floors and washing hair wasn't too bad of a job, and the salon's owner was my teacher's wife, so she rode his ass to be nice to me. Win-win in my book."

Bobby's hair was coarse silk under his fingers, with unyielding tight skin and bunched cranial muscles lying beneath his scalp. Starting at the connective points, Ichiro stroked back and forth, easing the tension along the stretch of knotted fibers.

"Okay, I don't give a shit if you drank all my tequila and peed on the hallway plant," Bobby moaned. "Just… don't stop."

"I peed on a plant? Really?" He looked around the loft, wondering if Bobby'd tossed his unfortunate victim. "I didn't even think you *had* a plant in here."

"I was joking," he muttered. "I'd have liked to see the look on your face when you heard that, but fuck it, this is too good. Shit, I didn't even think I had muscles there."

"Yeah, everyone's got connective tissue and muscles up until… well kind of like if your bone had male pattern baldness."

"I'm scared to ask you how you know that."

"Artist, remember? Can't draw something if you don't understand how it works." Bobby's skin tightened as he frowned, and Ichiro tugged at his hair. "Stop doing that."

"Doing what?"

"Making faces. Am I hurting you?"

"No." The denial was tentative, a low, growling tumble of sound and inflection. "Just trying to get... comfortable."

"Huh." He went back to work on Bobby's scalp, rubbing outward spirals from the center of his forehead and back down to his neck. As the tension eased slowly out of Bobby's body, Ichi teased lightly, "So this thing—the one you and I have—what exactly is it?"

"You want me to be honest?" Bobby's voice dropped to a husky rasp, and Ichi slowed his fingers in response.

There was something about the man's voice—something hard and steely he hadn't tripped on in another man before. There'd been others he'd sniffed at—leather jacket, hard-core bad boys who were more puff-of-air bravado than gritty integrity. Bobby Dawson didn't fit in that niche. He worked to keep his body brawling fit and his demeanor slightly prickly, sharp enough to ward off anyone soft from coming too close, even as his off-kilter, come-bend-over smile lured them in.

His hands and smile promised a hard, rough ride, even when he was rescuing princes in distress as they drank themselves into a stupor over lost somethings they couldn't name. The touch of silver in his brown hair and the slight burr to his face from hard-won years drew Ichiro in.

And as he caressed the man's strong neck muscles, Ichi began to wonder if Bobby tasted as molten hot as his rumpled suede voice swore he would.

"Yeah, be honest." He was going to throw it out there. Ichi had nothing to lose, and Cole—it wasn't like Cole had to find out he'd teased Bobby before the man tossed him out on his skinny ass. "Why would you change now? You think there's something between us? Like what?"

"You know there is. And fuck me, if it doesn't get me to wondering a few things sometimes."

"More things? Other than this one thing?" Ichi dropped his hands to his thighs, waiting for Bobby to make the next move. "Like what exactly?"

"Like whether or not you want to be bent over a bed or lying on it," Bobby purred as he tilted his head back. "You know, when I fuck you."

There was no mistaking the challenge in the man's darkening eyes or the cocky set of his grin as he twisted sideways to stare at Ichi over the back of the couch. It was a game Ichi knew well—one he'd played a thousand times before—the shoving out of a chest and the tossing of salt into a *dohyō*. It was a look he'd gotten right before he suckled down the gummy, hairy insides of a fertilized duck egg and shouted in triumph when he extracted the beak before he swallowed it. And it was a smile much like the one he'd gotten before he'd shot across a bed of salt flats in a broke-assed Harley held together with spit and a prayer.

Folding his arms across the back of the couch, Ichiro leaned in and gave Bobby a cocky smile of his own, tilting his head as he drawled slowly, "What makes you think you're the one who's going to be doing the fucking?"

CHAPTER SIX

"COCKY SON of a bitch," Bobby growled at the man behind his couch. "Let's knock that smirk off that damned pretty face of yours."

If there was a hell, Bobby expected his eternal torment would be the sweet taste of a demon's mouth, then a forever spent longing for more.

Ichiro tasted of that hell—a hot blast of sex, sweet, and trouble with a side of forbidden to spice things up—of fire and ink, and Bobby knew with the touch of that mouth on his, he'd be jonesing for that taste for the rest of his life.

It was no wonder the Devil threw off his wings and plunged into the depths of depravity.

They fought, tongues and mouths, with grappling hands tugging at hair and arms until their skin shone with the exertion of consuming one another. The sofa became a wall, then a desert between their lusting bodies, a separation Bobby knew he had to demolish. He hooked his arms around Ichiro's waist, then bent forward and yanked the man up out of his seat.

He dragged Ichiro over the back of the couch, long limbs catching on the cushions, and there was some moaning noise— either consent or grumbling at being manhandled—but he came over anyway, tumbling into Bobby's embrace. Ichiro's slender hands busied themselves with sliding under Bobby's shirt, his fingers raking over Bobby's back and catching on spots of abraded skin.

"Shit, watch the nails there, Sunshine. Your brother tried to get me killed this afternoon," Bobby muttered into Ichiro's open mouth, then dove back in, sliding his tongue past Ichi's sharp teeth and into the velvet heat beyond. "It's a bit tender there."

"Can we not bring Cole into this? Couch isn't big enough," Ichi grumbled back, angling his mouth for another kiss. "Fuck, you taste good."

Fisting his hands into Ichiro's hair, he yanked the man closer, savaging Ichi's mouth until he mewled and squirmed in Bobby's lap. Gasping, Ichi tried to pull away, shifting his legs to get his knees out of the cracks between the couch cushions. They fought for space and air, pulling back and moving in, delving into the fire building up between them.

Bobby's skin crackled from the friction of Ichiro's hands roaming over him. At some point, he'd lost his T-shirt, while Ichi remained clothed. There were too many elbows and odd angles for Bobby's satisfaction, especially when he tried to tug off Ichiro's shirt, but the man twisted about as he tried to angle in for another kiss, yanking the fabric out of Bobby's hands.

"Stay the fuck in one place, damn it." He made another grab at Ichi's shirt, snagging the hem. "You're like a shitting eel."

Frustrated, Bobby tugged and felt the fabric give, ripping under his pull. Ichiro's mouth moved down, tickling at his throat, and he arched into the younger man's body, digging his fingers harder into the shirt. The skin beneath the cotton was soft with steel underneath, and Bobby's knuckles glided over Ichi's light golden flesh.

Another shift, and Ichi straddled his lap, their cocks grinding together beneath layers of denim and zippers. Bobby growled low in his throat, futilely struggling to contain his want for his best friend's brother, but his will folded, and his lust was already raking in the pot.

"Screw this." He tossed more than caution to the wind. No, Bobby was picking up every piece of flammable scrap he had in him and throwing it into the flickering flames building up between them. Taking up another handful of fabric, Bobby tugged—hard—ripping Ichiro's T-shirt until the shreds dangled from his shoulders.

God, the ink. The colors. The images etched into Ichi's skin were vivid and sharp. Bobby longed to lick each line, trace every drop of ink left for him to find, but he burned too hot for Ichi's clench around him.

Raking his hands through Ichiro's red-streaked black hair, he pushed up and forward, toppling Ichi back into the couch seat. Their legs tangled, and Ichi kicked, refusing to submit to Bobby's maneuvering, but Bobby lowered his mouth onto Ichiro's and drank in the man's weakening protests, suckling at Ichi's skilled tongue, then toying his lower lip with small nibbles.

With Ichiro beneath him, the squirming wasn't half bad. Bobby slung his legs on either side of Ichi's, trapping the man's long body. Framing Ichiro's limbs with his own, Bobby held Ichi down, then bent down to dab his tongue at the edge of a dragon's muzzle cresting down Ichi's shoulder. He heard Ichi's gasp, and then he moved, snapping at the man's tight brown nipple.

If Ichiro's mouth was a sip of sweet hell, then his nipple was a touch of dark chocolate hidden in the recesses of paradise. Faintly perfumed with soap and musk, the nub rolled up tight when Bobby's lips daubed at it, pulling in on itself until it was firm and hard, easily flicked with Bobby's tongue. He teased the other one so it wouldn't feel neglected, rolling it between his fingers until Ichiro pressed his chest up into the heel of Bobby's hand, aching to stop the pain-pleasure working his nipple.

His dick was as hard as Ichiro's nipple and probably just as soaking wet as the one he'd had his mouth around. Digging his fingers past Ichi's waistband, Bobby came up short of his goal when his hand became trapped between Ichi's hipbone and stretched-out denim.

"Couldn't be one of those thug wannabes and wear your damned jeans loose enough to fall down?" Bobby muttered into Ichiro's ear. The lobe tempted him, and he suckled on it, drawing it into his mouth as he'd done Ichi's nipple. "Would have made this a lot easier."

"What? The guys you fuck are too stupid to work a zipper, so you only know how to get elastic down?" Ichiro lifted his hips, his fingers quickly undoing the top button of his jeans. "There, old man. Need a fucking map?"

"Want something for that mouth of yours?" Bobby snapped Ichiro's zipper down, their hands knocking together as the man struggled to open Bobby's fly. "Tell me you've got nothing on under these jeans."

"Tell me you've got something worth my time in yours," Ichi shot back. His fingers found what he was looking for, closing down on Bobby's dew-stung head. His other hand shook slightly while he placed it on Bobby's shoulders, his knees coming up as Bobby shoved down his pants legs.

They tangled again, slowing their kisses, their tongues gliding together in a slow waltz. He found underwear beyond Ichiro's fly, and Bobby sighed in disappointment.

"What kind of rebel wears briefs? You're supposed to go commando, Sunshine." Bobby snuck a peek at the underwear in question. Their color was alarming—cotton candy on faint amber skin. "They're pink."

"Yeah, I have red jeans, so… that happened." Ichiro shrugged. "You going to get those down, or are we going to talk about how I can't do laundry? Because you've still got too much clothes on, Dawson. Especially since I *know* you've got nothing past those jeans."

Bobby sat up, straddling Ichi's hips, and hooked his thumbs into the elastic of Ichiro's briefs. His own jeans were open, his crotch damp and uncomfortable as his cock strained to reach the man splayed out under him. He'd thrown on the first pair of Levi's he'd found on his bedroom floor when he heard the front door, thinking Cole had come by to check up on him. It'd taken him a moment to remember Cole had someone to come home to, and their traditional get-together to mock Cole's clumsiness was a thing of the past.

Staring down at Ichiro's beautiful, lean ink-covered body, Bobby's gut clenched, and something in his chest pounded as if he'd been punched. Flush with want, the man's cheeks were pinked and his mouth swollen from Bobby's lips and teeth. His ribs bore welts from a nail Bobby'd torn on the cement sidewalk during the supposed riot, slender, long streaks nearly as red as the ones in his hair. Creatures crawled under his skin, writhing through clouds, rivers, and scatterings of leaves and flowers. They moved as he breathed, his shoulders shaking slightly from the depth of their foreplay, and Ichiro's panting only deepened as Bobby's fingers traveled over Ichi's chest.

While not as heavily muscular as his older brother, Ichiro's chest and limbs were hard lines and lean curves with a dusting of soft, springy black hair circling his curiously flat belly button. His stomach muscles jumped and quivered while Bobby toyed with him, sliding his fingers back and forth beneath the pulled-up waistband until the sensitive skin beneath shivered from overstimulation.

Ichi's cock was straining its confines as well, the head sliding up from beneath its prison to tease Bobby's fingertips. Tamping his thumb over the damp slit, Bobby brought the taste of Ichi's spend to his mouth, keeping his gaze locked to the other man's passion-engorged lips and dark eyes.

"God... you are so damned... beautiful," Bobby whispered, unable to keep the words from spilling out of his soul. Ichiro's chin came up, and his eyes hooded, his sweeping long lashes casting shadows across his cheeks. "I—"

A familiar jingle—one keyed to a certain McGinnis—sang out from Bobby's phone, and they both glanced toward the cell jittering across the table.

"Don't—" Ichiro spat out. "Just—don't."

"Gotta, Sunshine. I never know when your fucking brother might need saving from himself." Bobby reached for the phone before it toppled over the edge. "If we're lucky, it's Jae asking for bail money because he finally strung Cole up by the balls. Now shut up. I don't want him to know you're here."

"Hey, thought it was going to go to voice mail," Cole rasped through the phone. He sounded tired, worn down even, and Bobby frowned, torn between the brother he had on the line and the one he had beneath him. "You okay? I didn't wake you, right?"

"No, I'm good." Bobby shifted, trying to slide off Ichiro's hips without hurting himself—or the man under him. "Just... shit. Hold on." Covering the phone, he hissed, "Quit moving."

"Fuck." Ichiro covered his face with his hands, rubbing at his eyes and cheeks. "Get off of me. I've got to take a piss."

"Cole, hold on—shit." Bobby slithered off the couch, trying to get out of Ichi's way. The man was off the sofa before he could turn around, and Bobby had to reach out to snag Ichi's arm before he got too far away. "Don't go anywhere. We're not done."

"Not to sound like a whiny bitch or anything, but I'm pretty sure I'm done." Ichi's snarl held as much of a bite as his words. "Go fucking talk to my brother. I'm going to take a leak and—"

"Don't go." A part of him withered inside, trapped between a man he thought of as a brother and a man who'd come into Cole's life with guns blazing, determined to break down any wall in his way. Ichiro tried to yank himself free, but Bobby held on tighter. "What do you want me to do? Beg?"

"Don't fucking bother. That's what I was doing before you answered the damned phone."

"Sunshine…." Bobby swallowed, taking his pride down with the gulp. "Please?"

"Dawson—"

"Please."

Ichiro stood silent and still for a long moment, long enough for Bobby to question if he was doing the right thing—begging. A half-held-in breath stretched out his lungs until they were about to burst when Ichi gave him a curt nod. Letting his lungs suck in another gasp, Bobby turned back to Cole as his friend's brother stalked off to the bathroom.

"Fuck." He pulled the phone away from his chest. "Hey, what's up? You okay?"

"Are *you* okay? Sounds like you've got company. I can call tomorrow."

The fatigue in Cole's voice was troublesome, so Bobby pressed on.

"Dude, you called tonight. Obviously it's important."

"They found Sheila—well, a uni in Santa Monica did."

"But?"

"The fucker let her walk. Dex called me. Said they're sorry—won't happen again. That kind of shit. Kid who did it was a newbie. Barely old enough to wear a shield or something—I don't know."

His stomach sank down to the parking and maybe beyond. The woman who shot Jae netted and released like some damned trout on a fishing trip, and deep down in his bones, Bobby knew Cole wasn't just going to let it go. Clearing his throat, he trod carefully. "And what are they going to do about it?"

"What can they do? Fuckers had their chance for the past six months, and she's still out there with a gun and probably bullets with his name on it. I can't have that, dude. Not Jae. Not—just not—"

"Not again," Bobby finished.

Ichiro stalked out of the bathroom, and Bobby held his hand up, pleading with him to stay. The pissed-off artist pointed angrily to the kitchen and pantomimed flipping something with a spatula. Not waiting to see Bobby's response, Ichi removed the meat he'd put in the fridge and began to rattle at the grill on the stove.

"Okay, I know that sound," Cole teased. "You should have let the phone go to voice mail. Go on, I'll talk to you tomorrow. From what I hear, you've got to go eat crow."

"Or something," Bobby muttered under his breath. "I'll call you in the morning. We can go for a run or something. Unless you're too injured to move your legs up and down. I saw that old woman take you out."

"Wasn't her. It was her fucking dog." His laughter lightened his words, and Bobby smiled, despite the trepidation he had about leaving Ichi alone in the kitchen with his recently sharpened knives. "And let's skip the run. Seriously, we can go grab a coffee and do manly talking or something."

"Fine. Since you're going soft and all." Bobby's bark didn't have any heat in it, and Cole snorted loudly.

"Coffee. At the Hairy Hippie. How about eight? We'll even bring Jae back some cake or something."

"Yeah, tomorrow's good. Later." He hung up and turned the volume down on his ringer. Bobby slid the phone across the table as he got up to go face the music. A few steps toward the open kitchen area,

Ichiro shook his head at him and muttered something in Japanese. Pursing his lips, he complained softly, "I don't understand you. If we're going to fight, at least give me a chance to know what you're calling me. I know you're pissed off—"

"Fucking Cole," Ichiro spat, hot bullets of sound meant to wound but not kill. "Jae called me while I was in the bathroom—"

"You talk to people while you're in the bathroom?" Bobby made a face. "That's disgusting."

"Jesus, my brother and you deserve each other."

"Hey, Cole's not that bad—"

"I was talking about Mike. He never shuts up and lets me finish either." Ichi turned the stove off. "Fuck it, we can order pizza. If I cook this, it'll end up burned. So, you going to let me talk?"

"Talk away," Bobby groused, folding his arms over his chest and leaning against the counter. "What were you and Jae talking about while you were holding your dick and pissing? Then can we talk about you being pissed at me?"

Ichiro rolled his eyes. Then his expression softened slightly until it resembled something Bobby would have called mulish. "Jae told me about Sheila. So yeah, fuck—you had to answer that."

"And you're still pissed off?"

"More at myself. Because, fuck, Cole needs you. He's your friend, and I—hell, yeah, while I'm his brother, I'm not—you." Ichi sighed. "So, shit, I'm pissed off because I got angry for doing what I'd want you to do. I was thinking with my dick—"

"Well, your dick would have seen some action, but it was your ass I was going to be aiming at." Trying for levity, Bobby sidestepped the swirling emotions coming up from his belly. Things had gone to hell in a handbasket before he'd blinked, and now he was facing the truth of what he'd almost done—fucking Cole's brother after his friend specifically warned him off. "Look, if you want to bail—"

"No, I'm going to make sure you've got some dinner or something in you and maybe tell you to take another shower. You've still got some sidewalk grit in your hair." Ichi held his hand up and made a show of dusting off his palm. "Either that or you've got the ballsiest dandruff."

"That's how we're going to end this? On a joke? Or are we going to just ignore what happened back there on the couch?"

The hardest thing he'd ever done was walking into a hospital room where another man lay amid the remains of his shattered life—a man he didn't know but knew of—and introducing himself as a gay man. Standing in front of that man's brother, Bobby realized he'd yet to learn the depths of his fears.

Men were disposable. Faceless after a time. Separated only by hair color and maybe mannerisms, but for the most part, he kept his dick happy with the equivalent of living dolls, falling in like maybe a few times but nothing more. Ichiro was going to be different. He was going to hurt, hurt someplace deep down inside of Bobby's core, and there wasn't a damned thing he could do about it but walk away now.

If only he could.

"Answer me something first. Why did you pick up the phone?" Ichiro skewed the conversation. "You knew it was Cole. Hell, I knew it was Cole because of that damned Queen song. It's an earworm. It's stuck in my head right now. And don't give me that shit about him maybe needing something. He was at home. Hell, you guys were *just* bailed out of jail. Why did you pick it up?"

"Because Cole's my first—" Bobby struggled to find the words for his relationship with the quixotic, death-defying younger man. Taking in a sharp breath, he stared Ichiro down and calmly replied, "Because Cole is my first *honest* friend. He didn't know me from jack shit before I came into his hospital room. I'd just retired from the force a few days before, and I was pretty fucking close to eating my own gun. Then someone—I don't remember who—called me to tell me what was going down in West Hollywood, and shit… changed."

"If you didn't know him, then why did you—you make no damned sense, Dawson." Ichi ran his fingers through his hair, working out some of the knots Bobby'd put there. "Why go down there if he didn't know you?"

"Because even if he was shot to shit, Cole lived his damned life out in the open. No apologies. He was either the bravest fucking cop around or the stupidest. And, well, maybe a little of both. Your brother doesn't stop and think about right or wrong—there's no question for him. Not a single damned hesitation about what path he needs to take. He's full bore while the rest of us dance around the edges of our lives waiting for something good to happen." Bobby exhaled the breath he'd been holding in—probably since before he'd walked into Cole's hospital room. "You know what I thought? I thought, fuck, here's this kid who just fucking lost everything, and he's fighting for a life he doesn't even fucking have any more. But here *I* am, whining to nobody about how rough my life is because I'm gay, and I'm too much of a chickenshit to tell anyone."

"You respected him?" Ichiro regarded him carefully, his dark eyes nearly lost in the shadows. "That's why you went down there?"

"Because I needed him to teach me how to be… fuck, I don't know, a man? At least an honest one. I'd lived my fucking life in so many damned closets I couldn't find my way out of a paper bag." Bobby grinned, remembering the first time Cole gave him a hard time for sampling more than one twink a night at a bar they'd gone to. "He's a good guy. I—wasn't a good guy. I'm still not, but hell, at least I don't want to snuff out the one that's here now. Before—can't say I was someone I'd want my own mother to meet. Well, if she were alive to meet me."

"Something else in common, then? Dead mothers?"

"Yeah, guess so."

It was his turn to rub at his face, and Bobby realized Ichi was right. Somehow he hadn't gotten all of the concrete dust out of his hair. Disgusted, he quirked a regretful grin at Ichiro. He'd hate to let him go. It was better for things. All around. Ichiro was more like his brother than Bobby realized—a serial monogamist, and that was something Bobby wanted no part of—no matter how much his dick and other parts of his body really wanted the other man. Dusting his hands off, he said, "This *thing* we've got—it's a really bad idea, you know that, right?"

"Yeah, I do." The shadows were gone from Ichiro's eyes, and they shone bright and dark, reflecting the lights of a city brewing its own chaos beyond the loft's open windows. "A really bad idea."

"I'll nuke some burritos. You should head out." He took a step toward the door, but Ichiro grabbed his wrist, holding him back.

"Cole doesn't have to know—about this. About us," Ichi murmured, his breath hot and slithery over Bobby's neck. "It's not like we're going to—get married or anything. It can be whatever it is until it burns out. No harm in it. We both know what we're getting into. No one needs to get their nose in it but us."

For a second, Bobby debated telling the man to let him get on with it, then. To get naked on the bed before he changed his mind and delivered what he'd promised Ichiro during their impromptu romp on the couch.

Because, God, he wanted to be so deep inside of Ichiro, the man would have trouble walking until he was ninety.

"No, Sunshine, I don't think so." He paused, taking one last look at Ichiro's slightly swollen mouth, knowing he'd brought that flush of sexual awareness to Ichiro's beautiful face. "Because I'm a really bad idea, and you deserve better. You need someone like… hell, you need what Cole has. A guy you can sit around with and have dinner. Or go walking around a fucking farmer's market and talk about different kinds of rice like it matters. You need that forever thing Cole's got. You really deserve that. And fuck, Sunshine, I'm not even your goddamn type."

"Yeah, see—" Ichiro's breath hitched in his chest. "—that's the problem. You're every damned bit of my type—including being a big fucking mistake. So yeah, if that's how you want it, then okay. I'll walk out of here."

"Just promise me, you'll… you can count me as a friend, Sunshine." Bobby skimmed his fingertips over Ichiro's mouth. "You can come here anytime if you need something."

"What I needed was to get fucked—preferably by you, Dawson." Ichiro let go of Bobby, dropping his own arms to his sides. "But sure, I'll keep that in mind. Especially when I need a pat on the ass and to be sent on my way."

"Baby, better a pat on your ass than you kicking mine," Bobby shot back. "Because that's what you'll do to me if I break your heart."

"Still so fucking cocky, Dawson," Ichi sneered. "What makes you think it's my heart that's going to be broken?"

CHAPTER SEVEN

IT WAS so different than in the movies.

So much quieter. So much more orderly.

And with a fuck of a lot less terror.

It was supposed to be a simple trip. He was going to talk to a Vietnamese woman named April, hoping to glean some information for his brother, Cole. A brother who was now crouched in against him, covering him tighter than any hug Ichiro'd ever been given—including from their mother.

To be fair to their mother, she'd also never shoved him facedown into greasy, filthy black asphalt speckled with glass fragments and cigarette butts.

Cole had his reasons. Small, deadly reasons cutting through the air above them and puncturing through cars and windows with little regard for the throngs of people cluttering the Los Angeles streets and sidewalks.

Fear tasted like blood. It filled his mouth with its thick, viscous cloyingness. Ichi thought he'd been shot through the lungs, but when he spat to clear his tongue, his saliva clung to his lips and face and was startlingly clear.

Because from the terror pouring through his marrow and choking in his throat, Ichi could have been bleeding out through his pores.

They'd just gotten out of the Rover when the first shots went off, and Ichi'd stumbled to the ground, panic driving him to cover. Cole shouted at him to get to the back of the car, and he'd half crawled on his hands and knees to find his brother waiting for him as more shots punctured the street's normal chatter of traffic and city noise. People were screaming in some kind of Spanish, panic puncturing through their words as messily as deep, booming pock-pock sounds of a gun going off. The windshield of an old Toyota parked behind them crackled into tiny, sharp pebbles as a bullet struck the car. A glassy shower sprayed through the air, a few far-flying specks striking Ichi in the face.

"Ichi! You okay?"

He put his hand up against the Rover's bumper, running his fingers over the stinging spots on his cheek. His brother met his stare, and Ichi wondered if his eyes were as glassy as the windshield's remains scattered at their feet. He couldn't focus on anything but the silence rippling over the street. He caught a sob in his throat, closing in on the sound before his brother could hear him, then flinched as another report of gunfire echoed through the broken calm.

His heart beat frantically, trying to keep up with the heaving breaths his lungs kept pushing out. Ichi put a hand to his chest, moving his fingers in small circles to calm himself down. It was no use. His heart tripped into another foxtrot and then swung into a full mosh when Cole pulled a gun out from under his jacket.

Cole patted Ichiro's shoulder and peeked around the end of the Rover. "Stay here."

"What are you going to do?" Alarmed, Ichi grabbed his brother's arm, his pulse racing and erratic. "You're not going out there."

"Kinda gotta." The amiable, charming brother he'd come to know and love was gone, replaced by a fierce, stubborn defender. Cole smiled gently, reassuring Ichiro with a quick wink. "Stay here. Get over there between those buildings; then call 911."

"Cole, *no*." Suddenly his heart stopped. Or at least it felt dead. There was another shot, and he jumped, startled by the sound. It was too near—too intimate—and he held on to his brother, refusing to let go. They'd come too far, had become too close. Ichi didn't want to lose Cole. Not now. Not ever. And he clung harder, refusing to let go of any scrap of family he had left to him. "Stay *here*."

The sounds of gunshots faded off, but the air was sharpened with screams echoing against the surrounding tall buildings.

Someone close had their world shattered, and Ichi stilled, wondering if he would be next to lose a piece of his heart.

He was about to pull Cole back down, ready to ignore the gun and anything else just to keep Cole safe, but his brother stopped him with a shake of his head. Cole cupped the back of Ichi's head, his fingers lightly threading through Ichi's long hair. He bent forward, kissing the top of his younger brother's head, and Ichi knew Cole would be leaving him there, alone, to face the nothingness of his fear.

Swallowing, Ichiro nodded when Cole asked him if he was okay.

"Yeah, I just… fuck." Cole's tenderness broke him, and Ichi resented the cowardice creeping up in him. Flushing guiltily, he let Cole go, sucking in the stink of the street's filth when he tried to control his shuddering breaths. "God, this must be how Jae feels every time he hears you're in the hospital."

"Yeah, you two can go bond over that later." Still reveling in his older-brother status, Cole shoved him away, a teasing push back, until Ichi's legs shot out from under him and his butt hit the dirty street with an inelegant plop. "Now stay here. See if you can get the cops to come. I'm going to check on what's happened."

"And if someone's been killed?" Ichiro asked softly as he pulled his cell phone out.

"Then it wouldn't be the first time that I've stumbled across a dead body." Sadly, it was the truth. "I'd say I'd be right back, but honestly, with my luck? If anyone comes up dead, it'll be the woman we need to talk to."

IT WAS too much to process. For Ichiro anyway. There'd been blood everywhere—or at least not where it was supposed to be. And as much as Ichi tried, he couldn't get the smell of burnt metal and hot skin out of his nose. He heard Cole speaking to the cops again, to the female detective about the women someone'd found in an apartment nearby. More blood. More death.

He'd stood over a woman's body—an almost woman—and amid the chaos and thunder of police, terror and crying, Cole became something different than what Ichiro knew. Staunch and unmoving but tender enough to console a crying Hispanic woman who'd witnessed the shooting.

The tenement was a slum. There was no other way to put it— not in Ichi's mind. It towered up around a tiny courtyard, its cracked cement edges prickling with dry grasses and weeds. A splash of blood beaded across a bright chalked-in sidewalk hopscotch game, purple and pink grit floating on drying brown dots. A hand moved him away from the blood, carefully guiding him clear of the scene. A glance told him it was a police officer, his voice a soothing but firm thread to cling to, but for the life of him, Ichiro couldn't make out his face in the rush of images and shapes coming at him.

A second later, Cole appeared at his side and, so American in his need to touch, wrapped an arm around Ichiro's shoulders to pull him in close.

It took everything Ichiro had in him not to pull away and step back behind his oh-so-familiar public face, distancing himself from his brother and the bloodbath around them.

"I still can't believe they took your gun." Ichi exhaled, a hot burble of air coming up from his belly. "You did *nothing* wrong. It's... *this*... is wrong. Why? Why would someone *do* this?"

"Because they can, little brother," Cole murmured, giving him another tight squeeze. "And I'm going to find out why. Or at least how it connects to Sheila. A lot of people have been hurt because of her. It's time someone put a stop to all of that shit."

ICHIRO THREW up after the short ride back to Cole's house—in the bushes, in Cole's downstairs bathroom, and finally a few dry heaves in the kitchen sink as Jae rubbed the small of his back.

"Your brother—he does things according to his nature— fearless and without thought but always for the best. It's why I fell in love with him," Jae murmured in Korean. "I know it's hard to understand why he does things. *I* don't understand half of the time—all of the time—but I know he has a good heart and he... can't stop caring about people."

"He could have gotten killed today, Jae-ah." Ichi spat a mouthful of water and bile into the sink. "I've got Megumi leaving me messages about naming her kid because she's happy she's pregnant and wants me to be a part of her daughter's life then there's my brother on the other side of things, trying to die. It's like Life and Death are circling me, and you're telling me he does it because he *cares* about people?"

"If you were that woman—if you were someone clinging to life and scared, wouldn't you want Cole to come help you?" Jae patted Ichiro's back one final time. "Come eat dinner. You'll feel better."

DINNER WAS congee, one of Ichi's favorite dishes. Sadly for his taste buds, it tasted more like paste than rice porridge. The flecks of frilled fungus too closely resembled lungs for Ichi's imagination, and he could only get a few mouthfuls down before he gave up and switched to beer.

He should have been comforted. There were familiar tastes, familiar sounds of his brother and Jae talking as their cat nudged him for bit of chicken.

But in the middle of the familiar—Ichiro felt like nothing would ever be the same again.

"Cole-ah, quit picking at the food and eat." Jae scraped at the bottom of his bowl. "There's nothing in there you haven't already had."

Even the admonishment was a common refrain as his food-cautious brother poked and picked at the food in his bowl. They'd set dinner up in the living room, using a massive apothecary chest set between a trio of sofas as their dining table. Ichi slumped back into one of the couches and rested his beer on his knee. Neko, Jae's tiny chinchilla-furred cat, spotted Ichi's lap and bounced her way across sofa cushions and a table edge to take possession of it.

Kneading carefully, she then squatted on Ichi's stomach and set her face to full smug, purring as loudly as her petite black body could.

"So you think this woman you're looking for—the one the cops are now looking for—April—do you think she will lead you to Ben's wife?"

"What?" Cole looked up from his congee dissection. "What about April? This stuff's crunchy. I didn't hear you."

"You're still going to look for April?" Ichi asked softly. "Even though you know someone killed the people she lived with?"

"Yeah. Kinda have to, dude." Cole spoke so casually about walking into a fire he couldn't control, and Ichi winced, recalling the drops of blood splattered over a hot sidewalk. Talking through a mouthful of fungus, Cole continued, "I can't just let it go. Especially since those people were killed. Something's up with April Bahn. It might not have anything to do with Sheila but—how can I just let shit slide?"

"Do you want him to do this, Jae?" Ichi looked to Cole's lover for support.

From the resigned look on Jae's face, there was none forthcoming from his corner of the room. He might as well have asked Neko to fetch him another beer.

"Cole-ah is going to do it whether I like it or not." Jae refilled his bowl from the congee pot set in the middle of the apothecary table. "So long as he doesn't get hurt, I can't say anything. But if he gets killed, then...."

"Then all this is yours." Cole gave a quick grin, sweeping one arm in front of him as if showcasing the living room for a game show.

"You already gave me the long storeroom for my studio. I don't think I need anything else." Jae shook his head. "I'd rather have you than the house."

"I'll do my best." Cole caught the pained expression on Ichiro's face and reached out to him. "Ichi, we're joking—"

Suddenly the air in the living room was too hot to breathe, and as his lungs filled with the scents of food, cat, and people he loved, Ichi felt his insides beginning to burn. They were so cavalier—too casual about talks of death, especially Cole's. Ichi couldn't take much more. It was too surreal, a Fellini scene cut from a movie too macabre and foreign to be shown.

"Do you know what my family thinks of Americans? What they told me when I said I was coming here?" Ichiro lifted the cat up off his lap and set her aside. "They think you're like children. Very dangerous, silly children with weapons. I used to think they were being naïve, but now I'm not so sure. What about your family? Jae? Me? The others? Don't you think about them?"

"I guess I think we're all kind of family," Cole said quietly. His brother's gaze was as wide-eyed as the first day Ichi met him, and what he'd assumed was an innocent gullibility now shone through for what it truly was—Cole's foolhardy conviction to throw himself into the middle of danger—even at the expense of his own life. "Whether we're blood or not. It's kind of who I am, Ichi."

"Even if it gets you killed?" Ichiro asked softly. His brother couldn't see—wouldn't see how scared Ichi was inside. Or it didn't matter. As if *Ichi* didn't matter. Or Jae. Or anyone.

For a second, Ichiro wondered if he'd merely switched from admiring one selfish man—his father—to admiring another.

"Even then, kid. Because someone's got to do it," Cole answered. "And that someone might as well be me."

"And you're okay with it, Jae-ah? Letting him do this?"

Jae-Min paused a moment before responding. "He wouldn't be Cole if he were any different, Ichi. It pisses me off and I worry, but that's who I fell in love with. That's what comes with love. You have to take the good with the worry."

Jae's willingness to let his brother throw his life away—for nothing, for no one he knew broke Ichi, and he stood up to dig his keys out of his pocket. "I… can't. This kind of thing—it's too much. I've got to go."

Cole followed him out to the front door, grabbing at Ichi's hand when he closed his fingers over the knob. Ichiro's anger blazed, seeing Cole's silent plea for understanding in his brother's light green eyes. Unable to get past the lump in his throat, Ichiro pulled his brother into a tight embrace, crossing lines he never thought he'd cross when growing up in Tokyo. Of the two brothers his mother'd left behind, Ichi knew he'd grown fiercely protective and fond of Cole. What he admired the most in his older brother was now a curse.

"Do not get killed," Ichiro muttered into his brother's ear. "I just fucking got you. Don't let anyone take you away from me. Just… don't."

WHEN THE phone rang late at night, Bobby always expected it to be Cole. It usually always was. Double-digit-hour calls were usually Cole, sometimes to talk or even to see what he thought about a line of inquiry he'd stumbled upon. He'd spent the day at the gym, his uncle's nursing home, and then digging up his neighbor Myrna's rooftop garden so the septuagenarian could grow her next batch of tomatoes.

Not that he for a moment believed the former burlesque dancer's resin-laden, pungent, leafy plants were ever going to actually bear tomatoes, but it was a lie they both agreed to.

And after Bobby'd turned down her offer of brownies, she'd forked over cases of local craft brews, claiming she'd gotten too old, and alcohol went to her head.

Funny enough, he'd gathered up around seventeen gin and vodka bottles during his rooftop excursion, drained sacrifices of Myrna's weekly get-together with some of the girls she'd shared a stage with.

They were up there now, their husky laughter coming in through his open windows. The air was fragrant with car exhaust, smoldering Purple Haze, and grilling tofu burgers. He'd been about to start on one of Myrna's gifts when the phone rang, and his life crashed into a confusing pile of emotions around his feet.

"No idea what the fuck I'm—" It was Ichiro. Bobby was certain of that. "Bobby, I… fuck."

"Hey, where are you?" Drunk came to mind. Or maybe roofied. Ichi was pretty, and he could see some asshole slipping something into the guy's drink. "I'll come get you—"

"No, I'm… downstairs." Ichiro was smoking. He could hear the other man pull in a drag on a cigarette and slowly let it go, only to draw in another right afterward. His breathing was shaky, hard across the phone line, and Bobby's heart clenched. "Do you mind if I come up?"

"What's wrong? Shit, I'll come get you. Is Cole okay?" The past twenty-four hours he'd tried to slough the man out of his mind, but no amount of hard work or beer seemed to be doing the trick. Now with Ichiro showing up on his doorstep, it didn't look like Bobby was going to shake his want of the man any time soon. "Are *you* okay?"

"Yeah. No. Fuck, Bobby. I'm… fuck." Ichi's words fragmented, dissolving into Japanese. Words Bobby *did* understand broke through, mostly death and tragedy. The clench turned into ice when Ichiro mumbled, "God, I'm so scared, Dawson."

A second later Bobby was out the door, his bare feet hitting the hallway at a brisk run. The stairwell was a blur, and he was through the foyer in a split second, his bare toes digging into the plush runner near the entrance. Panting, he emerged into the cool, humid air, looking around the parking lot for the broken man on the other end of his phone.

It only took Bobby a moment to find him, a long, slender figure leaning on a powerful Harley, straggly trails of smoke curling around his silhouette.

The walk across the parking lot was a short one but a trial of nerves with his bare feet. Bobby didn't care. A pebble bit into his heel, but he avoided what looked like a broken juice bottle lying near the curb. At some point he'd have to get on management about maintenance, but for right now, the only thing—the only person—he was focused on was the scared, hollow-eyed man whose trembling hands could barely hold up a lit *kretek*.

Ichiro crossed the distance between them in a blink. In the space of a glimmering moment, Bobby's arms were full of sweet-smelling, shivering man.

"I've got you, Sunshine," Bobby whispered into Ichiro's sweat-damp hair. "No worries. I've got you."

SHOCK TURNED Ichiro's skin to ice. His lips were nearly blue by the time Bobby got him up into the loft, and his teeth rattled when the warmed interior air washed over them. He'd been too heavy for Bobby to carry the length of the building, even if he'd wanted to unman Ichiro by carting him around like some princess in a video game. Instead he'd slung Ichi's arm over his shoulder and looped his own around the man's waist, taking most of Ichiro's weight. Once inside, Ichiro began to shake, his skin going clammy against Bobby's neck. Cradling Ichiro against him, Bobby gently walked him to the couch, urging the man to take just one more step.

"Cole.... God, there was so much... blood." Ichiro's words tumbled out of him in spurts. "Not Cole... but everywhere, you know? And they act like—nothing. Like it's nothing. And Cole's all ready to go right back into it—"

"Baby, let's get you sitting down and something hot in you." Bobby's shin hit the couch, and he nearly toppled over with Ichi in his arms. Swearing, he jerked back, righting himself, then removed Ichi's arm from around his neck. He laid Ichi down into the cushions, then grabbed a bright rainbow-hued afghan from a nearby chair to tuck around Ichi's body. "Stay here. I'll be right back."

It seemed like every second ticked off another eternity by the time Bobby was able to get back to the couch. Armed with instant Vietnamese coffee heated from the hot water spigot on his coffeemaker, he juggled the mug and a small bottle of Jack over to Ichiro's side.

"Thank you," Ichiro chattered through his teeth as he took the cup.

"That's my boy, polite down to the death," Bobby murmured, scrunching in to sit on the edge of the sofa's cushions. Brushing Ichi's hair from his face, he waited until Ichi took a good swig of the coffee, then offered him the whiskey.

"No. Too... much. Drunk already a bit." Ichi's fingers were cold on Bobby's wrist when he pushed away the offer. "Just coffee."

"Okay, just coffee. Mind if I finish my beer, and then you and I can talk about what's going on here, Sunshine."

The silence was broken with laughter—old women above them getting stoned and drunk, living well under the orange-tinted Los Angeles evening sky. Bobby leaned forward, about to get up to close the windows, but Ichiro held on, his fingers digging into Bobby's forearm.

"Please, don't go." The shivering was slight but still there, and Bobby felt it through his skin and into his bones. Fear lodged itself someplace deep inside of Ichiro's psyche and was spreading, taking over his usual calm and swallowing up the vestiges of anger lurking in the corners of his deep brown eyes. "I'm so cold inside. And I don't know why."

He was going to regret it, but Bobby knew a cry for comfort when he heard one. No amount of blankets would take away the chill Ichi caught, but touching him would... damn them both. He needed to be touched, to be told it was all right, and Bobby'd drawn the short straw.

Or the long one if his dick had anything to say about it.

"I'm not going anywhere, Sunshine." Draining his beer, he glanced up at the muted sky outside. "God help me."

Ichiro didn't hear him. The blanket was twisted around him, and he fought to get free of it. "I'm so fucking... lost here. I don't know what to do. Fuck, someone tell me what to do. What to feel—"

"Why don't we start with what happened?" Bobby put his bottle down, then tugged at the afghan, opening its folds so he could get closer to Ichiro. "Move over. Turn on your side so I can hold you while you talk."

"I'm not a damned girl. I don't need cuddling."

"Everyone needs cuddling. Even girls. And boys. Maybe the world would be a nicer place if more people did it. Now move the fuck over."

It took a bit of maneuvering, but the couch was wide enough for Bobby to lie out on—he'd made sure of that when he bought it—so other than the extra weight of Ichiro on him, they would fit. He pulled Ichiro on top of him, then lay still as Ichi squirmed and nudged, getting comfortable. Bobby's dick came up with a few suggestions, but he ignored it, trying to get Ichi settled.

"I shouldn't have... come here," Ichi confessed, mumbling into Bobby's chest as they shifted about. Sliding over Bobby's stomach, he lay half on and half off Bobby's body, cradled in a tightening embrace. "This thing... you and I... I just didn't know who else to go to. And... fuck, I needed this. Needed you."

"Talk to me, Ichi. Mouth moving. Words coming out. Talk." Bobby shifted, angling Ichi closer. "What the fuck happened? And yeah, you can come here any time. We'll work it out, okay?"

The tale spilled out—about death and bullets, of a young man trying to live his life in a different way and how he'd lost that life in the middle of a sunbaked courtyard, Cole's shadow stretching over his body like an avenging angel. He heard the shock of gunfire, heard for the first time up close and personal, and the terror those sounds made, knowing each *ping*, every *thwap* sound could be the end.

He'd been there before, wearing a blue uniform and praying to some God he'd broken up with years ago, but somehow in that moment, Bobby'd found the words to beg for some peace and calm in the middle of his death.

A death that walked by him and found someone else, their blood gushing out of their young bodies as the light faded from their eyes.

His first shootout ended badly, his partner at the time gruffly cuffing him across the back of the neck and telling him the kid got what he deserved. Ichiro was luckier. He wouldn't have to worry if it'd been his bullet that brought Thanatos's attention to a fourteen-year-old kid. He'd gotten comfort instead of the insult Bobby'd gotten when he lost his lunch in the back of a downtown alley, and the memory of the shooting would fade, instead of coming back to waltz around in Ichi's nightmares.

Bobby didn't say any of that. Instead he merely held Ichiro until he was talked out and sleepy, worn out from the emotional terror ride he'd taken. Only then did Bobby trust himself to stroke Ichi's back, letting his fingers trail down the dip of the man's spine and back up again.

"And Jae—he just... it's okay with him," Ichiro growled. "I want to take Cole and... fuck, I don't know."

"Kick his ass?" Bobby chuckled. "Good luck. Your brother's got a good right hook when he's pissed off. I've been on the end of it before. Not someone to brawl with if he's got a grudge."

"Probably spent his time beating Mike up as a kid." He grumbled in Japanese. "Or Mike beating him up. God, fucking Mike. I wanted to talk to him, but… you know how he is. Okay, so I didn't really want to talk to him, but he'd have been the logical choice. But he's—a dick sometimes."

"Yeah, he'd want to fix it," Bobby replied softly, his hand making another circuit down Ichiro's back. "Not what you want, eh?"

"No." He sighed, his muscles relaxing under Bobby's touch. The shivers and cold were gone, bled out during Ichi's rant. "I just needed… you. And it fucking pissed me off wanting you. Not even for fucking, because, you know, I want that too, but just—because I needed someone to hear me. Jae and Cole were like those bobbing head things with each other. *Yep yep, that's just how Cole is—gotta love him for it.* I wanted to punch them both until their brains came back."

"Thing is, Sunshine, that *is* how your brother is." It was regrettable but a truth. "Angels look at him and say, fuck, dude, kick it back a little bit. Shit, he knew Jae for what? A half second, and he went into a bombed-out building looking for that damned cat."

"He found her, though," Ichi murmured sleepily. Exhausted, he slithered into a boneless heap. Bobby could feel him relax, his body unclenching as he warmed up. "God, I'm so fucking tired. The Harley, I love it, but it's like riding a bone snake. I ache everywhere and not in a good way. I should have at least been fucked hard to feel like this."

"Not the best image there, dude," Bobby warned him gently. "You've got a Jeep. Shoulda driven that over."

"I needed space around me. Hell, I don't even know how long I rode around. But the thing's all rattles and jerks. Hard on the body, but I wanted to just go." He grumbled something Bobby couldn't quite catch, then sighed. "I left my helmet downstairs on the bike. Someone's gonna rip it off."

"Probably," he conceded. "I'll get you a new one."

"Don't need your money. Grandfather—my father's father—and my mother left me enough. I think he thought I'd turn out better. Maybe more traditional. Not a nice guy, but... I think he liked me well enough. Told me once I had to go out and see the world. My father told me I had to stay and root in Japan." Ichiro grimaced, turning his face up to look at Bobby. "It's not that I'm not Japanese. It's that I'm—I didn't fit. It was too tight on my skin. My father doesn't understand that. I don't think he ever will. Maybe Megumi will give him that son he wants. Or he'll like the daughter he's getting enough to make her his heir. Fuck, that poor kid."

"Things okay between you and Megumi? Will she let you see the kid? Or are they going to be assholes like Cole's dad?"

"Megumi and I were close—are close. She wants me to name her daughter, so I guess I'll want to see her. It's a little weird, you know? Fuck, she hurt me, but I think I was kind of relieved. I wanted out. She wanted... in. Sometimes I want to throw it into my father's face that he's with *my* leftovers, but that's not... hell—"

"Not you, man. That's not you. You're a pain in the ass, but you're not a dick."

"No, not to her." Ichi rubbed his nose against Bobby's chest. "But it's awkward. Family things are awkward. My aunts don't like her. Probably because she's young enough to be their daughter, but she married the head of the family. Lots of conflict. Tight smiles and backstabbing. So political, and everyone watches to see who'll stumble.

"If I were Megumi, I'd want a food taster, but she's not... bright in some ways. She's sweet, though. I'm more worried about her surviving the family than anything else." He yawned, stretching like a cat. "Fuck, look what it did to my mother. She could barely make a decision without worrying about what the family would think or do. It's a fucked-up minefield they've made to live in."

"I should move you to the bed," Bobby teased. "You're falling asleep on me here, Sunshine. And if you wake up sore, just remember, it was the bike. Not me. Although I wouldn't mind if it was me. I'd leave you rattled."

He regretted the flirtation as soon as he said it, but there was no going back. Playing snipe and tease with Ichiro was a habit, a very dangerous habit and one that was going to bite Bobby in the butt.

"Thought we weren't going to do that—*thing* thing. You kicked me out yesterday, remember? Now, shit... you and I, we've either got to go or stop here. One or the other." Ichiro propped himself up, sharp elbows digging into Bobby's ribs. He winced but kept quiet, startled by the dark circles under Ichi's eyes. "I go into your bed—even to sleep—and we fuck this up. Hell, I probably already did that coming here, no?"

"No," Bobby whispered. "You didn't fuck this up. You needed... someone, kid—"

"Not a kid, Dawson. I keep saying it, and yet you keep calling me that. It's like an excuse for you." Ichiro reached down and cupped Bobby's crotch, squeezing at the bulge he found there. "And this is telling me you don't think of me as some kid."

"You're the same age as my son, Ichi. Bad enough you're Cole's little brother. I could be your father." He moved his hands down to Ichiro's hips, intending to get off the couch. "And... shit, reasons. So many fucking reasons, Ichiro."

"Name *one* good one. Name one good reason we can't just... do what we want without anyone knowing. Why can't I just for once in my life do something—have someone like you—without the rest of the world poking their nose into it?" He exhaled, his breath a hot wind over Bobby's chest and neck. "Yesterday—shit, it was only yesterday you were pushing me away and telling me no. Today I spent a good fucking long time sucking on a piece of road hoping someone wasn't going to put a damned bullet in me, and then my stupid brother decides he's going to go be a hero and get into the middle of it."

"Same shit as yesterday, Sunshine. I'm a bad idea—"

"I'm covered in bad ideas." Ichi sat up all the way, straddling Bobby's hips. Shucking his sleeves back, he bared the ink embedded under his skin. "See these? They're supposed to be my idea of running into a burning building, because what I've done to myself is *everything* my family hates. The symbols, the ink—everything. But it's my decision, and I took the consequences."

"Nothing's changed since then," Bobby insisted. He didn't want to look at Ichiro's bared anything. Something about the man dug into him, and he was struggling to let it go. "You're still Cole's brother and—"

"Dawson, trotting Cole out like he's a cross and I'm a vampire isn't going to cut it. Age. My brother. None of that shit matters, and you know it." He leaned over, pressing his hands on the couch arm, his weight dimpling the stuffing. "I want you. I want to fuck you. You want to fuck me. I needed you, and you answered that need. And right now, I need… more than just a cuddle. I want to feel like I'm going to fucking live through this damned thing, because I'm scared. Today fucking *scared* me, and I don't know what I'm going to do with it. So yeah, I want… more than this cuddle. So give me that one good damned reason why you and I can't—"

"Because if I do this with you, Ichi…." It was a confession he couldn't stop. The words were coming up out of a scared dark place he'd buried years ago, but Bobby found himself staring down into the abyss, watching his personal Pandora's box crack open to release his demons. "Because if you and I go to that bed, and I get to do what I want with you, I might not ever want to let you go. Then what's going to happen to me when you get tired of it and walk off? Then what? I don't want to go through that again, Ichi. It hurt too fucking much the first time around."

Ichi's eyes moistened, and he lowered his face, brushing his lips over Bobby's parted mouth. He left a wet trail with his tongue under the breadth of Bobby's bottom lip, then whispered, "What makes you think I want to let you go? Take a chance on me, Dawson. Take a chance on both of us."

CHAPTER EIGHT

BEING IN the same room with Bobby, naked and writhing under his touch, hammered at Ichiro's senses. He'd stood once in the middle of a hurricane, young and foolish to face the wind and the pounding rain, hoping in some primal part of his brain the fury of the storm would wash away his sins and imperfections.

Trembling there in the dusky heat-brushed Los Angeles night and wrapped tight with the want of Bobby boiling up under his skin, Ichiro finally realized he'd been standing in the wrong storm.

He'd needed a hot, sweaty thunderstorm with a foul mouth and rough hands—one that whispered Ichi's name as if he were in the middle of a cathedral, and Ichiro was its altar.

God, those hands.

Hard and scraping, Bobby's fingers were scored with calluses and scars. Ichi felt every bump and bruise in Bobby's life raking over his back and shoulders when Bobby explored his body. The man wasn't gentle. Not by any means. He'd stripped his clothes off without a thought to seduction, perfunctory and practical, but his dark eyes were swallowed black with his arousal, and the jut of his thick erection as it sprang free from Bobby's jeans was a temptation all on its own.

The man definitely spent time pushing his body to its limits. It showed in every long plane of muscle sculpted over his broad shoulders and flat belly. Bobby's thick thighs rippled with power when he braced himself and pushed Ichiro down onto the bed, his tongue licking his top lip as if he were debating where to start on Ichiro's body.

Ichi didn't have to wait long to find out.

Clasping his hands on Ichiro's hips, Bobby tumbled down on top of him, chuckling when Ichiro's breath left him in a rush. Shoving at Bobby's chest, Ichi coaxed the man to turn over, then straddled his belly. The tickle of soft hair around his lover's navel teased Ichiro's cleft when he slid up Bobby's abdomen. Stretching his arm back, Ichiro found Bobby's cock, flicking his fingers over its soft head until it wept with excitement.

"Keep doing that, Sunshine, and there's not going to be enough left in there for you," Bobby growled, his voice deepening to a dark thrum. Ichiro felt the bass rumbling up from Bobby's chest, cupping his balls and traveling up his now rampant cock with every word the man spat out. Bobby's hands kneaded Ichi's ass, pulling apart his cheeks. The air on his hole was sharp and cold, a startling contrast to the heat building up between them. "God, I want to fuck you."

"Good. Kind of what I had planned. Next time, though, you're letting me do this to you," Ichi teased, bending to rub his lips over Bobby's mouth. Their tongues danced together, fighting, then retreating. Bobby's eyes shuttered, his lashes swooping down in a narrow glare. Mistrust built up, and Ichiro could almost see the walls springing up between them. Gently rocking against Bobby's rigid cock, Ichiro murmured, "If we're going to do this, it's gotta go both directions, Dawson. I'm not just going to be some hole for you to fuck."

"You're not a damned hole. That's what's getting me into this shithole I'm falling into," Bobby grumbled, his cock wedging itself into Ichi's tight cleft. Shoving his hips up, he ran the length of his erection along the crack of Ichiro's ass, his hands pushing in Ichi's cheeks, amping up the friction along their sweat-damp skin. "I've… hell, I haven't done that in fucking years, Sunshine. And the last time, it didn't go so well. But yeah, next time, I'm all yours."

There were no lies in Bobby's eyes. None in his voice either. Something dark slithered in his thoughts and wormed its way into his soul, and it peered back out at Ichiro, mocking the gruff tenderness he'd already experienced from Bobby's kisses.

Pressing his forehead to Bobby's, Ichiro whispered softly, "I'll take care of you, Dawson. Someone should, you know? And maybe that someone is me."

He didn't wait to hear Bobby's response. His tongue fit perfectly around the tip of Bobby's left nipple, and Ichiro took his time exploring the edge of the tightening nub. Bobby tasted salty-sweet, a hint of arousal blending into masculine skin. A drop of sweat ran down Bobby's neck, drawn out by the warmth of their rubbing bodies, and Ichiro chased it down with the tip of his tongue, following its trail down Bobby's throat to the hard curve of his side.

Bobby's ribs jerked when Ichi's mouth left butterfly kisses behind the drop, and he lost the smidgen of damp somewhere in the tumble of being flipped over onto his back. Bobby's heavier body pressed Ichi down into the mattress, and their cocks bobbed together, greeting each other in a wet slap of heads and prickling hair.

"You're killing me here, Sunshine." The growl was back, chasing away any shadows Bobby'd brought up between them. Raking his fingers up Ichiro's thigh, he left faint pink furrows along the pale skin as he bit into the softness of Ichiro's throat. The growl was replaced by a satisfied hum at hearing Ichi gasp, and Bobby pressed his hips down into Ichiro's crotch when his hips jerked up in response to the bite. "Damn, I could just eat you up."

The sparks of pleasure and pain continued. Bobby's teeth raked and scored down Ichiro's chest, stopping only long enough at a nipple to work it to a piercing bitter-sharp nub before moving lower still. He dug his hands through the short scruff on Bobby's neck, needing to guide the man to where Ichi wanted to be touched, but Bobby had his own ideas. He reached up, wrapping his strong fingers around Ichiro's wrists, and pushed his hands away, roughly shoving them against the slatted headboard.

"Let me do this." Bobby's tongue flicked over Ichi's still smarting nipple. "You just lie there and take it for a few minutes."

Ichiro tried to bury himself into his surroundings—anything to stave off the hot pleasure boiling up from his balls and through his body.

The air from the windows was filled with the sounds of the city. Soft laughter, husky and feminine, trailed over them, and, somewhere close by, a Mexican polka oompahed in encouragement to a boisterous party below them. Los Angeles flew past them, cars skimming out on the streets in a wash of soft white noise, but Ichi barely heard it.

His own ragged breathing drowned out everything but his mewling pleas for Bobby's mouth to finish what it started.

Cole might have been right. Bobby spent a lot of time with his mouth around dicks and on skin. If there was any question about that, it was answered as he teased and plied Ichiro's cock and balls with his tongue and lips. A soft sear of teeth on his balls made Ichiro jerk in response, but it was more to shock than hurt, especially when Bobby followed up with a skilled laving of the nipped area.

"Pay attention to me, Sunshine. Anything else—leave it outside." Bobby's hot mouth closed in on him, enveloping his cock head in a hard suckle. His hips rose, unwilling or unable to stay flat on the mattress, and it was all Ichiro could do not to grab Bobby's cock and shove it as far in as it could go.

Bobby, however, had other plans.

His tongue touched the edge of Ichiro's hole, and Ichi jumped, twitching in reflex at the soft, hot probe.

"Fuuuuu—"

There were other noises following that one, but none of them bloomed into full words. He tried. The universe knew Ichiro tried to mewl out his pleasure into something close to any language he knew, but he was lost in the sensations rolling over his skin and into his blood.

Then Bobby slid two thick, strong fingers through the tightness of his now wet hole, and Ichiro lost his damned mind.

He closed his eyes, falling into the dark. It didn't remain shadowy for long. The stretches of bone and flesh into his body held a promise—a raking, a splitting apart to follow once Bobby angled his heavy, lust-swollen cock up against Ichiro's ass and slid in. A wet smear streaked across Ichi's thigh, more promises—seed-laden fluid begging to run hot into Ichiro's insides.

More pressing in—deeper still—until Ichi wanted to scream in frustration. His fingers were numb, bloodless from tightening his fists into Bobby's sheets, and his ass ached to be filled. Hell, *he* ached everywhere.

"Dawson—shit, Bobby," he growled, unable to find a good purchase on Bobby's wide shoulders. His nails dug in finally, and Ichi knew he'd left a stinging reminder of Bobby's teasing in his skin.

"Want a bit of me, then, Sunshine?" Bobby's tongue worked around his head, drawing out the slip of skin around his glans.

The same tongue began another circuit down to his balls, and Bobby gently nipped Ichi's sac, pulling it down as his balls rolled and churned below Ichiro's hard cock. His fingers moved again, hooking up until Ichi thought his skin would envelop Bobby's palm. Then Bobby drew out, leaving him stretched apart and achingly hollow.

"Give me a bit of time, babe." Bobby tore a condom wrapper open, spitting out a sliver of foil stuck to his tongue.

The astringent smell of lube joined the night air, and Ichi's asshole clenched involuntarily, his body gearing up for the intrusion. Snapping the condom on, Bobby smeared the excess lube over Ichi's opening, then leaned over, covering his mouth with a savage kiss. Hooking his hands under Ichi's thighs, Bobby lifted Ichiro's legs and spread them apart, opening him up even wider.

"Hang on to me, Sunshine," he growled through another hot kiss, sucking Ichiro's breath out of his chest. "I'm going to give you the ride of your life."

SINKING INTO Ichi's tight, velvety heat was an exercise in patience.

There was no question the man'd gotten under Bobby's skin. Hell, if he could live the rest of his days with Ichiro wrapped around his dick, Bobby would die a happy man.

He'd even be willing to try having Ichi press into him.

The thought of a man other than—Bobby shook his head. The past needed to remain in the shadows, where it could lurk to its heart's content and not smear its ugly oiliness over the pleasure he'd pulled out of Ichi's body.

God, when *was* the last time he'd mourned the man he'd loved enough to break his life apart for? Bobby couldn't remember—hell, he wasn't even sure he felt any anguish over what Mark'd done to him after he'd broken his marriage and ruined his family.

He was freer for it—Bobby reminded himself as he drank in the sight and feel of Ichiro's young, primed body. Loving a man—this man—felt right. More than right. More than good. Running his hands over every inch of Ichi's body, Bobby wondered what kept him from having Ichiro. Fear of Cole finding out or—something darker and deeper welling up inside of him—a fear of wanting more than Ichiro could give.

Or just fear of wanting Ichiro to stay and rediscovering the pain of not being enough for a man to want in return.

He had to go slowly. Ichi was tight, nearly painfully tight, and no amount of stretching seemed to help. If anything, it drove Ichi into a frenzy, and he clamped down on Bobby, bucking and twisting to get more.

Every skimming touch along Ichi's skin brought out a growling sound or a slithering purr with Ichi writhing beneath him, begging for—no, demanding—more. Bobby intended to give him more. Give him as much as he could take and maybe even beyond that. The skin at the base of his cock tightened when he thought of how Ichiro's hole would kiss it, suckling at his cock's root until they both lost themselves in the fucking they'd danced around in the months since they'd first met.

"Damn," he muttered to himself, tightening his hold on Ichi's hips. "I just need to hear you scream."

Ichiro was damned gorgeous. Spread out over Bobby's bed, he was a sprawl of ivory skin inked to hell and gone with demons, birds, and swirls of color. Stories lay in his skin. A dip of a scar across his shoulder ran white through his faint golden tan. Ichi's dark eyes gleamed, catching a lamp's glow as he turned, mink studded with amber flecks, as if their depths hid slivers of a harvest moon. The faint light reflected off a dab of sweat on Ichiro's jaw, tracing its trail in silver when the drop grew heavy and surrendered itself to the curve of Ichi's throat.

They both shone with the wet of their efforts, muscles gleaming under a soft sheen as Bobby worked in and out of Ichiro's grip. His balls slapped and tickled Ichi's cleft, his cock growing slick with oil with each pound against Ichiro's hole. With each slide in, Ichi arched his back, sucking Bobby deeper in, then tightening, refusing to let the length of Bobby's cock slip away from him.

The strain showed in Ichi's thighs, his powerful, lean muscles rippling beneath their ink shrouds. A tiger on Ichi's rib cage leaped in time with their thrusts, its body undulating with Ichiro's hips rising to meet Bobby's cock.

His lover... God, Ichiro pistoned over Bobby's cock, and all he could do, all he wanted to do was revel in the feel of his *lover*. Something stronger than lust boiled up into his balls, cresting over his pleasure and frighteningly spilling out into his soul. Bobby didn't want *this*. He'd never wanted to feel that connection to another man. Men were... disposable. Holes and mouths who laughed and maybe kept him company but eventually wandered off like strays finding a new home.

He wasn't supposed to *want* to keep them. To soothe them or wipe their tears when their worlds were shattered by violence. The world was a tough place. He'd seen enough blood and death to stare it down until it whimpered away, but he'd never *wanted* to keep someone else safe from its looming, dark presence.

Until now.

And it scared the shit out of him.

His body feared nothing. Not when it was safe, warm, and suckled in deep by Ichiro's clench. No, his body and soul were running off without him while Bobby's heart skipped and churned, twisting to get away from the *reality* of the man he'd laid down on his bed and was—making love to.

Because as Bobby felt the ripple of lightning lick and curl at the length of his cock, he felt a tendril of... regret mingled in with his climax.

He wanted to fill Ichiro with his spend.

He wanted to wipe Ichi clean, wrap him in the sheets, and spend a sleepy evening laughing about the horrible music coming through his open windows.

He wanted to lick at the ink on Ichiro's body and ask him *why* this picture.

Bobby wanted—*needed*—to know the reason for each drop of ink, every smirk Ichiro threw his way, and the why of every hitch in Ichi's breath as life spun around him.

His cock released, bursting full gushes of come into the trap of latex around it, and Bobby bent over, letting Ichiro's thighs go so he could wrap his arms around his lover's trembling body. Ichi came, splattering the tight space between them with his hot release, coating their stomachs and tangling them together in a liquid kiss Bobby smeared as he lurched a few final, gentle thrusts.

"Fuck," Bobby ground out as Ichiro milked the last of his release from him. He didn't know what he was cursing—his resentful attachment to the man he'd needed since he'd first laid eyes on him or the knowledge he'd agreed to let Ichiro walk away from him. Either way, Bobby was screwed, and *fuck* seemed like too mild of a sound to explain the depths of his troubles.

"Yeah, *anata*," Ichiro gasped, his hair plastered to his cheeks and throat, damp from the sweat of their lovemaking. "I think we're in trouble."

ICHIRO WAS gone when Bobby woke up.

His bed was empty, but the coffee machine was on warm, fragrant and filled with a dark, syrupy roast Bobby knew would keep him buzzing all day. A quick trip to the bathroom turned out to be longer than he'd expected, because as he drizzled piss into the toilet bowl, he spotted a folded piece of paper taped to the mirror over his sink. Torn between wanting to yank the paper off the glass so he could read it and finishing his piss so he could walk without a limp, Bobby examined the situation—and silently berated his dick for seemingly taking its damned sweet time in finishing its business.

The note was more than three feet away, and while some of the ink bled through the other side, he couldn't quite make out what Ichi wrote. Stretching didn't help. It was too far away, and all it did was ensure Bobby would have to spend a few seconds wiping piss off the side of the bowl from trying to unhinge his shoulder joint to reach the damn mirror. He was about to give up and resign himself to mopping the floor when his bladder suddenly announced it was done and his dick sighed in relief, flopping back down into its space against his thigh, worn out from the previous night's calisthenics.

"Shit. Your handwriting is shit, Ichi babe." Bobby frowned at the scrawl of blue ink on a page torn from a legal pad he kept on his coffee table. "And you could have taped this to the coffee machine. Would have found it there. Holding my cock while thinking about you made me hard. Fucking impossible to piss when my dick's pointing at my chin."

Now that he had it, Bobby was scared to open the note.

"Like I'm a goddamn little girl in middle school," he snorted, tossing the note onto his coffee table. "I'm going to brush my damned teeth, get some coffee, and *then* read it."

The brushing of teeth happened.

The coffee didn't.

He didn't even bother to pretend he was going to pour a cup. After spitting the toothpaste foam into the sink, Bobby splashed water onto his face, then headed back to the living room.

The note sat there. Mocking him. Daring him to open it up so his heart could be broken.

"Pussy," Bobby scolded himself. "Man up. So what if it's a thanks-but-no-thanks piece-of-shit letter. Not like you haven't written them before."

Still, his fingers shook as he unfolded the piece of paper. Then his chest twisted and buckled when he read what Ichiro left him. Bobby went over it once, blinked, then focused again on the words swimming across the page. Huffing in a breath, he read it out loud, not quite believing what Ichiro left behind for him to find.

"Didn't want to wake you. Yeah, you snore. Been thinking about—us. Don't think there's any going back—you and me. Last night, both of us—I think we need to talk. Figure it out between us—if there is an us." He took another breath, exhaling hard. "And then, maybe see if we can tell Cole. I'm going out on a limb here, writing this, but life's too short. Yesterday—was it only yesterday? But Cole and the gun and shit, everything—made everything so real. So yeah, I want you, Bobby. Even if it pisses my brother off. I want you. Give me a call later. I've got to call Cole and apologize for being an asshole to him."

The ink on the back of the note wasn't bleed-through. Turning the page upside down, he chuckled and shook his head, foolishly grinning at Ichiro's surprising silliness. Tossing the note onto the table, he got up to get himself a cup of coffee and stopped short when he spotted another note on the fridge, Ichiro's now familiar loopy scrawl boldly darkening the page.

"I was serious about the cat," Bobby read. "You'll need something to keep you company when I'm not around. I worry about you being lonely. And I might be a little jealous about you spending so much time with my brother. Okay, mostly I worry he'll accidentally shoot you. And then who will I fuck?"

CHAPTER NINE

HIZOKU INK wasn't quite open for business, but it was already filled with laughter and music. An odd thing for seven in the morning for most inking studios, but Ichi's client felt better in the mornings, and he'd wanted to finish up the piece before they soft-opened the studio in a week.

The metallic purple coffee machine he'd bought for the shop had already spat out two pots by the time eight rolled around, and Hizoku was vibrant and busy behind its locked doors. A dual-cello rendition of "Thunderstruck" played through the shop's sound system, and the two artists Ichiro'd hired were setting their stations up and beaming over the new tattoo machines he'd given them as welcome gifts.

Both were young, but other than an insane amount of talent to put ink to skin, they were as different as any two people could get. Quaide was a tall, muscular man with braided long black hair and snapping sienna brown eyes. Dressed in a casual tank top as he organized his area, he flashed quiet smiles at his coworker, laughing as she teased him about the quirky artwork he'd chosen for his sleeves.

He took V's teasing well. They were both even-tempered, professional, and humble about their talents, traits Ichiro demanded for his shop. V was short, buxom, and full of laughter, tossing a mane of crayon red curls about, and her smiles were bright enough to deepen the lines crinkling at the corners of her bright blue eyes. Unlike Quaide, her ink was mostly hidden under her shirt and jeans, but as she moved, a peek of a feather folding into bright flames poked out of her collar, promising an elaborate, vivid piece beneath the fabric.

They chattered, already falling into a pattern of bantering, while asking Ichi if he needed anything as he worked on his client, Karin. She'd already sat for him three times before, and now, going into the final hour, they were both impatient to see the piece done but mindful of her body's stress. He dipped his needle into the cerulean he'd mixed up to highlight the scales of the nearly completed blue dragon winging its way over her shoulder and down her arm.

"You doing okay?" He caught a bit of movement out of the corner of his eye, watching intently as Karin worked her fingers in and out as much as she could while he daubed at some runoff near her bicep. "We can stop. I've got about ten or fifteen minutes left to go, but—"

"Oh no." The spiky-haired woman grinned up at him from her lounging sprawl on his padded table. Shifting so she could see over her generous breasts, she wiggled her eyebrows at him, laughing when Ichiro snorted in return. "Hey, my rheumatoid arthritis is just going to have to suck it up. How often do I get a pretty Asian guy leaning over me and rubbing me down?"

"I'd say pretty often," he teased back, winking when her grin grew broader. "I keep this going much longer, I'm going to owe you money for your company."

"Nah, I quit doing that. I kept giving it away for free." Karin chuckled. "Let's blow this puppy out."

"If you need to stop, you let me know, okay?" He bent back over her arm, edging his rolling stool away from her crimpled fingers and twisted wrist. "I'm going to be highlighting its tail down here. Adding some white spots, so breathe through it. White hurts like a motherfucker."

"Never did understand where that phrase came from," Karin hissed through the burr of the machine as it began to tick into motion. "Go for it, Ichi. They're kind of numb anyway. So, onward, Macduff."

He took nearly the full fifteen, laying down the white through the filigree swirls he'd dappled through the dragon's tail fluke. She bore the inking in silence—relative silence anyway, if he ignored the wolf whistle she gave when Quaide nearly lost his shirt on a coat hook as he hung a piece of artwork up in the hallway to the back door.

Wrapping Karin up, Ichiro sniffed derisively at her credit card when she dug it out of her wallet. "No, last session, this one is on me. You just let me take a picture of it after it's all healed, and we'll call it even."

Half an hour later, the studio was empty, and he slumped down onto one of the couches in the waiting area, toeing off his sneakers with a grateful hiss and wiggle of his toes.

His ass still hurt a bit—stretched out and satiated from the hours he'd spent with Bobby.

Bobby.

Dawson.

"Shit, I must have been fuck-drunk to leave him that note," he groaned, rubbing his face. "We *talked* about… fuck."

His phone burbled, and Ichiro froze at the tone. Grabbing the cell before it jiggled off the couch in its enthusiasm to vibrate and sing at the same time, Ichi answered it softly, poised for rejection when Bobby's deep, silky voice slithered into his ear.

"Hey, sexy," he rasped, bringing Ichi's cock up to full attention. "Wasn't expecting you to be up."

"Oh, you have no idea how much I'm up right now." Ichiro grinned despite the clench of anticipation in his guts. "It's almost eight thirty. I've been up for hours. Did you finally roll out of bed? You were snoring when I left."

"Yeah, some hot guy fucked me senseless last night, and I had to sleep it off." Bobby paused, drawing in a breath so deep Ichiro could hear it across the line. "Kinda was hoping he'd do it again—like soon."

"Did you get my note?" He was going to lay it out there. No dancing around things for Ichiro Tokugawa, not after he'd spent his life trying to be the good boy—the perfect son—and hiding his emotions behind a mask his family forged for him. It wasn't who

Ichi wanted to be—yesterday with his brother proved that for him. "Is this us talking?"

"It can be," Bobby replied gently. "I'd rather do it in person, but yeah, everything you... wrote? I'm—" There was something deep in Bobby's voice, a conflict Ichi heard in the husky sigh and sliver of desperation in his words. "I know we joke and call it this *thing* between us, but yeah, Sunshine, last night was something I wasn't prepared for but... I want to keep. So you and me, we need to figure it out and go forward with it, okay?"

"Scares me, you know," Ichiro admitted, nearly whispering into the phone. The stereo changed over, stomping out a dance track more suited to a rave than a discussion about relationships and fears. Grabbing the remote, Ichiro turned off the music, and the studio descended into a steeped silence, leaving him alone with his thoughts and the man waiting for him to speak his mind and heart. "I don't mean being with you scared me—fuck, it was just so intense, and I felt like—hell, I just *felt*, Bobby. I've never really *felt* someone like that before. Scared the hell out of me when I woke up this morning."

"So you booked. I get it."

"Booked?" Ichi wrinkled his nose, working out the slang. "Oh, left... ran away? Well, not because I didn't want to see you. I had to finish up a piece this morning. She's got joint problems, and sometimes later in the day is too hard for her hands. I did her up a sleeve but had to do some detailing. And I also hired a couple of inkers, so they came in to set up their areas and pretty much fuck around while I worked."

"Team Ichi, then." Bobby chuckled. "So you didn't run away from me, then."

"Nope. No running. No booking. No... isn't someone being arrested called being booked?"

"I don't invent the shitty slang. I just speak it," he laughed. "What are you doing tonight? I'd ask what you were doing the rest of the day, but your brother called me to come over. I think he wants me to run down with him to Santa Monica for something but hasn't gotten around to asking. Shouldn't be long."

"Is he still tracking down that April woman? I thought—oh wait, no. She wasn't one of the ones in the apartment. He thinks she's in Santa Monica? At that nail salon?"

"Yeah, I think so," Bobby agreed. "You said you were going to call him. You do that yet?"

"I was about to." Ichi sighed when Bobby called him a liar under his breath. "Okay, I was thinking about calling him. I just don't know what the hell to say."

"How about… sorry I freaked out. I'm Japanese, and we don't own guns?" It was a flippant suggestion, but Ichi had to admit it had merit. "Look, your brother's a pretty easygoing guy. He'll forgive you for just about everything."

"Except maybe for sleeping with his best friend."

"Yeah, well, I think he'd be more pissed off about his best friend sleeping with his younger brother." Bobby snorted.

"He's known you longer than he's known me," Ichiro pointed out. "I keep coming back to that, but no one seems to listen. I love Cole, but he's my brother, not my keeper."

"He seems to think I'd just toss you out when I'm done with you, and I've got to be honest with you, Sunshine, it's been pretty much how I've dealt with everyone I've fucked in the past. Cole knows me. Probably better than I want to admit, so let's face it, I'm not exactly looking like a winning deal for you here. So last chance here… you want to walk away? Or do we keep… figuring this out?"

"I think I've already got it figured out, *anata*." Ichiro tried to steady his breathing, staring down a path he never thought he'd take in his lifetime. "You and me—we—hell, Bobby, it's stupid that we're saying no, we can't at least try to… hell, what the hell do *you* want?"

"Truthfully—" Bobby's breath hitched, and Ichiro waited a long moment before he continued. "—I was kind of sad to find you gone this morning. It… hurt something inside of me, and I haven't felt like… I wanted someone like I want you in a long damned time. So yeah, I'm kind of pissed off I'm letting *Cole* tell me I can't give it a go with you. And… I'm fucking scared I'm going to hurt you."

"Are you scared I'm going to hurt *you*?"

"Fucking terrified. But… goddamn it if I don't want to take that chance with you."

"So then this thing? We're going to do it?" Ichi's nerves wept in relief, a numbness spreading out from his chest and into his limbs. "Because yeah, I'm in. And I've—"

"Going to have some explaining to do to your brother?" Bobby interjected wryly. "Because we're not going to be stopping this anytime soon."

"If ever," he replied in the silence of his studio. "I know it's crazy. Fuck, it was just one night, you know? I mean… shit. I keep asking *why*? Why you? Why me?"

"Because it's going to piss off someone we love. And that's kind of how the universe works, Sunshine." Bobby's sardonic smirk carried over into his voice. "Bread always lands butter side down when you're really hungry, and you always fall for the person who's the worst possible choice for you. You call your brother to say you're sorry for wigging out on him. Then you and I get together tonight and talk this out some more."

"Talk," he snorted derisively. "We're going to fuck like bunnies and then complain about my brother tomorrow morning."

"Okay, yeah, that too," Bobby agreed. "But we'll talk. We have to, because, baby, we're both going places neither one of us wanted to go, and we're doing it together. So go kiss your brother's ass, and then later on tonight, I might get around to biting yours."

ICHIRO DIDN'T trust himself to drive. Not after the phone call came, summoning him to a police station in Santa Monica. It was a short, terse call but one ripe with undercurrent and longing.

Cole was in trouble—*again*.

The call was too short for a lot of details, but one thing was clear, there'd been a gun—and it was the one used to try to murder Jae.

He threw money at the cabbie. It was too much, but Ichi didn't intend on waiting for any change. Slamming the door, he hit the pavement in a run, skidding around a couple arguing in front of the station's glass doors. A large shadow emerged from a small cluster of people in the lobby, and Ichiro was yanked sideways, drawn over by Bobby's grip on his arm.

"Is he okay? He wasn't shot, right?" Ichiro gasped for breath.

There were too many people, too much noise, and other than a brief brushing of Bobby's lips over his temple when he leaned in to whisper reassurances into Ichiro's ear, they were separated quickly by the rest of Cole's support group. Jae needed shoring up, his face pale and hands shaking even as he sat down to wait out the night. Mike prowled and pounced at nearly every detective walking by, pushing to get their brother released.

And Ichiro sat, stunned and cold, sneaking stealthy brushes of Bobby's hands on his whenever they could touch.

A couple of hours later, Ichi leaned over to Jae sitting next to him and said, "I'm going to go outside and get a smoke in. If something happens, come get me, okay?"

Jae nodded, mute and simmering with anger more than fear. His fingers were white, knuckles taut from gripping the chair seat. Scarlet's soft Filipino burble soothed the frantic tenseness in Jae's body, but she couldn't take away the worry building up inside of Cole's lover.

Cole wasn't bouncing back from this one, or at least it didn't seem like it from Ichiro's point of view.

He made eye contact with Bobby as he slipped through the glass doors, and his lover nodded, either acknowledging Ichiro was leaving for a few or that he had plans to follow him out as soon as he could get away.

Locating the smokers' area wasn't difficult. It was harder to find a spot not reeking of sour tobacco and desperation. There were other people shuffling their feet near a stone, sand-filled ash bin, the bleak expressions on their faces nearly a match for Jae's—as if they'd been issued a uniform mask to wear while they waited for word.

Cupping his hand around the end of a clove cigarette, Ichi lit the *kretek* as he sat down on a curve of bars meant to be used as a bike rack. Footsteps echoed through the walkway between the main station and the nearby buildings, warning Ichiro of someone approaching. He looked up, wreathed in fragrant smoke, hoping to see Bobby but instead stared down the piercing glare of his older brother, Mike, as he cut past the other smokers and headed toward him.

"Shit," he swore when Mike barreled in, cutting off Ichi's view of the front door. "Now what?"

"Why don't you tell me now what?" Mike growled, looming over Ichiro and blocking the light with his shoulders. "What's with you and Dawson making cow eyes at each other? What the hell do you think you're doing?"

"What I'm doing is none of your business." Ichiro took another drag off his *kretek* and surprisingly didn't choke on the smoke hitting his lungs. Cole losing his shit was understandable— Cole's world was a fragile one at times, and change was sometimes bad, but Mike's outburst came as a shock. Playing it cool, he blew out a plume and cocked his chin up, meeting Mike's angry stare. "I don't even know what cow eyes means, but I'm taking a guess you're talking about us—"

"Are you fucking Dawson?" Mike pressed. "Is that what this is?"

"Why is it everyone assumes Bobby's fucking me and not the other way around?" He stubbed out the clove, disgusted he couldn't smoke it in peace. "What do you guys want? Video? I can arrange it, but really, it's none of your fucking business, Mike. What goes on between me and Bobby—"

"You deserve better than that," Mike spat. "He's not good enough for you. I know he's Cole's best friend, but—"

"Mike, I'm pretty sure my English is good enough for you to understand me." Ichiro ground his teeth in frustration. "It is *none* of your—"

"He didn't retire from the force. He was kicked off," his older brother cut him off. "Or asked to leave. That's a better way of putting it. I found out a lot of shit about Robert James Dawson and not all of it good, little brother."

"You had him investigated? Jesus, and I thought my father was controlling."

"What else was I supposed to do? Here's some now gay ex-cop Cole *doesn't* know coming into his hospital room after Cole's just lost Rick and Ben? You fucking better believe I'm going to have him looked into. Cole's my goddamned brother, and right then—shit, even now—he's vulnerable. I wasn't going to have Dawson fuck with him, so yeah, sue me. I had him looked into, and you know what? I didn't like what I found."

"You have me looked into too?" Ichi felt the blood drain out of his face when Mike's expression turned to stone. "Fucking hell, you did. Wow…." He sucked in some air, trying to cool off the heat in his chest. "Fucking… hell. Just…."

"I have to protect my family," Mike said gently, his voice still edged in steel. "Then and now. So that includes you too, Ichi. Yeah, I had you looked into. Mostly because… shit, you aren't stupid. You know how people are. I had to make sure."

"That's how it is, isn't it? Cole takes everyone at face value, and you…."

"I don't take any chances," his brother admitted. "Not with Maddy, not with Cole, and now not with you."

"You can't wrap me up like I'm some teacup you want to keep safe, Mike. That's not going to work for me. And what the hell are you thinking? Bobby's not—"

"A man died—someone he knew—and Dawson had something to do with it. The cops covered something up, but sure as shit, Dawson knows something about it. It was one of his last calls. He found the guy, and the next thing on his record was his retirement notice. That isn't odd?"

"Yeah, you're right. A friend of his dies, and he leaves the police force. That *never* happens." Ichi mocked his brother, gasping dramatically. "Oh wait, our brother Cole did that too. You think *he* had something to do with Ben and Rick dying too?"

"Don't be an asshole, Ichi."

"Learned it from you, Mike. This is bullshit."

"Dawson was doing a welfare check on this Mark guy. No one called it in. He was doing it on his own. Cops called it a suicide—

but Mark, his friend, used one of Dawson's guns to do it, and it's supposed to be a coincidence that Dawson finds him on some welfare check? Tell me how that happens."

"He loaned him the gun for something?" Ichi argued. "I don't know. It's not something I'd ask for, but lately I've been getting the feeling passing guns around here in America is like borrowing a cup of sugar. How the hell is that Bobby's fault? If there was something off about him, Cole wouldn't have him around. You just don't like how close he is to Cole. And now you're pissed off because he's close to me. Why don't you worry less about Dawson and spend more time trying to be less of an asshole. Your brothers might like you better."

"I'm not jealous of Dawson. Not by a long shot." Mike shifted, pushing into Ichiro's space, and he steeled himself not to take a step back. "By the time I got enough information on him, he and Cole were already friends. So I backed off."

"So his friend kills himself, and that's Bobby's shit to carry?" Ichi stood up, going toe to toe with Mike. "What? You're afraid he killed this Mark guy and what? Going to kill me or Cole? People die, Mike. Hell, I was reminded of that—shit, *yesterday*? Bobby probably had nothing to do with it. Christ, he's in there... being a damned good friend to our fucked-in-the-head brother, and you're out here giving me shit because I'm starting something with him?"

"I don't want you with—"

"You're not going to get what you want. Not always, Mike. Maybe Cole puts up with your bullshit, but I'm not. If I want to screw Bobby Dawson on the damned front desk of that police station, I'm going to. So unless you can show me he killed his friend Mark, you need to shut the hell up and mind your own business."

"Yeah see, babe, your brother's right." Bobby's shadow stretched over them, dousing the wobbly orange light coming from a flickering sconce on the main building. "I did kill Mark. Sure as shit might have put the gun to his head and pulled the fucking trigger."

CHAPTER TEN

"NOT HOW I wanted to have this conversation, Ichi, but shit, if you want it now, I can do it." Bobby shoved his hands into his jeans, rocking back on his heels. Ichiro was hard to read; inscrutable wasn't even on the ticket. Stone-cold was a nearer description, although granite ready to be carved into the faces of four presidents with some left over for a kitchen counter came to mind.

"If you want to talk about anything, I'll listen," Ichi replied softly. "But not with *him* here. Like I keep saying, it's none of his business what goes on between the two of us."

"You want to get lost, Mike?" Bobby stared down at Cole's older brother. "This is between me and Ichi."

"I'm not...."

Bobby had to give Mike credit. Shorter and about fifty pounds under, Cole's older brother was determined to hold his own. He knew Mike was a muscular block of strength under his suit and tie, but the man ran a security firm—armed with high-tech weapons and exit strategies. Bobby would lay his hardscrabble, cop's kid street upbringing against Mike's polished fisticuffs any day.

And if today was that day, he was more than willing to step in.

Ichiro might have had something to say about him tearing off Mike's head, but from the disgruntled scowl on his lover's face, Bobby thought he had a pretty good shot at having help burying Mike's body.

"Mike, go." Ichiro's tone was flat, and his eyes burned as they raked over his older brother's face. "Send someone out if Cole gets loose and we're still out here, please."

"Fine," Mike ground out. He took a step toward the station, shoving his shoulder up against Bobby's. Pressing into Bobby's side, he growled softly, "You fucking hurt my brother—either one of them—and there won't be a big enough piece of you left for anyone to find. You got that, Dawson?"

"And here I thought you loved me," Bobby shot back.

"Oh, I like you well enough," Mike replied as he walked off. "That's why you'll be dead when I chop you into pieces."

A blur of white noise settled on them, a layer of humming tires on cooling asphalt and murmuring chatter from people gathering at the edges of the building. Ichiro tapped his foot on the ground, a slow beat of time as he waited for Bobby to begin speaking.

He needed to say something.

Anything.

But Bobby was frozen in the tangles of a convoluted past, unable to find the end of a thread to take him back out of the labyrinth.

"I—fuck, this is just not where I wanted to talk about this," he grumbled softly. "Your damned brother—"

"Both of them, really." Ichi grinned suddenly. "Cole's off assaulting hobos, and Mike's shoving his pointy nose into everything, but what he needs to be taking care of—is getting Cole out. Look, Mike's the one who forced this on you, and right now, can I be honest?"

"Always, Sunshine."

"I'm not in a headspace to talk about this Mark guy. I'm not sure if you are either." He reached out, tangling his fingers into Bobby's. "Look, you want time? I can give you time."

"I've got to at least tell you I didn't kill Mark." Glancing at the building, Bobby's anger simmered back up. "Fucking Mike. He just layered that in, didn't he?"

"Yeah, he's a master at the subtle dig. If I didn't know better, I'd say he was my father's son."

"Well, their dad's no fucking treat either." Bobby tightened his fingers around Ichi's. "Mark… shit, it's complicated."

"Like I said, we can uncomplicate it later, okay?"

"I don't want it to... hang over us," he admitted softly. "Mark—fuck, Mark."

"There's a coffee shop across the way." Ichi nodded toward the street. "We can go there if you want. If you think we've got enough time. I don't know how long it takes to spring someone out of jail. Most places I've been it's either really easy and quick, or there's no hope you'll ever see them again. No clue about America."

"Well, with your brother, God only knows." Bobby glanced over his shoulder. The place was quiet, and with each encroaching second, the evening darkened, lessening their chances of springing Cole. Anyone who had any say on the matter would either be gone or hard to hunt down, no matter how hard Mike pulled on his strings. They'd probably have time for Bobby to tell his entire life story.

He just didn't know if he could handle it if Ichiro walked out on him after hearing it.

BOBBY WAS nervous.

It didn't take a psychic to divine he had a lot on his mind, and Ichiro wasn't sure if Bobby was even willing to listen to him when he said it would be okay.

Because as far as Ichi was concerned, whatever Bobby did that pissed Mike off, the ex-cop was probably beating himself up for it, and Mike tossing in his two cents was about as good as pissing on a burning bush in the middle of a Southern Californian firestorm.

The coffee shop was a haven of bearded men and sloppily dressed woman smelling faintly of florals and incense. A few stalwart trousers-and-polo-shirt wearers shored up a long bar-style top against one wall, huddling over their recycled paper coffee cups and muttering about the unwashed masses around them.

Surprisingly, one of the shop's niches boasted a beat-up red velour love seat, and Ichiro claimed it, dragging a low table over so they had something to set their drinks on. His lover arrived as Ichi plopped into a corner of the sofa, its springs squeaking loudly when he moved about to get comfortable.

"Here. Got you a misto with soy milk." From the glum look on Bobby's face, Ichi guessed he'd gotten Ichi a coffee while Bobby went for the arsenic and old lace special. "Check your cup for floaters. This place is worse than the Hairy Hippie across the street from Cole's."

"Scarlet's going to text me if he gets out so we can head back over." Ichi left his phone on the table, then took the coffee from Bobby. "You don't owe me anything. Just because Mike—"

"Can you just let me get through it?" Bobby sat down on the edge of the sofa's seat, rubbing at his eyes with his free hand. The coffee cup shook slightly in his grip as he set it down, and Ichiro patted the small of his back. "God, don't be nice. Wait until you decide whether or not you want to walk out on this, okay?"

"What can you say that I don't—" The beleaguered look on Bobby's face put Ichiro's shoulders back. "Shit, I don't think you killed that guy."

"Might as well have," Bobby remarked harshly, wringing his fingers around his wristwatch. "Cole's not... look, your brother's got a good heart, and unlike Mike, he hardly ever crosses the line. So when he told you to steer clear of me, he was doing you a solid. I'm not good with... fidelity, Ichi. Fuck, I haven't been faithful to anyone in my entire life—including myself."

"Dawson—"

"Let me finish, then... let's see, okay?"

"Okay." Ichi turned sideways on the couch, facing Bobby as much as he could on the cramped seat. "Go ahead."

"I was married... before." He paused long enough to take a sip out of his coffee, wincing at its taste. "God that's strong."

"Less coffee, more talking." Ichi waved his hand forward. "Complain about that later. You were married. Did you love her? Trying things out? What?"

"I got her pregnant," he admitted softly. "It was stupid to sleep with her and even dumber to marry her, but that's what guys did back then. You *married* when you knocked someone up. None of this baby daddy shit. People don't realize how fucking much marriage ties you up, I mean legally. You don't get married, and it's a damned fight for every little thing if one of you dies, especially if there's a kid. Insurance—hell, everything. I get why everyone wants the right to marry. You have to if you want your family taken care of."

"No, I get that." His coffee was getting cold, and it smeared a film over his tongue when Ichi sipped at it. "So you married her. And you've got a kid. How old? Do you have weekends with him?"

"Ichi, I've got a kid your age. Jamie's—James—is twenty-seven. And fuck, he hasn't wanted to see me in years." Bobby's hands were over his face again, scouring away either the tired or the shame he was holding in them. "Jesus, I married her—but I wasn't faithful. Fuck, I didn't even try. I screwed her—Marsha—because I was trying to prove I wasn't gay. Hell, Ichi, I fucked any chick who looked my way back then, and when it got too damned much of a lie to choke on, I went back to fucking guys."

"So that's what you're worried about? Fidelity?"

"Sunshine, if I'd been faithful, maybe Mark would be alive right now," he ground out. "And you and I wouldn't be having this conversation."

MARK. SHIT, he'd buried Mark years ago. Even before he'd found Mark slumped over a ratty couch with his brains splattered all over a wall in a cheap, knocked-together condo in WeHo, he'd buried Mark in his memory.

He'd buried Mark the day he'd come home to find Marsha choking on her tears and anger as she waved pictures they'd taken on a weekend trip down to Mexico. A few days filled with sex, tequila, and tight asses, documented all in living color.

Cum-splashed, suntanned living color.

The last time he'd seen those pictures, they'd been in Mark's hot little hands. Hands he'd let grab his dick and work him off while they'd joined the mile-high club coming back from Cabo.

Right before Mark told him he'd never come out of the closet—never join in out in the open where they could have a real life instead of sneaking off behind closed doors.

He'd been so fucking willing to crack his life apart and bleed for Mark.

"Bobby, you don't talk, I don't understand," Ichi prompted, nudging his knee with his knuckles. "So talk. Or wait. I'm okay with it."

"Yeah, I'm... fuck." He exhaled the heat building up in his lungs. "Where the hell to start?"

"How about anywhere I wasn't there? Good place."

"You can be an asshole, you know that, Sunshine?" He eyed Ichiro, who responded by flashing back a cheeky grin.

"I was aiming for dick, but asshole seems to be okay too."

"Yeah, good job, then." His coffee'd cooled too quickly for his liking, but he sipped at it anyway. "About fifteen—shit no, sixteen years ago—I'd hooked up with Mark at a club down in WeHo. I liked him—a lot. I'd been fucking around behind Marsha's back since... hell, since we'd said I do."

"You weren't out, though, right?"

"Hell no." He chuckled, trying to imagine the captain who'd been in charge of him dealing with an out cop. "Back then, that kind of shit could have gotten you shot in a back alley all accidentally like. You kept your mouth shut. Safer and easier that way."

"They must not have been ready for Cole." Ichi laughed under a smirk.

"Babe, I don't think anyone's ready for Cole, least of all LAPD," he said, shaking his head.

"So Mark?"

"Yeah, Mark. He wasn't out either. I'd seen him before. He was a resident down at one of the big hospitals. I'd seen him there. A lot. I can't tell you how many times I'd had to drag a bum choking on his own vomit to the ER, and there was Dr. Tight Ass, giving me a hard time for not treating them like they were glass unicorns." He pulled up his shirtsleeve to point out half-moon blemishes under his skin. "I've been bit so many fucking times by those assholes, I look like a giant squid got hold of me and tried to *hentai* me. Wait, did I use that word right?"

"Perfectly," Ichi assured him. "Katsushika Hokusai's *tako to ama.*"

"Some guy wrote about squid tacos?"

"I'll explain… forget about the *tako*. So you and Mark didn't get along?"

"Nah, he was always riding my ass about police brutality. Fucker didn't even know me and accused me of beating up some guy I'd found down on the tracks." He shook his head, recalling Mark getting up into his face and shouting him down. "We went at it and… got to be honest, Sunshine, he was hot. Fighting with him turned me the fuck on, so as soon as I got off my shift, I headed down to one of the places I went to get some, and there he was."

"And you guys hit it off?"

"Hell no, we were both pissed off at each other, so I fucked him up against a wall in the back room." Bobby snorted when Ichi shook his head. "He wanted it. I wanted it. It just sort of happened. Then… it kept happening until, well, shit… I was digging through downtown looking for assholes I could take in just to see him."

"Did the two of you end badly?" Ichi took Bobby's cup away from him and set it down on a table. His hands suddenly felt too empty, and Bobby rubbed his palms on his jeans. "How did you get from angry sex to…?"

"Him shooting himself a decade later?" He puffed out his cheeks, staring off into the evening as the traffic lights blinked red and green through the coffee shop's tinted windows. "We were together for about a year. Maybe a little bit more, but you know, I… fuck. I was stupid. I thought… I thought he wanted the same things I wanted.

"See, Sunshine, I was sick of the fucking lies by that time. I was lying to everyone. Marsha, him… myself. I told my wife I was working late when I was fucking Mark, and I told Mark I had things to do with my kid when I was home trying to convince myself the whole gay thing wasn't real." Bobby closed his eyes briefly, then continued slowly. "Wife didn't have any complaints, but shit, not like we... I wanted out. I wanted to... fucking breathe. You know?"

"So what happened? With all of it? Did Marsha find out?"

"Worse than found out. Mark and I went down to Mexico with a couple of friends to some gay resort. And it wasn't like... we hadn't fucked other people before, but he acted like it was an all you can eat for a dollar ninety-five buffet. I didn't want that. Shit, I even told him beforehand, I'd just wanted to hang out and do... tourist things."

"What did he say when you told him that?"

"Actually, I told him I wanted it to just be the two of us. From that point on. No more clubbing. No more... any of that shit. I brought it up, and he looked at me like I was crazy."

"He didn't understand you wanted just the two of you guys and no one else?" Ichi cocked his head. "What's wrong with that?"

"Yeah, apparently it was worse because I told him I wanted to find a place and move in with him." He could barely get the words out. It seemed like a lifetime ago, but the punch in his chest was just as hollow... just as hard. "I told him I wanted to split from Marsha. Just... fuck, end that whole life I'd being lying in and shake it off. You know what he told me?"

"I'm going to guess I'm not going to like it," Ichiro murmured, sliding in closer.

"He said the only reason he was fucking me was because I was married. Because he *knew* I wasn't going to want something more than what we had. Hell, Ichi, I hadn't slept with Marsha for two months before that trip, and it took everything I fucking had to get that out of me." He rubbed at his chest where the burn began to spread up from his stomach and into his heart. "He jacked me off on the plane ride back and then said it was over. Last time I saw him... before that night... was at the airport as he got into a cab. Then I went home and acted like nothing happened.

"Until Mark decided to drop on by the house a couple of days later and hand over photos people took of us in Mexico." It was still a bitter pill to swallow. The foolishness he'd dreamed up of a happy-ever-after between two men stuck somewhere under his breastbone, refusing to be dislodged by common sense or self-loathing. "She lost her shit. And I can't blame her for it. I'd have lost my shit if I were her. Man, we had a fight. I let her… shit, she threw everything she could lay her hands on at me. Fucking waffle iron cut open my head, but I never touched her. Not once. And when the cops showed up, I stood there and let them handcuff me while they talked it out with her."

"Wait, you were bleeding, and they handcuffed you?"

"Yeah, you can go on about gender equality, but first thing cops are going to do is grab the guy and put him down." The apologetic murmurs he'd gotten from the uniform stung his pride a bit, but he'd been cooperative. "Someone calls in a domestic, and they're going to go for the guy first. Standard. And hell, a lot of cops do shit to their families. We're not the best kind of partners for that. Shit, they did that to Cole, remember?"

"Yeah, I remember. Did she out you? To everyone there?" Ichi frowned, creasing his brows together. "What… hell, I don't even know what to say."

"Say she was right, and I fucked her over," Bobby replied softly. "Because it's the truth. She didn't say shit to the cops about the pictures. Just that she'd caught me cheating and was mad, but she didn't tell them it was with a guy. They asked me if I wanted to press charges, and I said no. Everyone shook hands, they left, and she told me to get the fuck out of my house. That's when I found out Mark'd come over in person to throw our shit into her face, then didn't even have the balls to stick around and face me. A week later, I got served, and part of the divorce settlement was me getting tested. Didn't blame her for that either."

"What about your son? Jamie?"

"Marsha's a good mom. I don't have any complaints about how she raised him. She always takes care of him first. She'd sent him to a friend's house for a sleepover, but I think he knew. Fuck, how couldn't he have known?" The tension building up along his shoulders was intense, and Bobby rolled them back, trying to work them loose. "She remarried a couple of years later. Shit, Jamie was… sixteen then? Barry—the guy she hooked up with—wanted to adopt him, but she told him no. Actually, she said hell no, because he's my kid. We've done okay by Jamie."

"So she's all right with you... being gay now? What about your son? Is he?"

"Things between me and Jamie weren't always good. I stayed in the closet until... well, you know when, but he.... Jamie doesn't know. It's better now, but he's got a lot of shit on his plate that I dished up. I never told him about me being gay." Bobby grimaced. "I've got an uncle... the one I told you about in assisted living. He's... old-school cop. Hell, I haven't told him either. I think he'd shoot me if he ever found out."

"So how... why did he...? Mark...." Ichiro got hung up on his words, his eyes hooded in the shadows flung down from the hanging lamp above them. "So why did he do it? And how did he get your gun?"

"I didn't know why he did it until he called me at the station that day. The gun was one I'd given to him as a gift." He grinned at Ichiro's wrinkled nose. "Don't give me that look. Cops... hell, people give each other guns all the time. I'd taken him out to the range—"

"Not going to happen with you and me," Ichiro cut in. "Just saying."

"I figured that. I keep them locked up tight. You won't even see them." Bobby crossed his chest with his index finger. "Mark worked in a shithole. I felt better knowing he at least could handle himself. There are a lot of crazies out there, and some of them would think because he was a doctor, he'd be carrying drugs or something. So... a gun."

"Scary crazy," Ichi muttered. "So it was what? Over ten years later, and then he calls you to say what? Sorry?"

"He wanted me to... I don't know what he wanted. The note he left was... a bit crazy. He wasn't a happy person inside, Sunshine. And you know I'm not one of those tree-huggers who's going to say we need to sit around the campfire and talk about our feelings, but... he was *sick* inside."

The blood was old by the time he walked in. The message from Mark was several hours old by the time he'd gotten around to hearing it, and by the time he'd broken in through the fragile door to the address Mark'd left him, his ex-lover was a feast of maggots and gore.

"Did he blame you for something?" Ichiro shook his head. "He couldn't have. You didn't do shit to him. He's the one who fucked with your life."

"*I* was the one who fucked with my life," Bobby corrected gently. "He just pushed me out into the open with it. And still, I fucking hid who I was. Everyone thought I was some asshole prick who slept around on Marsha—but giving me high fives for having a piece of ass on the side. No one knew the piece of ass had a dick on it. Would have been different, then."

"Did his note tell you why he… killed himself?"

"He was tired. The note was… rambling. Talked a lot about how he tried to fuck me out of his brain but couldn't. Like he hated loving me. Didn't want to love me. Hell, I don't think he even knew what that meant, but I'd been… a normal he'd pissed away." Bobby spread his fingers, working out a cramp in his hands. "I think he was done hiding too, but he couldn't see a way out. I think Mark *liked* the secrets. He gossiped and hid things. It was… just a part of who he was. Thing is, he *hated* being gay. Even as he was sucking some guy's dick, he hated it. I wanted him to have a life with me, and he looked at it like it was a prison sentence.

"Biggest fear I had before I walked through that door was someone on the force finding out I was gay," he whispered, his heart pounding. "When I walked out of that place, my biggest fear was that someday, that was going to be me in there."

"So you handed your badge in? Why not stay? You liked being a cop."

"I liked being the cop I was. I needed… space? Time?" He struggled to recall why quitting the force had been a good idea at the time, but then the sense of relief when he'd clocked out for the final time hit him. "I own a couple of businesses—JoJo's does well, and there's a few sandwich shops that pretty much run themselves. I've got a pension and money my folks left me. It's enough for me to take care of my Uncle James and the building—the loft's paid for.

And if Cole keeps getting me shot up, I'll be able to claim disability soon. I like being... my own man. Having the time to do things I want. No regrets on that."

Ichiro sighed and leaned back into the couch, tapping his fingers on his thighs. "So that's why Mike thinks you're a shitty guy? Because some asshole killed himself?"

"He thinks I'm a shitty guy because I have a zero track record of being a good boyfriend," Bobby pointed out, then grinned at Ichi's derisive snort. "He's not wrong, Sunshine. I suck at it, but I'm willing to try."

"All I can ask. Hell, that's all I want." Ichi looked like he was about to say more when his phone buzzed a path across the table. Snatching it up before it fell off, he frowned. "Sure, *now* my brother's ready to get out of jail. Scarlet says we have about fifteen to twenty minutes. Jae's going to go outside and smoke, so we can go meet him there."

"So then, what do you want to do? Here. Us." His stomach twisted up, reminding Bobby he'd only filled his gut with coffee and regret over the past twelve hours, and it was coming back to haunt him. "Now's a good time to walk away, Ichi. Before it goes any deeper between us."

"Yeah, you're not getting rid of me that easy, Dawson," Ichiro said, standing up. "Only thing you and I are going to do is... well shit, tell Cole. Because I'm not going to sneak around behind his back. Shit, I don't owe him any explanation and neither do you. We're adults. You and I—we work on some level, and hell, it either goes well or falls apart, but that's for us to decide. Not anyone else."

"Okay," Bobby agreed, a tingling excitement eating away at his anxiety like a firestorm through dry brush. He'd been holding his breath... hell, his heartbeat, until he was sure Ichiro was crossing over the line with him, and now, with the way clear between them, he was nearly giddy with relief. "Just... let me tell him. I've known him longer than you have, and to be honest, I've got a way with words. I can break it to him gently. Just wait and see. He won't even blink."

CHAPTER ELEVEN

IT WAS a farmers' market like any collective sprawl of produce, baked goods, and junk hawkers. The Los Angeles sun was out in a halfhearted attempt to bake its victims off the broad stretch of black asphalt and concrete pads. At some point, a building of some sort squatted on the lower block of downtown LA, tucked into Little Tokyo's armpit, a forgotten cement skin tag grown heavy with neglect. Either fallen to blight or a failed redevelopment, there was little to remind anyone about what once stood stretched out between two uneven parking lots, only its mottled concrete foundation, its surface cracked and speckled with determined clumps of weeds.

Caught in a no-man's-land of warehouses and a depressed manufacturing market, the lot lay empty most days until the weekend—when the city declared it was open season on wallets and threw the gates open to local farmers, snotty hipsters hoping to fund their vinyl collection by selling off junk, and vendors looking to fleece people with cheap salad spinners and knock-off purses.

The air was filled with voices and the smell of cooking food. A line of food trucks took up residence against the far end of the lot, and the crackle of grilling meat tempted Bobby as his stomach groaned at the idea of adding another bite of food on top of the breakfast they had at a diner near his loft.

A very typical farmer's market, one Bobby might have strolled through countless times before. With one exception.

This time, he was holding Ichiro's hand.

And he didn't feel like letting go.

"Hard to believe this thing with Sheila's done." Ichi stopped to look down at a glass case filled with crudely cast silver rings. "It's weird to imagine Cole's caught his white whale. That's the one, right? Moby Dick?"

"Yeah about the whale but fucking God no about that crap you're holding in your hand. That shit will rot your wrist off." He snorted in disbelief as Ichi held up a bracelet made up of grinning metallic skulls. "I find it kind of hard to believe your damned brother didn't get plugged full of holes. Who the fuck but Cole goes to scope out a cheap motel and have OK Corral break out?"

"You guys are the ones who told me that's how his life is." Ichiro handed money over for the bracelet without haggling.

"You could have gotten that for at least a couple of bucks less if you'd wanted."

"Yeah, but I didn't want to waste the time." Ichi squeezed his hand. "Not when I could be walking around with you."

"Smarmy." Ichi unmanned him. He flung out small drops of affection, more invasive than any water torture Bobby could imagine.

"What does that mean?" The confusion in his lover's eyes made Bobby smile. "That's an old word, huh? Like saimin to ramen."

"Yeah, I guess. Means… hell, it means smarmy. We'll look it up when we get home." His heart jumped at the word, tightening when he realized Ichiro practically had moved in, and he'd welcomed it.

Cleaning out a drawer or two led to actually having another dresser delivered to the loft, identical to the square black one he'd purchased a year ago. His apartment smelled different—looked different—with complex smells coming from the kitchen and the sudden appearance of tattoo machine parts Ichi left on a small drafting table he'd maneuvered up from Bobby's storage space in the downstairs garage.

They'd been inseparable since Cole's arrest, living in one another's pockets in an effortless flow of time and space. The peace he felt inside left Bobby wondering when it was all going to end—and how badly. And whether or not he'd survive it.

Still, Ichi crawled into bed with him every night, and sometimes they even woke up together, the gurgle of the coffeemaker pulling them both out of sleep. They had sex nearly every morning—slow blowjobs and rubbing—and Bobby's cock was now primed to get hard at the smell of roasted beans, a hazard every time he walked into a coffee shop to get a fix.

"We have to tell him. Don't we?" Ichi murmured. "My stupid brother. The other one already knows, and Mike's only got so much patience."

"Not his shit to share. If I found out he wore frilly panties, I'd keep that shit to myself. Not my business."

"Mike's not good on secrets in the family—whether they are his or not." It didn't need pointing out. In the days since Mike'd tracked Ichi down outside of the police station, he'd given Bobby the evil eye nearly every time they'd seen one another. "Now that Sheila's in jail, I think we should tell Cole and get him used to the— he's going to lose his shit, isn't he? Maybe it's too soon? Shit, I hate hiding… this. I just want him to know and get it over with."

"Dude, it's been… what? How many days?" Bobby peered over his sunglasses at Ichiro. "We've got to talk to him. He'll catch on. He's not stupid."

"He ran into a gunfight."

"The shooting happened after he got a hold of Sheila."

"Not that one. The one before that. The one I was in." Ichi sighed. "Dawson, it's pretty bad when I have to clarify which one of Cole's gunfights I'm talking about. Think he can go a week without getting shot at? Why doesn't he ever get knifed? Or maybe just spat at? Hell, I'd settle for someone throwing a cup of hot tea in his face."

"Nah, he's too pretty. He'd scar, and that'll piss Jae off."

It was like summoning Satan with a handful of glitter and a cup of goat blood. A too familiar bob of black hair popped through the crowd, and Bobby's face froze into a tight smile. Jae spotted him nearly immediately, and Bobby only had time to shove Ichi between the pavilions, nearly decapitating himself on a clothesline filled with tie-dyed caftans in an attempt to reach Jae first.

He didn't like the sound of Ichi's *oomph* or the rattle of pans when he hit, but if there was one thing Bobby did know, it was Jae's willingness to bare all to his lover, a newly found honesty that, while cementing the bond between him and Cole, put Bobby in a precarious spot.

Especially since they'd not even agreed on *when* they were going to tell Cole they'd hooked up.

Jae's beauty was breathtaking, nearly ethereal in some ways, with a healthy dose of sin. He couldn't help comparing Jae to Ichiro, deciding he preferred the inker's hardscrabble look and cocky, wicked mouth to Jae's porcelain beauty. Still, he wasn't hard to look at, and his smile was carefree, with no sign of the troubles he'd been through. Accompanied by his gender-bending best friend, Scarlet, they were a pretty sight for a sunny day, a pair of swans gliding through an ocean of plastic and debris.

"Hey, you two." He sounded too cheerful, and the grin he plastered on his face was nearly Cheshire in width. Toning it down a bit, Bobby leaned over and kissed Scarlet on the cheek, winking at Jae's *nuna* when she tousled his hair. "Hello, gorgeous. Does God know you're taking a day off? And where'd you stash your wings?"

"Oh, you are bad. And look at how long this is! Makes you look younger." She purred and took another kiss, pushing at Bobby's chest when he blew a raspberry on her neck. "*Aish*, stop that. You'll leave a mark, and then *hyung* will have to kill you."

"He'd make me suffer first," Bobby teased. He let Jae give him a quick hug, thumping his back and surprised to feel the muscle there. "Doing yoga still? You feel... bigger."

"Maybe toned?" Jae cocked his head slightly, adjusting his sunglasses. "A little bit of muscle, but I think that's mostly eating Cole's cooking for a few months. I had to work off the fat."

"He does like his bacon, grease, and butter." There was more rattling of pans, and a woman's voice cut through the crowd's noise, a rapid-fire Mexican glut asking someone if he was all right. Bobby raised his voice, hoping to drown out Ichiro's response if he spoke up. "What are you two doing here?"

"Getting things for the barbeque. You're coming, right? Cole will want you there. He's visiting Sheila today. I don't know what he thinks he's going to get out of her, but... you know him." Jae held up a few plastic bags, rattling them playfully. "I was going to do a vegetarian grill, but I think Cole would kill me. We're stopping to get some steaks on the way home."

"Steaks. Good," Bobby murmured with a short nod. He was resisting the urge to glance over his shoulder to see if Ichi was okay. "Need me to bring anything? Beer? Cake? Antacids?"

"Anything you want. We always end up with more food than people, so maybe some of those take-out trays you brought last time so we can pack up the leftovers." Wrinkling his nose, Jae batted at a gnat trying to land on his face. "See you in an hour?"

"An hour sounds great. I can get some stuff together by then." He was about to say more when Jae piled his bags into Scarlet's hands.

"Wait here. There's the cheese booth. I want to get some of that brie for Maddy. She's got cravings." Jae shook his head. "God, Mike as a dad."

"Cole as an uncle." Scarlet's husky laugh teased Bobby's ear. "That poor baby is going to learn how to play video games before it can walk."

"And swear in about seventeen languages." Bobby was talking to Jae's back. He lost the man in about a second into the crowd. Turning to Scarlet, he shrugged. "Damn, he's quick."

"Not as quick as you," she purred, tucking a stray lock of hair behind her ear. "You and Ichiro... I think I like that."

"Shit." Bobby bit back another curse, finally looking behind him. His lover was nowhere to be seen, and when he turned around to face Scarlet, he saw a cunning grin slide up over her face. "Oh, fuck me."

"I would, but ah, I've found my heart, no?" She tapped at his cheek with a polished nail. "I wasn't sure it was him until you panicked. Have you told Cole?"

"Are you kidding? You'd have seen a mushroom cloud or a crater in the middle of Los Angeles if I had." He sighed, then rubbed at his face. "I need to. I want to. I don't like hiding this kind of shit. It was one thing when it was… casual, but it got serious—real fast."

"It's nice." She trailed her finger down Bobby's throat and over to his chest. "I could tell you the heart wants who it wants, but—he's your best friend. Do you think you will be asking him to choose between the two of you?"

"No… yes," Bobby admitted. "I don't want that. Fuck, I don't want Ichi to be in that position either. It's… complicated."

"Well, he'll be mad at you." Scarlet pursed her mouth, a crimson moue in her tanned face. "But he'll get over it. He loves you both too much. Cole needs to learn he's not the center of the universe—although I don't think he believes that."

"No, that's Jae." They shared a quick smile; then Bobby sobered up. "Yeah, I'm going to tell him today. I'll get him away from the others and talk to him. He won't kill me if there's people around."

"Just do it quickly," she advised gently. "Because neither one of you should be hiding. Not from Cole."

"No, not from Cole," he agreed. "But he's not the only one I'm hiding Ichi from. He's just the only one I can tell."

IN RETROSPECT, Bobby realized he should have perhaps rehearsed what he was going to say to Cole, but instead his dick and mouth appeared to have had a discussion on the matter, leaving his brain out of the conversation. There was an eternity of horror, regret, and sheer outrage firing up sparks in his skull when his tongue went rogue, and he made quite possibly the biggest mistake he'd ever made in his life since he'd married Marsha and promised her a forever he couldn't deliver.

"There's no easy way to tell you this, Princess, but I'm fucking your brother, Ichi."

He couldn't have stopped the words even if he tried. They spilled out like a tightly held release, and he'd stuck his brain in some glory hole to be sucked off by a whirlpool. The vacuum between his nervousness and Cole's proximity needed to be filled, and his stupid tongue seemed more than willing to spew out the worst thing he could have said.

Then came the silence.

The cold, hard silence, and a rigid chill slammed down over Cole's face.

It was surprising to find what he could hear in the spaces between friendship and condemnation. The babble of the two women sitting across the street, chatting about the obese basset hound snoring between them. The buzz of a bee as it sucked on flowers spilling out of hanging pots set under the porch eaves was nearly as loud as his breathing, perhaps even louder, because Bobby's vision was beginning to speckle, and he had to gasp in some air to shoo off the black spots beginning to float across his eyes.

"You're fucking my brother," Cole repeated flatly. "*Ichiro*."

"Well, it sure as shit wouldn't be Mike." His brain apparently continued to not only be on vacation but apparently had thrown in the towel and jumped off a high bridge in despair. The remaining bits of his sanity scrambled to smooth things over, but he didn't have much hope. Especially since the best thing he could come up with after that gem was, "'Cause you know… he's married. And straight. But mostly married."

"Didn't think that would stop you. The married part. But okay, we'll agree not Mike." The cold arced over to glacial, and Cole's warm hazel eyes went flat and bottle green. He seemed to struggle to find something to say, finally deciding on the obvious. "How long? You and him? How long have you been…? *Shit.*"

"A while." Bobby tried counting back the days since he'd first kissed Ichiro, if that counted. "But I'm not doing this right, Cole. Let me—"

"Shut up right now," Cole snarled, pressing into his personal space.

Bobby took a step back, suddenly unsure of the fury in Cole's expression. The happy-go-lucky charmer he'd teased and prodded was gone, replaced by a tangle of emotions and barely held-in anger.

"Look, this is between—" He held his palms up when he noticed Cole's hands clenching and unclenching at his sides. "We didn't do this to hurt you. Shit, Princess, I swear to God, this isn't even about you. I—"

"You want to talk?" Cole shoved at him, smacking the flats of his hands against Bobby's chest. The force of the blow staggered Bobby back, and he struck the porch rail, its wide, flat top digging into the small of his back. "What the fuck are you thinking, Bobby?"

His brain finally kicked in. Unfortunately it joined the battle in full retaliation mode, and suddenly Bobby didn't care if Cole was his best friend or even how often he'd pulled the man's ass out of the fire—so many fires. He edged Cole back, getting up into his friend's face to push him back and get some air between them.

"I was thinking maybe I could get some happiness out of it. Hell, maybe even make Ichi happy too," he snapped back. "Not everything is about you, Princess."

"No, it's about Ichi. Fuck, it's even about you!" Cole countered, his breath hot on Bobby's face.

"What? I'm not good enough for your baby brother? Is that it? I'm sure as fuck good enough to be your best friend." He was going to the mat with this, disregarding everything he'd built up in their friendship. "Or do you think I just want a piece of your ass too and am just waiting for the chance to get to it?"

Suddenly Ichi seemed worth losing Cole over, and as much as a trembling fear whispered the doom of his brotherhood with Cole, Bobby threw in with a wild hope Cole wouldn't abandon him when it was all said and done.

Providing his temper didn't leave the entire relationship in ashes at his feet.

"Fuck, you're not good enough for *you*," Cole spat back. "Goddamn it, Bobby. You think I wanted you away from Ichi because you're a fucking whore? Because I think you'd fuck him and then dump him? Yeah, I do… and because doing that would be the worst fucking thing you've ever done in your damned life. You'd fuck up a good thing because you don't think men can be together… be in love."

"I don't—"

"Over the past few weeks, every time I even fucking talk about two guys hooking up, you piss on it like it's on fire. And all this time, you've been fooling around with my younger brother?" Cole stabbed a finger into Bobby's chest. "You don't think that's a problem? For either of you?"

"Look, I—"

"You shit on my relationship with Jae. Hell, from the beginning when I first saw him, you were the first one to tell me not to get attached." Cole held his hand up when Bobby tried to say something. "Yeah, you're a great friend, but you're a shitty boyfriend, Bobby, and you *like* being a shitty boyfriend. You take pride in it."

"It's different," he protested. "Fuck, yeah I've been an asshole about it lately because… fuck, I didn't… we weren't ready to tell everyone we were… I don't have a word for what it was. What it is."

"Yeah, see, that's another problem. You aren't honest with what you do with your life. Bobby, your own kid doesn't know you're gay. And you're okay with that." Cole snorted. "I'm not. I'm not fucking okay with you lying to everyone outside of this little circle we've got. Yeah, it's your business. I get that. I get that no one should be out if they don't want to, but fuck, what about when you sit down for dinner and you've got to explain who the pretty Japanese guy is to your family? Or are you going to hide him in the closet with your shoes?"

"I haven't told Jamie because it—" He should have told Jamie. If he owed his son one thing, it was the truth. Marsha hadn't spilled the beans. For all the crap he'd shoveled her way, she'd kept their son out of it, leaving Bobby to clean up his own mess. A mess he'd left to stagnate and rot instead of facing it head on. "Okay, yeah. I should tell Jamie. I'll admit to having to man up to that."

"I get you not telling your uncle. Hell, he still calls blacks the *N* word to their face. I'm surprised someone there hasn't injected him with antifreeze yet," Cole growled. "But Ichi… he deserves to be loved out in the open. His father shoved him down enough in his life—enough for five lives—and here you come along. You think I'd want him living in the shadows because you can't grow big enough balls to be honest with the family you've got?"

"Shoving Ichi down... not going to happen," he snapped back. "You think I don't know what he's given up just to be... hell, just to be who he wants to be?"

"The worst of it, Bobby? You're a fucking coward. You're scared to admit you want to be loved. Or have someone in your life. You'd rather burn it all to hell than commit to having someone in your life, and that's a crappy way to live," his friend ground out. "Shit, you're going to screw yourself up more than Ichiro, and then fucking what? Where the hell are you going to be when you break your own goddamned heart?"

There was more silence—this time, filled with stunned breathing. The women were still talking about the dog—as if the hound was the most interesting fucking thing in the world—and not even noticing Bobby's world shattering in front of them. Another buzz took over for the bee, and oddly enough, it had a slight Korean hint to it. Turning, Bobby saw Jae taking the porch steps in a fierce march with a worried Ichi hot on his tail.

Ichiro looked from his brother to Bobby, his eyes widening slightly in shock. Gulping like a goldfish for a second, he finally sighed wearily and muttered, "So I guess you told him."

CHAPTER TWELVE

"DID YOU know about this? About them?" Cole's fury ran hot, burning the air under the eaves. It turned its flames toward Jae, and he flinched, visibly hit by Cole's wrath. "Did he tell you?"

"I didn't—wait, don't make this about me or you." Jae's snarl was just as fierce, shoving back at Cole's assault. Mounting the last step to the porch, he went toe to toe with his lover, a slender, ferocious reminder of the man he'd fought to become. "No, I didn't know, but fuck that. *You're* not a part of this. *I'm* not either. This—"

When Ichi'd come up the sidewalk after parking the car, he'd spotted Bobby first. It didn't take a lot of brains to figure out what they'd been discussing. Not when he could see the murderous look on his brother's face. Jae meeting him at the end of the sidewalk was a fluke. Now they were both hip deep into Cole's anger and struggling to get a word in edgewise.

"Look, yeah we should have told you," Ichiro interrupted, sliding in between his brother and Jae. "When Mike found out, that night—"

It was definitely a slip up. Not having siblings up until a year or so ago, Ichi wasn't prepared for the landmines he sometimes found along the way. By the chilling grit of Cole's teeth, he guessed he'd hit one.

"Mike knows? Oh, this is getting better and better." Cole threw his hands up. "Anyone else besides me you've left in the dark? How about the dog over there? He invited to the wedding? Maybe going to be the best man?"

"Why are you doing this? Why do you think you have this right?" Jae squared off again, stepping closer to Cole, his lip lifted into a snarl. "Ichi and Bobby don't have to answer to you. They don't have to answer to—"

"What the hell are you all doing up here? *You*, get up there." A rumbling alto spiced with a dash of maternal grit drew them all up, and Ichi found himself being shoved up the steps by a forceful push of Claudia's right hand. He stumbled, astonished at the strength in the enormous black woman's arm. The porch went silent, dropped to a deathly quiet barely broken by their breathing. "Boy, do you have your keys? We are *not* doing this out here. You have *guests*."

There wasn't a question who she was talking to, and Cole patted at his jeans, shaking his head. "No, I left them in the house."

"No, I left them in the house, what?" Claudia's nostrils flared, and she tilted her head back. "Right now there'd best be a ma'am or a momma at the end of everything you say from this point out. Do you hear me?"

As quick as that, Ichi saw his brother fold in and settle into himself. Claudia took another step forward, her flats barely making any noise on the porch planks. Bobby shuffled back and forth on his feet, his hands shoved deep into his jeans. No one seemed able to make eye contact. Even Jae looked guilty and contrite when Claudia raked a glance over him.

She stood still among them, a Gorgon arriving to decide which of them she wanted in her garden—and she owned a murmuring of acid-shitting pigeons with diarrhea.

"Yes, ma'am," Cole muttered, looking down at his feet. "Um, no, I left them in the house, Momma."

A curious Scarlet and one of Claudia's teenaged granddaughters trailed after her, but the woman clearly didn't need any reinforcements. With her broad shoulders set back, she sailed up the porch and cut through their argument with a force strong enough to back up her steely glare.

"Sissy, you go get Nana's keys from her purse and bring them here. When you're done with that, you go tell those women to get their asses off the sidewalk and go get some food. Bring that damned dog too. Poor thing's going to get sunburn on that lily white belly it's got. It can sleep in the shade." Nodding to Scarlet, a small, soft smile cracked her hard reserve. "Scarlet honey, can you keep everyone out back over there while I get these boys' shit straightened out? Unless you're wanting a piece of their asses to chew on, because Lord knows, there's enough of it to go around."

"No, I am fine," Scarlet murmured sweetly, but her eyes narrowed when she glanced at Cole. "I'll take what you've left if I need to."

If Claudia's harsh tone wasn't enough, Cole's face paled to a pasty white as Scarlet turned around and headed down the sidewalk to the backyard.

"Not going to be much ass to kick when I get done with you all," Claudia muttered. Sissy came back at a full run, bolting up the stairs to hand her grandmother a set of keys. "Thank you, honey. Now go talk to those fools across the street and then get something to eat. Jae, you go on with her. None of this is on you."

"*Nuna—*" Jae began to protest.

"This isn't a discussion, Jae-Min. You get your ass out back, and you go make nice with the people who came here to eat and have a good time. And sucking up to me by calling me *nuna* isn't going to do you one bit of good. One of you needs to go back there and play host, and from the looks of things, you're just getting dragged into this mess by your fool boyfriend. So get." She stomped across the porch, opened the screen door, then fit a key into the office's front door. Unlocking it with a twist, she growled at Cole. "*You* go undo that alarm. Ichiro and Bobby, you two head in and find a chair to plant yourselves in. We're going to have this out right now."

Ichi stood there, stunned and senseless, as his brother nodded once, then headed into the section of the Craftsman house he'd turned into an office for his detective business. Bobby began to follow but stopped in front of Ichi.

Holding his hand out, Bobby gave Ichi a warm smile. "Come on, Sunshine. Let's go get our asses chewed out."

"Robert Dawson, are you mocking me?"

"No, ma'am." He shook his head, but his smile grew when Ichi entwined their fingers together.

"Well, that just sounded nasty," Claudia harrumphed. Standing nearly as tall as Bobby's shoulder, she was a stone-faced sentinel as she held open the door. "Get in. And all of you, sit down and you listen. Because we're not going to be doing this again. Or so help me God, you shall feel my wrath and wish the Lord had given you locusts and floods instead."

AS ASS-CHEWINGS went, Bobby had to admit it was a spectacular one.

There was very little talking on their parts. Claudia cut through their arguments with a sharpened word or a look, her offhanded comments a shiv to the hot-air balloons they used to lift their anger. She jabbed, prodded, and with a few harsh reminders of their mortality, reduced their fight to a few choice points.

Most of which, Bobby had to agree on. Especially when she began to question his sanity. And Cole's. But mostly his.

"Ichiro, you tell me one thing before I go any further. Do you love him?" Claudia crooked a finger up, stopping them from bursting in. "Don't give me any crap about not knowing or not telling him that yet. You tell me whether or not this thing between the two of you is serious."

Bobby met Ichi's wavering gaze. It was silly for them—three grown men—to be called up on the carpet like children, but in some small way, it gave Bobby a sense of relief. Clearing his throat, he spoke up before Ichi could.

"I'm serious," he interjected. "About Ichiro. I'll say it first. I don't give a shit if anyone knows it. We've got a good thing going, and I want to… see where it leads. I don't think Cole—"

"We're not talking about Cole right now." Claudia shoved his argument aside with a wave of her hand. "I'm asking about how things are between the two of you. Ichi, you feel the same?"

"Yeah, I do." His lover fidgeted in his chair, bumping his knee against Bobby's. "It's been… good. Nice."

"Nice?" Bobby gasped teasingly. "Shit, I've got to work on my game—"

"It's not a goddamned game, Bobby," Cole grumbled. "That's my baby brother."

"Brother yes, baby no," Ichiro corrected. "Why are you being like Mike here? Maybe I thought you'd be happy for me. For Bobby—"

"Ichiro, now's when you go help Jae." Claudia jerked her head toward the door. Ichi raised his eyebrows and stole a look at Bobby. Catching him, Claudia sniffed. "Don't go looking to him for permission. I tell you to do something, you get to doing it. You're not needed here."

"Um, Cole's—" His argument came quick and was shot down even quicker.

"I know who Cole is to you, and I know who Bobby is to you, neither of which have anything to do with what's going on between them. You're just a bone these two dogs are chewing over, and we're going to put a stop to it." Claudia glared at Cole when he looked up from the chair he'd claimed in the rush to get inside. Standing in front of them, she blocked the way out as effectively as a Sherman tank, barely turning to let Ichiro out. "Ichi, go on. I'm going to be right behind you. These two can go work out their problems without you, and then the brothers can deal with their own things at their own time."

He appreciated Ichiro's willingness to go to the mat for him. Even as outclassed as the little boy from Tokyo was to the Dupree clan matriarch, he was game—as if Godzilla tearing apart his city gave Ichi any street cred when going up against Claudia in a full rant.

Still, another nod from Bobby and Ichiro was out the door like he'd been shot out of a cannon. When the screen door banged against its frame, Claudia turned back to them and put her hands on her hips, glaring down her nose.

"I'm going to tell it to you straight, Robert Dawson." Her voice was low, crooning to a sweetness Bobby didn't trust. "I don't have a lot of faith you're not going to hurt that boy. Yes, he's a man, but he's looking to you for love, and other than Cole here, you've not got a lot going on in that heart of yours."

"I don't need that spelled out to me, ma'am." He tacked it on quickly, keenly aware of Claudia's wicked backhand and how his head was very tenuously attached to his neck. "It really is between me and Ichiro. Cole's just—"

"No, this is between you and Cole," Claudia pronounced, slapping Cole's shoulder when he turned in his chair. "There's a lot going on here. There's a lot at stake between you. If it goes badly with you and Ichi, where does that put Cole? Suppose he has to choose between you?"

"I wouldn't—"

"And you think Cole isn't maybe jealous of you and Ichi?" She cocked her head when Cole jerked to attention. "Don't tell me you aren't. I know you. I know how that little green monster burns inside of you. Hell, you used to be jealous of that damned cat."

"The cat hated me. And I'm allergic to it," Cole pointed out. "I'm *not* jealous of Bobby and Ichiro."

"Maybe not on the surface, but it's there. He's your best friend, and son, let me tell you the truth, you might know a lot of people, but very few of them are your friends—not like this man here. And it scares you that you could lose him. I'm here to tell you both to stop being stupid and talk to each other. Now I'm going to go outside, and when you come out—both of you better be smiling and hugging, or I'm going to decide who Ichi's going to be left with. Understand?"

"Yeah," Cole muttered.

"I'll let that one go because I love you. Just like the two of you love each other." Claudia patted Cole on the head. "Now I'm going to go and get something to eat. You both come join us when you're done. I'll save you some pie."

"I'M *NOT* jealous." Cole was the first one to break the heavy silence, cracking it apart to sear and bubble on the hot anger they had lingering between them. It spat, then faded, dulled by the cold, hard truths Claudia laid out before them. Grimacing, he continued, "Okay, not really, but yeah, I thought about how things would be if you guys broke up first—instead of how great it was the two of you might have something together."

"I'll give you that." Bobby rolled the chair back an inch, squeaking its wheels across the floor. "I'll admit to kind of liking sneaking around behind your back with Ichi." He cut Cole off before his friend could say anything. "Not that I'm ashamed of him. It was kind of fun. And well, you can be an asshole sometimes."

"Shouldn't have lied to me."

"Didn't lie. Just didn't tell you everything," Bobby clarified, but he caught the hurt look in Cole's hazel eyes. "You want me to be honest with you?"

"Yeah." Cole leaned his chair back until it struck his desk. Biting his lower lip, he looked too much like Ichiro for Bobby's comfort. "For once, Bobby, tell me what the hell is really going on with you."

"Your brother scares the living fuck out of me," he admitted, gently tearing apart his soul so Cole could see inside. "He's way out of my league and… kind of frighteningly smart. I'm just some ex-cop with a shit ton of baggage and so fucking fresh out of the closet I've got coat hanger marks on the back of my neck. What's someone like Ichi doing with an old man like me?"

"Hey, you're not that old," Cole argued. "You can beat the shit out of me in the ring, remember? Guys half your age can't do that."

"But guys half your age aren't fucking guys half their age either," Bobby pointed out.

"No, 'cause that's illegal." Cole cocked his head at Bobby's grin. "And kind of immoral."

"I've pretty much tried to define immoral… without drifting into the illegal, mind you." Rubbing his hands over his thighs, Bobby stared at his best friend. "I'm not saying I'm perfect—"

"Well good, 'cause that's a shit-faced lie."

"Shut up for a second here. I'm trying to be serious." He nudged Cole with his foot. "Your brother's gotten under my skin, and I can't get him out. Hell, I don't want to get him out. Dude, I didn't tell you because I knew you'd react as shitty as Mike did. And you've got more cause than Hedgehog Head does. You've seen me at my worst—"

"I've also seen you at your best." Cole rolled his chair over until their knees bumped. "Yeah, I'm pissed off because you should be telling me shit like this. Even if it was Ichi—okay, shit, I can't believe it's Ichi—but you should have given me that fucking chance."

"Yeah, I should have." It was hard to admit, and the words stuck in his throat, dry and scratchy, but he forced them out. "So, we good here? You willing to let me try it with your brother?"

"With Mike, yeah. Maddy deserves better, but he got her pregnant, so I'm guessing she wants to keep him."

"You're a dick, you know that?" He reached over to slap Cole on the arm.

"You should tell your kid. He should know. It's not fair to him or Ichi." Cole barely budged at the smack, and Bobby grimaced at the shock waves going up his elbow.

"You work out too much. Getting too beefy."

Cole chuckled, and Bobby joined him.

"I'm serious. Me and Ichi, we're not going away, Princess. You're going to have to deal with it."

"I can. Deal with it, I mean." He shrugged, his broad shoulders lifting gracefully.

For the years since he'd first become friends with Cole, Bobby felt… scared. Frightened of losing a man he'd first come to think of as a casual friend, then his best—his only true—friend. There were men he knew to call for a cheap fuck or even to help him move on the promise of pizza and beer. There were guys he could share a pool table with or catch a game at the stadium, but Cole was the one who reached out to *him*, and he found the fear of losing that trust overwhelming.

He'd already seen that loss in Jamie's eyes. Hell, even his uncle looked at him sideways sometimes, and the man'd raised him, but never once had Cole wavered. The fear of it choked him, and it brought up a sting of bile to his throat.

"I can't lose you, man." Bobby reached for Cole's hands, then clamped them into a tight grip. His world went wet, smearing about the edges, and he blinked, trying to clear his view. "But I can't lose him either. Not… now. Not if… fuck, I think I love him, Cole, and that scares the fucking shit out of me like you don't know."

"Yeah, I know." Cole returned his grip, a fierce, quick tug on his fingers. "You're not going to lose me, and if this… if you and Ichi go belly up, I'll be here. But I'm hoping—really hoping for your sake—it doesn't. Go belly up, I mean."

"It sucks wanting someone so fucking bad you can taste it at the back of your soul." He pulled one hand free and dug the heel of it into his eyes. "He's so damned young."

"Ichi is about as young as a rock," Cole scoffed. "I think he was a thousand years old when he was born. Naïve as shit but old. Not who I'd expect you with, but hell, maybe it was meant to be. Maybe you need someone older inside, because, dude, you are one messed-up fucker."

"Yeah, I am." He exhaled, releasing the hot sour inside of him. "But maybe I'll be okay. Shit, I can't be worse."

"You going to talk to Jamie?" Cole cocked his head, searching Bobby's face. "Because dude, really. Closet. Aren't you getting sick of jumping in and out of it?"

"Yeah, I am. I just need to figure out if I'm going to tell my uncle."

"I don't know about that one. He's pretty…. What's a good word for it?"

"Old-fashioned?"

"I was going to say bigoted."

"Set in his ways."

"He called me a gook." Cole eyed him skeptically. "To my face."

"He has issues, left over from 'Nam," Bobby countered.

"Your uncle was never in 'Nam."

"The war hit him hard. Lost um… fuck, okay, so he's an asshole. All of the Dawsons are assholes. It's like our family motto."

"Just don't be an asshole to my brother," Cole grumbled.

"So are we? Good, I mean?" A weight hung in his chest, threatening to drop into his belly, but Cole nodded, and he could breathe again. "I didn't… fuck. I never meant this to hurt you, man."

"You broke the rules, you know. Sisters—and brothers—are supposed to be off-limits." Cole rolled his chair back again, putting space between them. "Isn't there like a code you're supposed to follow? I'd never touch your brother."

"I don't have a brother. Or a sister for that matter," Bobby amended quickly, "Okay, maybe I could because my dad was kind of a whore. I've got cousins, though, but they're pieces of shit who don't even take care of their own father. Tell you what, how about if I give you a free shot? Just to get it in, and we call it even."

"And no retaliation? Free shot?"

"Totally free. Just one. Anything past that, and it's fair game." He made a big deal of looking around the office. "Place could use a little redecorating if you want to go for it."

"Nah, Claudia really likes her desk." Cole grinned. "Stand on up. I don't want to hit a man when he's down on his ass."

CHAPTER THIRTEEN

"WELL, THAT went well," Ichiro muttered as he flung his car keys onto the kitchen counter. "I can't fucking believe he hit you."

"I can't believe he only hit me once," Bobby replied, closing the front door behind him. "If he'd at least shoved me, I could have gotten a shot in. Never knew your brother had that much self-control. I can usually count on that asshole to leap off buildings after kittens and shit. Who knew?"

"Are you guys okay? He wouldn't talk to me about it." Unpacking the bags Jae'd shoved into his hands, Ichi tried to find space in the fridge for the leftover food. Neither of them would probably feel like eating for a few weeks after the afternoon they'd had, something Bobby silently seconded when he reached over Ichi's shoulder and snagged a couple of beers from the icebox.

"Yeah. For now. He's got conditions. You heard him." A bottle hissed when Bobby twisted off its cap. He bent the soft circle in half, then chucked it at the trashcan, hitting the rim once before it bounced in. "And before you argue, he's right. I've got to tell my son. Hell, I should probably even tell my uncle, because it'll piss him off, and he'll call one of his kids to come get him. Which they won't. Because they're assholes like he is."

"Go sit down. I'll get you another ice pack to put on your face." Ichiro studied Bobby's jaw. "Hell, are you sure it's not broken?"

"Pretty sure," he mumbled as he moved his jaw around. "I don't know. I've never broken my jaw before. I'll be pretty pissed off if he did. Going to make giving you blowjobs a bitch and a half."

"Probably why he hit you in the face." Rooting around in the freezer, Ichi found an ice pack buried under an enormous opened bag of peas. "Here, put this on your jaw. I'll grab you some ibuprofen."

"Can't I just grab you instead?" Bobby teased, snagging him as he went by. "Maybe you can kiss and make it better?"

"That ever work?"

He could drown in Bobby's eyes, their silky depths so much like the shadowed waters of his family's communal hot spring baths. Ichi tried shoving away the sting of pain growing to a throb in his chest, but it resurfaced, flaring up when Bobby brushed gentle fingers over his mouth.

"Where'd you go, Sunshine?" His lover tugged at Ichi's lower lip between a pinch of his fingers. "What'd I say?"

"You didn't do anything. Didn't say anything. Just... maudlin? Is that a good word?" He rubbed at the spot where Bobby's fingers touched him, sending the tingle in deeper. "Melancholy... maybe?"

"Good words. Let me wipe them off of you, though. So he tapped me on the face. I asked for it. He gave it to me. Tell me you don't do stupid boy shit back in Japan."

"No." Ichi laughed, pulling up his jeans leg to show Bobby a small white cat with a bow near his ankle. "Losing bets to other tattoo artists there can be dangerous."

"What did you bet on?" Bobby leaned over to inspect the ink. "You know I can't really see it. You might have to take off your pants all the way. You know, for full examination."

"Pervert."

"That's what you like about me," his lover reminded him. "Seriously, what was the bet on?"

"That I could eat two buckets of Kentucky Fried Chicken." Ichi shrugged at Bobby's recoil. "It was Christmas. It's what you do there. You get together and eat KFC, get drunk, and then do stupid things like pretend to be Samurai X in the middle of a busy intersection."

"Okay, suddenly leftover turkey and cranberry sauce sandwiches for a week don't sound so bad." Bobby slid his hands down Ichi's back, stopping at the rise of his ass beneath the denim. Squeezing Ichiro's cheeks, he pulled Ichi close until their bellies touched. "How far did you make it into the buckets?"

"Four pieces. But they were huge! I thought I'd start with the breasts first. That was a huge mistake." Ichi grinned at the memory. "I always did like breasts."

"Miss them?" Bobby walked him backward, shuffling them to the bedroom.

"Breasts?" He chuckled. "No, not really. I never knew what to do with them. Most Japanese girls are small, you know. Well, they start off that way, and then the ones I knew go out and get this huge melons put there. What do I do with that? And I can't ever... I don't know how I'm not supposed to remember it's squishy plastic. Weirds me out a bit. Only the really big ones. Normal sized, I can handle that. It's when they're bigger than a prayer bell that gets me worried."

"I'm more worried you use a prayer bell as a comparison." Bobby stopped his shuffle, angling Ichi away from a table.

"Are you trying to get me to the bedroom?" He glanced over his shoulder. "Because at the rate we're going, it'll be morning before we get there."

"I'd pick you up but...." Bobby made a show of eyeing him. "You're not a girl, and I don't think you'd get into that whole carried over the threshold thing. I didn't even do that to my ex-wife."

"Life lesson, when trying to seduce a guy, don't bring up your ex-wife," Ichi suggested as he broke loose from Bobby's embrace. Grabbing his lover's wrist, he tugged Bobby along. "Come on. You can try to convince me my stupid brother didn't damage your face."

"Hey, you okay? With Cole. Did you guys talk?" Bobby tackled Ichiro when they got close to the bed, and he grunted, gasping when the air whooshed out of his lungs.

"Dude, heavy. Ouch, get off," Ichi choked, wiggling out from under his lover's bulk.

"Yeah, you're kind of scrawny. More red meat for you." Bobby's fingers were making quick work of his jeans' buttons, and the denim was being tugged down Ichi's hips before he knew it. "And cheese."

"I'd be sicker than when I ate all that chicken." He slapped at Bobby's busy hands. "Stop that. I can get undressed by myself."

"You take too long." He tried to block Ichi's pinch to his nipple but failed, squeaking low in his throat when Ichiro caught Bobby's nub in a tight clench. Rubbing at his chest when Ichi let go, Bobby flopped back into the bed to watch Ichiro undress. "Seriously, you okay? With Cole? He was just being… well, shit… an older brother. You'd probably react the same way when that sister of yours gets old enough."

"Doubt it." Ichi sat down at the edge of the bed to tug his socks off. He rolled them up then tossed the ball into the pile of jeans and T-shirts he'd made in one of the space's armchairs. "I'm probably never going to meet her anyway."

"What are you talking about? It's like a plane ride over. Hell, I'll go with you."

The bed tilted as Bobby got onto his knees and came up behind him. The older man's hard cock pressed up along the ridge of Ichi's spine, and he shivered at the wet smear Bobby's precome-dampened underwear left on his back.

"Okay, so we don't have to tell them we're… you know, together or anything, but shit, she's your baby sister."

"She's going to be my father's daughter. One he's having with my ex-fiancée—my very traditional ex-fiancée. I can tell you exactly what her life is going to be like. She's going to be educated just enough to be a good corporate wife—just like Megumi was—but not so smart that she'll have her own opinions." He tried not to sound bitter, but the hatred of who he'd been, how he'd let them control his life until he'd finally broken free of his father's manipulations still burned a hot fire inside of Ichiro. Megumi was just the tip of the iceberg, a shadowy betrayal amid countless disappointments and humiliations.

"You can't be serious—"

"I am. How do you think Megumi and I met? We're commodities. My father not only married the daughter, but he also bought out the company her father ran. We're like amoebas, eating each other or spawning off identical replicas. I just didn't want to— be that kind of man. Not anymore. He—my father—is not worth that kind of sacrifice of self." Ichiro almost laughed at Bobby's horrified expression.

"That's... fucked-up." Bobby's hands were hot on his skin, rolling over his tense muscles, and Ichiro leaned into the man's touch, drawing strength from him. "Yeah, I know. Different culture. Different... everything. Cole's always getting on my ass about that, but shit, baby, that's just not right. Who'd do that to their kid?"

"Trust me, as soon as he can, he'll arrange a marriage between her and either some other corporate kid or some guy who he considers worthy of being his son. Because that's what's going to happen to whoever marries my sister. They're going to win the lottery. My father's going to put him on the family registry and have that perfect Japanese son he's always wanted."

"Fuck that," Bobby growled, pulling him down onto the bed, flopping them both onto their sides. "If my kid turned out half as good as you, I'd be okay with it."

"Kind of went to the weird there, Dawson," Ichi teased. "But thanks. Icky weird, but thank you."

"Admit it, you kind of like me weird." Bobby did a few calisthenics on the mattress in an attempt to shed his clothes without getting up. Sighing heavily, he finally gave in to physics and sat up.

"Yeah, I do," Ichi agreed, tracing Bobby's spine with his fingertips.

There was power in Bobby's body, a core strength he'd built on. The interplay of muscles along his back and hips was a tight ballet of lean threads and hard curves. A spray of freckles dappled his hips, and he'd gotten a scar along the edge of one rib, probably from something Cole did to him. Ichi was fairly sure of that. There were other blemishes, leftover reminders of a life lived hard and a bit too fast.

The age difference between them showed in the grit of Bobby's hard, muscular body and the light sheen of silver flecks in his soft brown hair. Stubble roughened his square jaw, frosted more than the tousle across his scalp, and the faint silken strands across his chest and down his belly were a tawny mink on his tanned skin.

But it was the sardonic quirk of his grin that grabbed Ichiro by the balls and twisted them up into desire. There was a dash of cowboy and pirate in Bobby Dawson's swagger, a bravado hiding the sometimes-tender soul within. Here was a man who worked his body into a sweat wearing gloves and a mouthpiece, pounding the hell out of his opponents—the same man who sprawled out onto a comfortable couch while the rain beat away at Los Angeles's grime-ridden streets and read Ichi passages out of sweet gay romances.

"What are you looking at?" Bobby paused in midwiggle, his briefs tangled up around one knee. "Better yet, see anything you like?"

"Everything," Ichi whispered, reaching over to slide the offending piece of underwear off his lover. "You were everything I was looking for."

KISSING ICHIRO was possibly the best thing Bobby had in his life. Being inside of him ranked closer to heaven, and his body burned with a whispering need he'd chased for decades. It'd been years since he'd let another man in him. He'd hidden his desires behind a cloak of secrecy, and with those secrets came shame and, worse, ignorance.

His sex life during his marriage was either furtive or unfulfilling—through no fault of his ex. What little he knew about sex with men was gleaned from back rooms and filthy corners, unseen faces and rough hands with little use for lube or foreplay. He'd come of age in a time of hard cocks, detached pleasures, and remote, aloof interactions.

Sex was just that. Sex. A live and learn the hard way thing he sometimes walked away from with more bruises than if he'd fallen off a tall building. He'd broken skin, rules, and trust along the way, and now, having come out the other side, Bobby wanted more than what he'd found before.

He wanted Ichiro—in every way he could.

"Make love to me, Sunshine." It was a soft whisper, barely audible over the pound of his own heartbeat in his ears, and for a second, Bobby thought it'd been lost in the sounds of the Los Angeles night bleeding through the open windows. "I want to feel you... in me, Ichi. Will you?"

Presumed lost until Ichiro replied just as softly... as gently as the kiss he'd left on Bobby's throat, "Are you sure?"

"Yeah, babe, never been more sure in my life." He went for honesty. Ichi deserved it. Baring every part of himself, he said, "Never been more fucking scared in my life either."

Sliding back, Ichi lay on his side to face Bobby. "When was the last time you—did that?"

"Bottomed?" He searched his memory and gave up after tumbling back to before he'd divorced. "Years. Fucking years ago, Sunshine. It wasn't... great, but hell, back then, we all just wanted to get our rocks off before someone saw us. Closet's too tight of a space for foreplay and kisses. Just... go slow."

"Like... a sleep-deprived sloth," Ichi promised.

"Can we not bring animals into it?" Bobby cracked a smile. "Not an image I want to take with me into this."

"Well, at least not sloths," Ichi murmured as he slid over Bobby's sprawled body. "Have you seen the claws they've got? Wicked damage there, and I like you as you are right now."

Their fingers were slick from spit and the crowning drops on their cock heads, and as Ichi explored the heft of Bobby's sac, he left a damp trail along the ridge beneath the churning skin. Bobby flinched when one of Ichi's nails lightly scratched at the edge of his hole, then shivered as goose bumps ran over his shoulders and down his stomach.

"Fuck, that... tickles a bit." Huffing in a breath, he waited for Ichi to push in, then groaned in frustration when the man merely teased at his rim. "You're killing me here, Sunshine."

"Did you… know you were going to do this? Want this?" Ichiro growled as he bit into one of Bobby's nipples.

He hissed at the sudden pain, and his hips rose off the bed, knees drawing in involuntarily when the prick of pain brought his cock to full salute. For a second, Bobby wondered what Ichi was asking him, then remembered the time he'd spent in the bathroom, alternating between worrying about Ichiro plunging deep into him and preparing for it.

"Yeah, I knew," he gasped, aroused by a rake of teeth along his ribs.

"Then a first for you… and one for me," Ichiro whispered. "Turn over, *anata*. Onto your stomach. I want to see how you taste."

Turning over was easy. Lifting his hips up and resting his weight on his knees and shoulders was harder, mostly because the angle splayed Bobby open, exposing him to… everything. His heart fluttered, frightened at the steps he was taking in trusting the slender Japanese man he'd taken to his bed, and his brain clenched at the thought of his body being invaded. Clamping down on his whispering thoughts, Bobby focused on the one thing—the one person—that mattered in that moment.

Ichiro.

He was sure of Ichi. More sure than he'd ever been in his entire life. Something in him *trusted* Ichiro. Bobby found greater faith in Ichiro's steadfast presence and slightly quirky view of the world. Beaten at the seams by his own family, he'd emerged stronger than he'd expected and still sought out brothers he'd known about but never seen. It was a risk. The McGinnis boys could have spat on his existence—hell, it was close with Cole, but Ichiro kept pushing, reminding him the sins of the parents did not rest on their shoulders.

Just as the sins and pain of Bobby's past encounters didn't lie at Ichiro's feet.

If anyone would take care of him, it would be Ichiro.

And he had to own the slithering dark need inside of him—a want to be taken care of, to be desired as he desired. To be possessed as fully as he'd pleasured Ichiro even as his body rippled with the memory of how he'd been used before.

It would be different this time.

Because his lover was Ichiro.

The flick of Ichi's tongue on his crack startled him, and he pulled his cheeks in, unable to stop himself. Ichi pressed in again, and Bobby forced himself to relax, allowing his lover to push his tongue down against his ring. Then Ichiro slid in, and Bobby lost his mind.

The sheets weren't enough for him to get a grip on. They slid about in his hands, working out between his fingers, and he writhed, wanting Ichiro to press in farther as his body jerked away in response to the laving. When Ichiro's hands closed over his hips, Bobby groaned and fought to keep still, but it was nearly impossible. His body was too attuned to the tingling rakes of Ichiro's flicking jabs, and then in a moment, everything in him shifted, turning inside out when he felt Ichiro breech his ring, sliding a long finger into his depths.

It didn't hurt. Stung more—like a light slap of a branch across his chest or a glove glancing off his cheek during a bout, but combined with the electrical pulses of his body's nerves rolling in pleasure, the slight irritation was easily endured. A snap of a bottle echoed in the room. Then Bobby felt the cold dribble of lubricant flow down his ass crack, and Ichiro worked his ring, pulling the oil in as he stretched Bobby open. The touch of Ichiro's tongue around his own fingers, all delving and dipping into his center, broke Bobby, and he rocked his hips forward, fucking himself on Ichi's hand.

"Can't, baby. God, just… damn, I want you in me," Bobby groaned. "Please. Fuck me. I can't—"

"Let me get—hold on." Ichiro spent a moment playfully biting Bobby's firm ass, then suckled at the spot, probably leaving a mark behind. The snick of a condom wrapper punched a tremor through Bobby's belly, and he tensed, anticipating and dreading the coming stretch.

Ichiro crawled up over his hips, pressing against Bobby's upraised ass. Sliding his hard, latex-cocooned cock along Bobby's wet crack, Ichiro rubbed at Bobby's spine with long, graceful strokes. Bending over, he gave Bobby's shoulder a gentle kiss, then fit the tip of his cock into Bobby's pulsing hole.

"You ready, *anata*? Because I'll stop at any time." Ichiro's promise soothed Bobby's fears, drowning them in a gentle warmth.

"Yeah, don't stop until you coat the inside of that condom with your come." He tried not to push back, but the urge to have Ichiro in his ass was too much to take. "Hell, you and I—we're going to have to go make sure you can fill me without that thing, because, Sunshine, fuck if I don't want to feel you get off in me."

He'd thought he was ready. He was sure of it. Yet nothing had prepared Bobby for the long slide of Ichiro's dick into his body or the press of hard flesh up against his ring. Shock warred with his panic, and he reached back, nearly toppling over onto his face in an effort to slow Ichi down.

"Take your time, Bobby," Ichi murmured, running his hands over Bobby's back. "You tell me when."

It was forever before Bobby could get his body under control. Between the feeling of being torn open and the tingle of shock waves rocketing up his spine, he had to steady his breathing before dropping his hand back down to the bed. Sliding his hips up, he rode onto Ichi's hard dick, taking more of its length in.

It felt… good. Too damned good for his mind to wrap itself around. When he growled for Ichiro to continue, the man pushed in until their balls slapped in unison, and Bobby unraveled, breaking apart under the bursts of hot, stinging pleasure rising from his ass.

They fought their way up, moving and slapping their bodies together. Ichiro's fingers dug in deep, scoring furrows and welts into Bobby's heated skin, but he didn't care. He wanted Ichi to mark him. He wanted to carry something away from the night they spent after the hurricane they'd made together. Caught up in the swirling sensations of his body's keening needs, Bobby wasn't ready for the cresting white noise of his skin tightening and his balls pulling up.

It was so different than when he was inside Ichiro. The *now* of their sex settled in over him, a blanket of shifting vibrations and emotions shielding him from time. His release hit him hard, drowning Bobby in its intensity.

He could feel Ichi's hand around his cock, but the pull of his lover's fingers down his shaft and over his head was nearly too much for him to handle. Caught between the plunge of Ichiro's dick and the clench of his hand, Bobby's climax churned, frothing up out of his balls to splatter the cramped space beneath him.

If anything, he was falling. A tumble down a long, dark hole following a White Rabbit who teased out of him more than he had to give. His spine jacked and arched, bending under the spasms in his groin, and Bobby had enough of a split second to wonder if he'd ever stop coming before another roil took him over.

His ass felt hot from the inside out, and he gasped, realizing the heat was coming from Ichiro's cock gushing down into its latex sheath, trapped and kept from painting the inside of Bobby's body.

God, he wanted that too. Gasping for air and trying to survive the tremors taking over his skin and nerves, Bobby found he wanted more—anything—everything Ichiro could give him. And in the reluctant slide of Ichi's waning cock from his ass, Bobby mourned more than the pull and emptiness.

"Love you," he murmured, catching up Ichiro's face and kissing his lover's slightly swollen lips. "I don't know if you'll believe me, but I do."

Ichiro's eyes were dark, his pupils blown out and swallowing up the color around them. Smiling, he pressed his mouth against Bobby's and whispered, "I—"

"Dad?"

Bobby froze, captured in the sliver of ice crawling up from his belly and into his brain. The clatter of keys hitting his kitchen counter was a distinct warning, as was the deep, rolling voice—so much like his own—calling out for him, getting louder as footsteps crossed over the loft's hardwood floor.

"Hey, Dad, I saw your car when I pulled in so I came on up—"

Jamie's face would have been comical if he hadn't looked so damned much like his mother—especially on the day when Marsha flung a packet of incriminating photos at his head and swore he'd never see his son again because she *knew* he'd touched Jamie when she wasn't looking. His son's mouth dragged open, impossibly gaped in shock as Jamie stared through the bookshelves at Bobby and Ichi, naked and entwined on a sex-drenched bed.

"Jamie—" Bobby gathered up the bedsheets he'd crumpled in his hands a few moments before. "Hold up—"

"Hold up?" Jamie's voice broke as his chest worked hard to catch up with its breathing. "What the fuck is this? This why you and Mom… holy shit. Uncle James was right. You're a goddamned faggot."

CHAPTER FOURTEEN

"SHIT, JAMIE, wait." Bobby was up out of the bed before Jamie could turn around. His son blocked out most of the ambient light coming from the living room, and the flicker of neon orange street lights, and whatever else blinked outside of his loft's windows wasn't enough for him to find a pair of pants.

The dark shape that was Jamie moved off, quickly lost behind the bookshelves and screens around his sleeping area. His son's response was short and quick, thrown out as he disappeared. "Fuck. You."

"What do you want me to do?" Ichi scrambled off the bed. His lover sounded… calm. Maybe with an edge of panic but nothing like the thin razors slicing through Bobby's belly.

Bobby found a pair of cutoff sweats on the floor, then jammed his legs through the holes as Ichiro tugged his jeans on. Glancing at his lover silhouetted against the bank of windows, Bobby hopped into the cutoffs and broke into a run, catching a glimpse of Jamie's shoulder as he slammed the front door behind him.

After sprinting to the front door, Bobby turned the handle and flung the door open. Jamie glanced once over his shoulder, his face sour with disgust, then ducked into the elevator as the doors opened. Calling back to Ichi, Bobby shouted, "Grab my keys!"

The elevator dinged, closing the doors behind Jamie before Bobby could reach them. Swearing under his breath, he weighed his options and only found one rational thing to do. A small glass case next to the elevator protected alarm and stop buttons from a casual touch. As slow as the elevator was, it would hit the first floor before Ichiro could get to the foyer. Gritting his teeth, Bobby knuckled down for the pain he knew was coming and smashed his elbow into the glass door, then punched the elevator's emergency stop button.

His elbow spurted a bit of blood, and Bobby pulled back, shaking off the tingling shooting up into his fingers and over his shoulder. Twisting his arm, he quickly assessed the damage, flicking off a few specks of glass embedded in his skin, then waited as the indicator lights above the doors wavered between floors.

Gears and pulleys ground to a halt, and somewhere in the building, a tinny alarm rang off, warning the inhabitants of a possible emergency in the elevator well. Ichiro reached Bobby's side with the keys, panting heavily.

"Tripped over the couch. Feels like I broke a toe." Holding out the keys, he bent over to catch his breath. "Oh shit, there's glass. What did you do? Did you break that?"

"Yeah, it's a trigger to stop the elevator." Bobby watched the numbers above his head, satisfied he'd caught the car before it'd hit any of the lower floors. "Watch your feet."

"Are you sure you should be going after him?" Ichi carefully picked his way clear of the scattered glass. "Maybe he needs time to cool down?"

"No, I fucked this up. I should have told him way before this. God knows what he's... he's my kid. Finding his old man with another guy's dick up his ass isn't how he should find these kinds of things out." Bobby grimaced when he heard himself. "Not that your dick's a bad thing—"

"No offense taken." Ichi waved away Bobby's apology. "To be fair, my dick had left said ass by the time he came in."

"Okay. Elevator's stopped, and I've got to find that damned key on here. I'm going to go fix this. Should have been honest with that kid from the beginning. Stopped him from thinking that the shit that came out of his mouth is okay. I fucked my son up, Sunshine. This one's totally on me." Bobby rifled through the keys on his ring, shaking his head. "God, I hate it when Cole's right. Fucker."

"God, your landlord's going to be pissed off."

"Yeah, I *am* the landlord."

"Oh." Ichiro blinked, an owlishly confused look on his face. "Huh. Um. Well, at least you won't get into trouble about the glass."

"Pretty sure either Jamie's going to kill me, or I'm going to die of a heart attack looking for this fucking thing."

"He's probably not going to be happy when he gets out of there."

"Yeah, I know that too. Why do they make these keys so fricking small? I can't find it." He finally found the tiny silver fob he was looking for. "There we go."

"How are you going to get it going again?" Stepping onto the runner in front of Bobby's door, Ichiro scratched at his bare chest, rippling the splashes of ink on his pale skin.

"I'm not. You are." Bobby fit a slender silver key into the locking mechanism under the button. Switching the lock over to Off, he shut off the alarm and then nodded toward the front door. "You go get some shoes on. I'm going to head Jamie off in the garage. Wait thirty seconds so I can get down the stairs and then turn this to the On position. The elevator's got to go down to the garage to reset. I'll catch him there—and well, that's probably where his car is."

"How'd you know he was going to take the lift?" Ichi muttered as he grabbed at Bobby's elbow. "And you're bleeding."

"He just got knee surgery. Can't do the stairs." He took another look at his arm. "Shit, your brother's done worse to my face. Thirty seconds, babe. Then switch it on, okay?"

"Okay." Ichi hugged himself, goose bumps crackling over his chest. "Okay now, shoes and shirt. It's fucking cold."

"Yeah," Bobby grunted, stealing a quick kiss. Running barefooted down the hall, he caught the edge of a welcome mat with his toe and almost tumbled. Catching himself on the stairwell doorframe, he stopped long enough to give Ichi a wink and tossed back, "Oh, and yeah, I love you too."

He took the stairs at a full run, catching at the railings to propel him around the well. His ass hurt, reminding him of what he'd just been doing, and his left foot throbbed at the spot he'd slammed it against the hallway wall. Three full flights down and the sounds of the elevator starting up rumbled through the stairwell. The garage door stuck a bit when he pressed down on its release bar, but a quick shove pushed it out, and Bobby was standing in the building's dim, murky garage.

"Got to get someone to add more lights down here." He looked around, catching his breath. "And fuck, I've got to do more cardio. Should have kept that damned StairMaster."

Bent over, he nearly missed Jamie emerging from the elevator. Shaken and pale, Jamie stumbled out, gasping slightly when Bobby grabbed at him.

"Hey, I got you. You okay?" Bobby hugged his son tightly. The thin sheen of sweat on Jamie's cheeks and forehead worried him. "Catch your breath, kid."

"Figures. *You.*" Jamie shook him off, pulling away from his father with a jerk. "Get your goddamned hands off of me."

They were too much alike in all the bad ways. Staring at his son—nearly eye to eye—Bobby wondered where his little boy had gone. Swallowed up by the broad-shouldered man angrily glaring at him, he took a step back, giving Jamie some room to breathe.

The mop top of curls he'd had as a toddler were now ruthlessly cropped short to his skull, but his tawny eyes and milk-tea skin were reminders of the young boy who'd beg Bobby for his police cap. Feet once small enough to fit into Bobby's hands grew, first large enough to be shuffled across the floor in Bobby's work boots, then sprouting out so far Bobby debated just buying Jamie shoeboxes to wear until he stopped growing.

He'd stopped, now taller and as broad as his father but sadly as closed-minded as the old man he'd been named for.

"I needed to talk to you about… what you walked in on upstairs." Bobby wanted to start off simple, easing his way into the mess he'd made. "There's things… shit, come upstairs. We can talk about this."

"*This?*" Jamie wasn't having any of it. He took a deep breath, leaned into Bobby's space, and took his shot. "*This* is why you dumped Mom, isn't it? Because you were fucking guys. She should be damned lucky she didn't catch anything from your sick ass."

"Over the line, boy," Bobby warned him.

"Boy? I am not your fucking *boy*. Is that some kind of crack because of Mom? To show how hip you are? Taking back the word because you're all down with whoever is around?" he snarled. "Mom wasn't exotic enough for you? That why you went gay?"

"What the hell are you talking about?" he growled back.

"I saw the kid you've got up there. You've got a thing for variety, then? Maybe Mom's too mixed for you, so you pared it down a little bit? That kid's—what—what is he? Shit, who's that gay friend of yours? Cole? Did he hook you up with—Hell, you're fucking that guy up there because you can't have Cole, is that it?"

"Jesus. You're like a fucking squirrel on a xylophone. Your mom—hell, this has *nothing* to do with your mom. And that kid's—Ichi's your age." Bobby kneaded the air with his hands, and Jamie caught the motion, cocking his head as he nodded down to his father's fists. "Will you shut the hell up and listen to me?"

"You going to hit me?" His chin jutted out. "That's what you're finally going to do?"

"That's what you're waiting for? You're pissed off because I didn't beat the shit out of you like your friends' dads did? What the hell is going through your head?" Bobby gave up his calm, throwing it aside to wrap his fingers into Jamie's shirt. "I have never in my life laid a hand on you. I worked my ass off to make sure you and your mom were okay and our marriage—and how I fucked up your mom's life—that's on me, but it's also none of your goddamn business. And trust me when I tell you, I'm as sick of saying that as much as I'm sick to death of having people decide what I should or shouldn't do."

Jamie fought him, but Bobby had too good of a grip on him. He pushed Jamie back until his son was up against the garage wall, and his shoulders strained to hold him there, letting Jamie fight it out until he grew tired.

There was a skill to holding back a fighter with blood in their eye, and Bobby'd learned it well. He'd handled riots and angry, enraged men wanting to hurt the world as much as they'd been hurt, but nothing wounded him more than his son's spitting fury and weakening attempts to break free of Bobby's hold.

It'd been too long since he'd held his son close.

And holding him still so Jamie would just… listen… hurt more than any injury or gunshot he'd ever gotten.

"Stop." He shook Jamie lightly. "Just… listen to me."

"Give me one good damned reason I should." Jamie spat as he spoke, peppering Bobby with wet disgust. "Give me one reason—"

"Because I love you," he said softly. "And yeah, I should have told you this before. I should have, but this… how you're acting… this is on me too. This isn't how I raised you—"

"You *didn't* raise me." Jamie pulled free as Bobby uncurled his fingers, releasing his shirt. "How damned often did I see you as a kid? And then after… you and Mom divorced, it was even less. What part of me do you think you raised?"

"Every damned part of you." He stepped back to study his son, frowning when Jamie shook himself loose. "I rode your ass as much as I could—"

"Yeah, bad choice of words there, Dad. Although knowing what I do now, maybe I was just lucky you were too damned tired when you came home from work. Or do you expect me to thank you for not—"

"Swear to God, if you finish what you're going to say there, that whole never hitting you is coming to an end 'cause I'm going to break those teeth I spent so much damned fucking money straightening." Bobby had to take another step away, distancing himself from Jamie and his own anger. "I can't even believe that was about to come out of your damned mouth. Really, Jamie? Fucking really? *That's* what you believe? And you'd think *I'd* do—"

Jamie's words were like a punch through his chest. Bobby'd expected things—rank things—to be tossed at him in anger. Expected yes, but to have his son's thoughts stray to… *that*… made him sick to his stomach. If he hadn't already been shaking with adrenaline, Bobby was sure he'd be puking his guts out at Jamie's insinuations.

Bobby held his breath, then sighed. "You are *not* the man I wanted you to be. You're supposed to be better than *that*. Better than my dad. Better than your Uncle James. Shit, better than *me*."

Something deep in Jamie cracked. Bobby could see it on his face. Jamie's rage burbled and seeped out through small things; the shifting of his weight on his feet and the flicking of his gaze across Bobby's face as if he was thinking about the best place to punch his old man. There was more than a little resentment in Jamie's face, and it hurt Bobby's heart to see it there.

Maybe, a small voice whispered in the back of Bobby's breaking heart, *your love just isn't enough for him. Maybe, he just doesn't love you like you love him.*

"I'm sorry." Jamie's voice broke, crumbling down to a teary whisper. He could nearly taste the shock rolling off Jamie's body, and his son caught his breath, finally comprehending what his rage drove him to say. "Shit, Dad. I'm—God, I don't know where the hell that came from. Shit, I'm—"

"There's a lot of things I've done in my life. Things I'm not proud of, but I've always been... you've been one of the very few things in life I can look at and say, shit, I'm proud of that kid. He turned out to be a good man." The tears in Bobby's eyes burned, but he refused to let the fire spread. If that hurt took hold of him, it would sear away his soul, and he fought it back, swallowing his rage. "I am so damned *not* proud of you right now."

"I shouldn't have.... God, I *don't* think like that. I know better than that—"

"I am so pissed off at you, I can't even think. I have never, *ever* raised you to believe that about any gay guy. Ever. Even before... this. You can be disappointed in me for all sorts of things, but I'll be damned if my kid's going to—"

"Dad, I am *sorry*." Jamie swallowed hard. He rubbed his face, then scraped his hands over his head. The anger was gone from his face, replaced with a contrition thick enough to fill his eyes with shame. "God, I was just... so damned pissed off at you. I wasn't... shit, I wasn't even thinking."

"When you're angry is when you *should* be thinking the most. Didn't I teach you that?"

"Yeah," his son sighed. "You did."

"If you need some time, I can give you that." Bobby growled at his son. The little boy who stole a cookie or two was tucked somewhere inside of the man standing in front of him. "You and I, we talk things out as much as we can. It's never been easy, you and me. But that's on me. I get that. I've kept shit from you that you should have known about. This... me... gay. I'm not blameless. It just seemed easier and hell, the truth wiggles out from whatever wall goes up in front of it."

"You should have told me. It's... I don't think I'm ever going to forget what I saw upstairs. Worse than finding out Santa wasn't real." Jamie nodded, shuffling his feet back and rolling his shoulders. "Why the hell wouldn't you tell me about... all of this? Hell, until Mom married Uncle Barry, I figured you and her would... you know, get back together."

"Oh, that's *so* not going to happen." Bobby shook his head.

"Well, yeah, I know that *now*. It was just... something a kid thinks about. You know?"

"Your mom... I'm not saying I didn't hurt her, only that I'd never meant too. Hell, I hurt her deep—and you too. I know that, and I don't know what I was thinking back then. Maybe I thought I could deal with it. I hid it. From her. From you. Shit, from myself for a long time too. I *was* going to tell you, Jamie. I guess the universe not only hates lies, but it's pretty damned impatient too."

"Have you... shit. I can't deal with this right now. I just—" Jamie sighed. "I need some time. To work through this crap in my head. I don't know... this changes *everything*, Dad."

"This changes nothing," Bobby replied gently. Quirking a slight grin, he said, "Okay, there might be some funky-ass food at Thanksgiving dinner, but Ichi's pretty okay."

Thanksgiving. Christmases. Hell, Fourth of July BBQs suddenly stretched out in front of him, and Bobby—didn't mind. Shit, he grinned, he was kind of looking forward to it. Stupid romantic things like getting a tree and arguing about the decorations. Everything he'd merely handed over to Marsha because it'd been her family—*her* happy little domestic scene—and now Bobby had someone he wanted to share those stupid special Hallmark moments with.

If he wasn't careful, he and Ichi would end up with matching purse dogs and calling each other Boo.

"Fuck, you're serious about this guy. Like serious *serious*. Or… is he just the first boyfriend I've known about?" Jamie looked like Bobby *had* punched him. He rocked back on his heels, studying his father with a trepidatious stare. "Shit, Dad—are you going to get married to him? He's just a *kid*—okay, maybe not jailbait but—"

The word *married* brought a quick end to the tinsel-hanging and heart-shaped boxes of chocolates floating through Bobby's thoughts.

"How about if you work on how you feel about the whole Dad's gay thing and let Ichi and I worry about whether or not you're going to have to choke down Jordan almonds any time soon?" Bobby held his hands up to stave off Jamie's questions. "So, we good? Or as good as we can be for right now?"

"Yeah," Jamie grunted, nodding. "I just…. Dad, I just need to wrap my head around it. It shocked the hell out of me. I mean, you don't *look* gay."

"Really? I'm not even sure what gay looks like." He wanted to hug Jamie, but his son was pacing off his energy, eating up a square of concrete as he listened. "But we can work on that. At least you're not a bigot like your Uncle James."

"Kind of hard to be. What *aren't* I? Mom's black, Persian, and Chinese, and you're Irish and whatever. What's left?" Jamie's snort sounded exactly like he did, and Bobby's grin grew. His son grew serious, and he reached out, placing a hand on Bobby's shoulder. "I just…. God, I'm kind of pissed off and sad… and a bunch of things I don't even have words for."

"No, I get that." He sighed. "I felt that way too. Shit, sometimes I *still* do."

"Let me head home. I'll call you tomorrow maybe. Just… give me some time to work out my shit." Jamie dug his keys out of his jeans. "Okay?"

"Yeah, okay." Drained, Bobby exhaled, then turned as Jamie was about to walk past him. "Hey, one thing—why'd you come by? What did you need?"

"Me? Shit." Jamie's grin ate up his face, wrapping up broad and white. "I just came by to tell you that you're going to be a grandpa."

THE ROOFTOP was cool, and despite the blaring spangle of music coming from a taco truck a block down, relatively peaceful. Ichi'd cleaned up the glass from the lobby, using a wet mop to catch any stray slivers only to find one with his knuckle when he bent down to pick up the filled dust pan. Waiting in Bobby's loft drove him insane after ten seconds, and Ichi'd headed up to the top of the building, hoping to find some solace in a *kretek* and a tumbler of iced coffee.

His lungs twinged when the spiced smoke hit them, then shuddered into a calm when the nicotine kicked in. The coffee chaser was a good idea, especially since Ichi could still taste Los Angeles in the air despite the cloves and tar.

It was strange to stare out onto a cityscape and see its edges. He'd apartment hopped in Tokyo but always in the central districts—always where cement, steel, and glass bristled upward toward the sky. He'd grown up used to being surrounded by its sea-urchin spines rising from the streets, and the bustle of crowds was a familiar comfort, snippets of languages and lives he could almost predict merely by watching people go by him.

Los Angeles was different. Here it was like casting fortunes at the temple. He never knew what was going to come up, and most of the time, it took him a while to figure out what the perplexing sliver meant.

Now he couldn't imagine living anywhere else—or being without the man he'd just been with.

"You're Dawson's boyfriend, aren't you?" A man's aged voice boomed out behind him, a sonorous, British pour of tea, cigar smoke, and fog. "Tell me you brought a lighter up here with you. I plum forgot."

Startled, Ichi turned to see a tall egret of a man approaching him from the rooftop access door. Despite being slightly stooped and leaning on a cane to help him cross the uneven rooftop, the older man towered over Ichiro. His shock of white hair caught the sparkle from the faerie lights someone'd strung up over a large space near the door, and his fierce Roman nose threw a long shadow down his strong, long face. Even in the night's faint dusting of light, his light blue eyes held a fierce spark of life in their watery depths.

"Sure, yeah." Ichi fumbled at his pocket, finding his Zippo. "Here, let me—"

"I'm coming. No need to stir yourself." Holding up a cheroot, the elderly man made a brisk progress toward Ichi, his cane thumping in time with the swing of his stiff leg. Sticking the raw-ended cigar into his mouth, the man cupped the other end against the wind, then held still as Ichi flicked the Zippo's flame back and forth under it. The leaves caught, smoldering at first, then glowing a deep cherry once he sucked on the cheroot a few times. Pulling back, the man blew out a mouthful of fragrant smoke, then stuck his free hand out to Ichiro. "Charles Howell. I have one of the corner ends on the first floor. I've seen you around with Dawson. Heard him making a racket coming down those stairs while I was taking the trash out. Thought maybe you two had gotten into a tussle, but here you are. Or did he go the wrong way and should have gone up here instead?"

"Ah, no, Mr. Howell, It wasn't me he was fighting with. We're good."

"Please, call me Charles. Mr. Howell makes me sound like I should be stuck on an island with a bunch of incompetent sailors and a bevy of pretty women. Now why are you up here and that boy isn't?"

"Okay, Charles, then. I'm Ichiro." He grinned at the Brit, catching the man's wink. "He was trying to catch up with his son. They… have to talk about a few things."

"Let me guess," Charles said around the end of his cigar. "That boy of his found out his father's not one for the girls?"

"It's like you can see through walls." Ichiro motioned toward a cluster of Adirondack chairs near them. "Did you want to sit? Maybe get off that leg, sir?"

"Sir's just as bad as mister." He leaned a bit more on the cane. "No, I'm fine here for now. Stretch my legs. You get to sitting too long, and your body forgets to move. How'd the boy take it? The whole Band of Thebes thing? I like Dawson. He's a good man. Son should know that about him."

"Yeah, I don't know. I was waiting downstairs and just... couldn't stand there doing nothing. Came up here to pollute my lungs." Ichi leaned back against the short wall running around the roof's edge. "You okay with... us? Me and Bobby?"

"What? You think an old man can't be open-minded? Hell, some of the wildest people in the world have snow on their roofs and a fire in their belly." Charles shot him a playfully scornful look. "Besides, every generation's got a struggle they have to fight. In my time, it was me marrying a Chinese woman from Jamaica. God, did I ever hear the whispers behind my back. Here, this is from when we first met. Oh, more decades ago than I care to count, but tell me... have you ever seen a more lovely woman? You'd have married her too if you were... you know, that way."

He pulled out a leather wallet, its folds creased and comfortable. Flipping it open, he turned a flap so Ichiro could see an old black-and-white photo stashed under a protective plastic layer. The woman was caught in midlaugh, her ebony hair teased up into a fall to add a few inches to her petite frame. His wife's sleeveless jacquard shift dress exposed her bare arms and her skin shone with faint healthy gold. With her head thrown back, her cheeks pulled up into plump frames for her sparkling dark eyes. She was beautiful, carrying a pair of cats-eye sunglasses in one hand and a pineapple-embellished drink in the other. She was surrounded by faint blurs of movement and out-of-focus people, but her attention was clearly on the person taking her photo.

"She's gorgeous," Ichi agreed. "And I can definitely appreciate a gorgeous woman."

"Thing is, most men those days—they treated women badly, especially if the women weren't... white. And if there was one thing I could not stand, it was to see any woman being treated as if they were dirt. Was a time when I spent more time defending my choice of bride than I spent loving her. It was damned nice to see that time slip away, let me tell you." Charles nodded at him as he put away his wallet. "It's the same with the two of you. Back then, I never would have imagined I'd think any differently. You called a man a ponce or a nancy boy, and it was a surefire way to get your nose knocked right off your face. Now some of the best men I know are ponces. And I'm glad to know them. Hell, probably some of the best men I've known in the past were too, but they hid. Don't hide, son. It eats everything up inside."

"No, hiding's not my style," Ichi agreed.

"Dawson done hiding too?"

"Yeah, I think so." He drew on his *kretek*, but the end had gone out. Lighting it again seemed like too much of a bother, and the woodsy scent of Charles's cheroot seemed to be enough for his body to suckle out what it needed. "I hope so."

"Good, because that man needs someone in his life. Other than that insane friend of his who keeps trying to get him killed. God, what is that boy's name?"

"Cole," Ichi murmured. "Unless Bobby's got another stupidly insane friend in his life I don't know about."

"That's the one. Cole. Good-looking boy but the common sense God gave a dead iguana kicked up into a lorry's grill. You know him well, then?"

"Yeah, he's my brother."

"Oh." Charles sniffed, then eyed Ichi. "Sorry about that, then. No offense meant. Or disparagement."

"No, you've got it about right. Trust me."

"Surprised Dawson isn't up here yet. How long do you think it takes to argue some sense into a son? I had two girls myself with the wife. Don't even try arguing sense into women. You always lose because you find out you're the one who's off his rocker, not them." Charles exhaled again. "Unless you're one of those tech kids who's forgotten how to write properly and you don't know what a pen and paper is for. 'Course these days, my own hand isn't too easy to read either."

"Oh shit, a note." Ichi choked on his own spit. "I didn't write a damned note."

"Well then, young man." Charles tapped the floor with his cane. "You better get your damned ass back downstairs before you break that man's heart. He's going to think you've left him."

"Nah, we talk stuff out. Or at least I do. He grumbles under his breath, then spills the beans when I poke at him." He pulled himself up, reluctant to leave Charles alone on the roof. "Want some company going back down?"

"Nope, I'm sitting right here and seeing if I can find some stars through all this crap above us." The older man eased down into a chair. "You go and pull Dawson's head out of his ass if he needs it. I'm going to go look for my wife's smile in the sky and tell her about my day."

CHAPTER FIFTEEN

SILENCE DOMINATED the loft, a heavy blanket of what-if and what-now settling in the air as Bobby walked through the empty space. There was no note, nothing to tell him where Ichiro'd gone, except his clothes were still on the floor, and his keys were missing. But then so were the pumpkin-pie-scented cigarettes he liked to have once in a while.

"Fuck… this day." Bobby sighed. "God, I'm so damned tired."

Flopping down on the couch, he reached for his phone, then stopped. He wanted to call Cole. It was such a damned ingrained response to dial up his best friend and rage about the shit around him. Touching his jaw, he had a very painful reminder of why he shouldn't call Cole. Hell, they'd spent the afternoon avoiding each other while everyone around them pretended not to have heard the fight coming from the front of the property.

"Screw it. I'm calling him." The phone rang three times before Bobby realized it was almost one in the morning. He was about to disconnect the line when Cole answered, his voice soft and grumbly.

"Hey, what's up? What's wrong?" It was a comfort to hear Cole's worry. "You okay?"

"Yeah, sorry. I… didn't know it was so damned late. Go back to bed, Princess," Bobby reassured him. "I'll call you in the morning."

"No, dude. It's okay." There was a murmur of Korean-accented English, then the squeak of a mattress before Cole spoke again. "Going downstairs. Jae asked if you needed us over there. I told him I didn't think so, but dude, if you need—"

"No, nothing like that." He tried to get a handle on the flow of thoughts and emotions swamping him, but Bobby felt like he was sucking more muddy water than clarity into his brain. "It's been a fucking shit day."

"Ichi? You guys okay?" More concern, heavy and without censure. "I didn't fuck things up between you, did I? 'Cause if I did, I'll fix it. Promise."

"He and I are good. Ichi—your brother's a lot like you, you know that? Talks the shit out of things." He laughed, recalling Jamie's accusing eyes when his son flung a supposed unrequited lusting for Cole at his face. "Ichi's good. I think he went up to the roof to catch lung cancer. I'm going to see if I can break him of that habit."

"Good luck," Cole grunted. "I got Jae to cut back a lot, but sometimes... I think it's 'cause everyone over there in Korea smokes. Or it seems like they do. Maybe it's that way for Japan too."

"Maybe." Bobby's words were caught in his throat, and he tried to clear away the lump lodged behind his tongue with a hard swallow. "So you know that key I gave Jamie?"

"The one you weren't sure he was going to use?" Cole laughed. "Let me guess, he used it... and caught you and my brother doing things he's going to have to bleach his eyeballs out to get the image out of his brain."

"Fuck, got a crystal ball over there, McGinnis?" Bobby chuckled as he stood up. He headed into the kitchen, then pulled a bottle of water out of the fridge.

"How did it go?"

"Not... good," Bobby admitted, tucking the phone against his shoulder so he could open the bottle. "This is where I tell you about how right you are and you can gloat."

"No gloating," Cole murmured. "Can't be any worse than me telling Mike. *He* punched me so hard I almost lost my front tooth. Wait, he didn't punch you, did he? I mean, dude, that'd be twice in one day."

"No punching… at least not with fists. It got kind of scary there. And shit, he about called me a pedophile for a second, then—"

"Bobby… no way. No *fucking* way."

"Yeah, but he was pissed off, and I think his head took him someplace he didn't really intend to go. Imagine that, saying shit without thinking. You'd think I was his old man or something."

"Fair enough. You've definitely said some shit without your brain being connected to your tongue. Today for instance. Good example there."

"Yep, that's at least one time I was thinking about."

"But you guys are okay? Ichi? He okay?"

"Jamie and I are. Your brother?" Bobby took a long gulp of water. "I don't know yet. I think so. He was okay when I left, but he's had time to think about this. Might be too much—"

The front door creaked open, and Ichiro walked in, his mouth turning into an O when he spotted the phone against Bobby's ear. Ducking his head in a quick bow of apology, he mimed brushing his teeth, then headed to the bathroom, walking a few steps backward so he could make elaborately campy fish lips at Bobby.

"Or he could be just fine. He snuck in smelling like a chai latte." He listened as Ichi splashed about in the bathroom, the sound of running water coming through the open door. "I'm going to go see how he's doing."

"Sure." Cole's yawn was loud enough to be heard over the phone. "Shit, sorry. I'd just gotten to sleep when you called. It's been a long fucking week."

"Tell me about it. Hey." Bobby caught Cole before he hung up. "*We* okay?"

"Sure, why wouldn't we be? Okay, so you're screwing my younger brother, and if you guys fuck it up, I've got to decide who I'm going to kill, but other than that, it's all good," Cole teased. "No, we're good. I thought you knew that."

"Just making sure, Princess," he murmured quietly. "I don't want to lose you, man. You mean a lot to me."

"Wow, must have hit you harder than I thought." He laughed at Bobby's soft invitation to go fuck himself. "Well, you mean a lot to me too, dude. I'll talk to you later. I'd say tomorrow, but it's already that."

"Hey, one last thing." He shook his head, still unable to believe the drop-and-run bomb Jamie'd laid on him. "Apparently, while you're going to be an uncle, I'm going to be a grandfather."

"What the fuck?" Cole choked. "Jamie?"

"You know any other kid I've got? Because, dude, if you do, that'll be even worse, because I got Marsha knocked up when I was a damned kid myself. Yeah, Jamie. His ex-girlfriend, Sara."

"Oh, man, I liked her. She's his ex now? How long? What happened?"

"Yeah, a couple of months now. Apparently they wanted different things. He wanted to move in, and she wanted to move on. Didn't see spending her life with him." Ichiro padded out of the bathroom, and Bobby smiled at his lover, mouthing he'd be right off the phone. Ichi gave him a quick nod, then headed into the bedroom, disappearing behind the wall of bookshelves. "I think he's actually okay with it. She had it right. They were more friends than lovers. He was just… comfortable with her."

"Well, now she's not going to be able to get rid of him." Cole chuckled. "Dude, you're a grandpa. That's awesome."

"Yeah, let's see if your brother thinks so. He might not want to be around now that there's probably going to be diapers and vomit in his near future."

"Dude, at your age, he'd be dealing with that shit in a couple of years anyway."

"Say good night, Princess."

"Good night, Princess," Cole rasped. "But really, I love you, man, and congrats on the kid. You're going to be great for it to have around. Kiss my brother for me… but no tongue. 'Cause, you know, that would be weird."

THE SHEETS were still cool when Bobby came in from the front of the loft. Ichiro lay staring up at the open ductwork and listened as his lover checked the locks on the doors, then turned off the lights, plunging the loft into semidarkness with only the sleepily murmuring city outside to illuminate the cordoned-off spaces. Ichi found himself regretting drawing closed the curtains in the bedroom as Bobby shucked off his clothes, then stretched, working the kinks out of his muscles before climbing into bed.

If there was one thing Ichiro loved to do, it was watch a naked Bobby Dawson move.

His eyes adjusted in time to see Bobby slide his cutoffs down. The fabric rippled down Bobby's tight ass, shadows pooling in the recessed dimples as he bent over to pull his legs free. Washed in faint blue-and-gold light, Bobby's muscles bulged and stretched as he moved about the area picking up his cast-off clothes, then tossing them into an open hamper near the wall.

He turned and caught Ichiro studying him, smiling when Ichi rumbled an appreciative purr. Bobby climbed onto the broad bed, then slid up the length of Ichi's body, his hands leaving behind warm trails where he'd run them over Ichi's skin.

Bobby was about to kiss Ichiro's mouth when Ichi pulled back and grinned up at him. "So, you're a grandfather now? I feel a bit dirty seducing you. Like you might not survive the sex."

"Oh, I'll show you how well I can survive anything you dish out, Sunshine," Bobby growled, then bit Ichiro's neck, making him gasp. "See if you can keep up with the old man, baby. I'm going to teach you things you never even dreamed of."

"I grew up on manga," Ichi teased. "I can imagine quite a lot."

"No octopuses, okay?" Bobby pulled back. "That shit's just weird."

"*Tako* is for eating, not fucking," he agreed. He was naked under the sheet, and Bobby let loose a low whistle as he unwrapped Ichiro's body.

"Damn, you are pretty." Working his fingers through Ichi's, Bobby pulled their hands up over Ichiro's head, pinning him to the bed. "Oh, I told your brother I'd give you a kiss for him, but—"

"We've already had your son in here. Let's not bring Cole into it too." Ichiro groaned as Bobby's teeth caught on the ridge of his neck. "Uh, Bobby…."

"You know, I like hearing you call out my name. Silly, huh?" He bit down again, this time hard enough to leave a mark, and Ichi writhed under him, squirming to get free. "Nope. Stay there."

"Active participation." The protest sounded weak, even to Ichi's ears, and Bobby chuckled.

"I want to just look at you for a bit, Sunshine." He sat up on his knees, straddling Ichiro's hips.

There couldn't have been enough illumination for Bobby to see much, maybe skin washed with blue from the lights outside and tinted tangerine where the streetlamps bled through, but Bobby still took his time staring down at Ichiro. After a long minute, he shifted, uncomfortable at the scrutiny, and Bobby's smile cut through the shadows on his rugged face.

"I'm glad you're here, Ichi," Bobby whispered, running his hands up over Ichi's belly. His fingers prowled over Ichi's stomach, then tickled at the ridges of his ribs before flicking over Ichi's nipples. "Sometimes I wonder… fuck, not even sometimes… *all* the time, I wonder what you're doing here with me—"

"Because you piss me off," Ichi replied softly. "And I love you for it."

No one'd ever gotten under his skin like Bobby had. For too long Ichi'd held himself above the fray of wanting or needing someone else. He'd sought out his own little rock to stand on once Megumi'd become his father's wife, and nothing—no one—came close to his heart.

Not until a gruff, silvering handsome man eye-fucked him while he'd been meeting his favorite brother.

And even then, Ichi half hoped he would never see that man again—because the light in his eyes burned right through Ichiro's defenses and into his soul.

"It's hard to say that, you know? I love you." Bobby nodded, ducking his face back down into the shadows. "I mean, I love my kid—I might not have liked him a couple of hours ago, but I love him. Your brother too. And yeah, I'm bringing them in here just for a second. Just so I can tell you—fuck, Sunshine, I just want you with me. Okay?"

"Yeah, okay." He pulled his hands off the pillows and raked his fingernails through the trail of hair running down Bobby's stomach. Ichi stroked at the thick root of Bobby's cock, then followed the length of his lover's dick until he got to its damp slit. Smearing the wetness he found there onto his thumb, Ichi circled Bobby's head, working it up to a sturdy girth. "Anything else you want to get off your chest? How much you hate traffic? Or crunchy peanut butter?"

"You're driving me crazy there, baby," Bobby growled. "Here I am trying to be romantic, and you're—"

"I'm thinking this part of you is too far away from my mouth or my ass." Ichi cocked his head, quirking a grin at the frustrated man. "Or did I ride you too hard earlier?" Frowning, he studied Bobby's face. "Are you okay? I didn't—"

"I can handle anything you dish out there," he teased, lowering himself down to stretch out over Ichi's body. "Anything at all."

Bobby's heat chased everything away, including Ichiro's worries. Their hands tangled as their mouths met, tongues sliding against open lips, and Ichiro slid his knees apart to wrap his legs over Bobby's hips. He couldn't get enough of Bobby in his mouth or on his skin. One inch would be satiated, then left aching when Bobby's lips or fingers moved on to somewhere else. A tug at his nipple cascaded down to his taint, and his ass clenched at the shock riding his nerves.

They went at each other hard and fast. He fumbled to get his fingers around Bobby's thick cock, its shaft already slippery from Bobby's leaking slit. His own dick wasn't any better. Its skin was painfully tight, and if his balls roiled up into his groin any more, he'd have to yank them back down just to walk. And when Bobby's hand slid up between his asscheeks, Ichiro heard himself groan and beg for more.

His delirious, aching cry was in Japanese, his English lost under the press of Bobby's spit-slick fingers to the edge of his hole, but his lover caught the intent behind his words.

And pushed in.

Nothing in the world—*nothing*—came close to the feel of Bobby's flesh sliding into his body. The man seemed to know exactly what to do—how to twist his fingers or drive his cock in— and Ichiro's body sang in anticipation of Bobby taking him over the edge again.

"Need me here?" Bobby's husky whisper gilded Ichiro's want.

He couldn't speak. Hell, Ichi couldn't even find his tongue in the dry confines of his desire-slackened mouth. He could only ride down Bobby's fingers, trying to feel as much as he could of the man sliding between his legs.

Sex was... different. Larger, fuller... more than what it'd been before. Ichi wished he could slow down time so he could feel every bit of it before it whispered away into the past. He wanted to revel in the catch of Bobby's nails on the crinkled velvet of his sac, and even the pinch of the man's fingers sliding around his rim was a sensation Ichi could relive forever.

But the night slipped off around them, and with each passing stroke of the clock's minute hand, Bobby ratcheted up Ichiro's burgeoning want. Two fingers became three in a slide of flesh and the cold addition of lubricant. The slush of oil hit Ichi's ring, and his ass clenched at the sudden chill before Bobby stoked up the heat again.

He was fuller than he'd ever been. For a wild second Ichiro wondered if Bobby'd slipped his entire fist into him—then oddly, a passing regret of emptiness as Bobby pulled free.

"Need to be there, Ichi," Bobby warned him.

He didn't need it—the warning. Instead, he needed an eternity of the man sliding deep into him, hitting spots of pleasure until Ichiro could no longer see the difference between light and dark.

And with a single plunge of his sheathed cock against Ichiro's hole, Bobby was in, and Ichiro felt himself falling.

Bobby folded his arms around Ichi's shoulders, pulling him up close. His cock was trapped between them, rolled through the sweat and spent seed they'd caught on their bellies. The tickle of hair around his cock head nearly made Ichiro laugh, but the press of hard, velvety steel through his hole kept his body too overwhelmed with sensations for him to do anything more than ride the smashing waves cresting over him.

"Hold on to me, Sunshine," Bobby ordered.

He rode Ichi. There was no other word for the hard, rocketing plunge of Bobby's cock into his heat. Ichi clenched in, trying to milk Bobby along, but soon all he could do—all he wanted to do— was lift his hips to slam his ass on Bobby's shaft. The bed creaked, swaying with their movements, and someone—one of them—cried out with the ache of tightened balls.

Ichiro was pretty sure it was him, but it was difficult to tell. They'd become a single lurching beast, each carrying the other across a threshold neither one of them had known existed before their mouths touched for the very first time.

The pull of Bobby's cock stretched him, and every downward stroke pushed Ichi further toward the edge. He clung at first, then dug his fingers into Bobby's shoulders, tearing at the man's skin. A thick musk of male rut filled the air, and Ichi drew it into his lungs, savoring the aroma of sex and his lover in his core. Bobby's thrusts were throwing Ichiro back into the mattress, and he strained to take more of Bobby inside of him, pushing open his ass to swallow the man whole if he could.

"Going to shoot," Bobby grunted, reaching up from under Ichiro's arms to grab at his shoulders.

Pulling Ichi even closer, Bobby slammed their hips together hard enough to rock their bones loose. Bowing his head, Ichi tucked himself into the crook of Bobby's neck. His cock was too close to spilling, and their bellies met, then parted, dancing around his dick in an elaborate push and pull of skin over skin. He was about to reach down, but Bobby beat him to him. His shoulder was suddenly free of its clenching shackle, and then his cock was engulfed by his lover's rough, callused hand.

Bobby reached down to the root of Ichi's cock and pulled up, drawing the course of his climax from his balls and up to his head. A few strokes were all he needed. The raspy yank of burred skin on his shaft combined with the muttering heat of Bobby's filthy mouth was good enough to make him release, but when Bobby's cock thickened in warning of his spill, Ichiro finally lost it and flung his body up to take everything Bobby was giving him.

His body surrendered, and Ichi's air burned away under the firestorm Bobby unleashed inside of him. The turn of his cock in Bobby's grip was lost under its spasms, his hot cum seeping out from between Bobby's fingers. His mind flew apart, and Ichi's skin felt as if it was peeling up from his flesh, leaving him open to Bobby's ravenous plunges. Vulnerable and exposed, his eyes snapped open as Bobby's cum-damp hands cupped his face and their mouths met in a savage kiss.

The forever he wanted wrapped Ichiro up tightly, and he slipped into its grip, unable to stop his body from shaking out its spend. His ass ached from Bobby's hard cock, but he didn't want Bobby to leave him. The heat of Bobby's shaft began to slip out, and Ichiro murmured a protest, his voice cracked from the screams he didn't remember stretching up to the ceiling.

"I'm not going to go anywhere, Ichi," Bobby promised, easing them both back into the mattress. His hands were off Ichi's back for a second or two, then returned, his cock free of its latex prison but sticky with its release. "God, we're going to be a sticky, hot mess in the morning, babe. I should carry you into the shower, but I'm too damned worn out."

"Tomorrow," Ichi promised. "So we stick to the sheets. Too tired."

"You going to be here?" Bobby whispered into his hair, spooning up behind him.

"Tomorrow?" He cuddled back into Bobby's embrace, chuckling at the squeak of their skin rubbing together.

"Good," Bobby sighed. "Then you can help me do laundry. Because, Sunshine, I've got a feeling that with you around, I'm going to be washing a fuck ton of sheets."

CHAPTER SIXTEEN

"ARE YOU sure about this?" Ichi leaned away from Bobby, his eyes hooded and cautious. "It's a big damned decision."

"Yeah, pretty sure." He braced himself against the chair's arm. "Go for it."

That'd been hours ago. The low buzzing warned him, as did Ichi's fingers on his malleable skin, but Bobby's stomach still clenched itself up into a ball when the needles hit his flesh. Since then, it'd been the longest day of his life, even with breaks in between for him to chug down some orange juice and then piss it out; each passing second was punched under his skin, an indelible reminder of his need to grace his life with a token of his love.

All of his loves.

Hizoku Ink hummed and thumped, its brightly painted floor squeaking with tennis shoes and rolling chairs. A rock band Bobby didn't know played over the sound system, a raspy velvet-voiced singer telling a tale about Chinatown, wrought-iron staircases, and sin. One of the other artists, a tall man with flashing eyes, teased a smile out of the other as she worked, her head bent over a slender blond woman bearing the pain for a delicate dragonfly winging over her shoulder blade.

The hours were beginning to wear on him, and not even a sneak of whiskey slipped to him from other artists was helping much. His skin stung and smarted from being worked with heavy color and his insistence of Ichi taking a break every hour. Lost in his own world, Ichiro said very little as he worked, oblivious when the other inkers came to peek over his shoulder to watch his progress.

Much like the artists, Bobby couldn't wait to see it finished, especially since the piece seemed to be pouring out of Ichiro's soul straight into Bobby's skin.

He'd asked Ichi for something Japanese in style, wanting— needing—to have his lover of almost a year with him at all times. They'd discussed elements, discarding some and agreeing on symbolism. The result lay with Bobby's trust, since Ichiro decided to loosely freehand the design with markers directly onto Bobby's upper arm.

The torture began in the early hours of a Saturday morning, and the shop's traffic flowed in and out, with Bobby paying little attention to anything but the stabbing burn of needles dragging across his skin, Ichiro's seductive proximity, and then after an hour or so, the numbing relief of an anesthetic spray picking off most of the sting.

Most. Definitely not all. Especially not where the midpoint of his arm jumped and jived when Ichi's attention strayed in its direction.

The phoenix rose out of his skin, slowly forming out of curling clouds and waves. Dappled red and orange feathers were touched with blues and greens, its wings spraying outward to wrap around his shoulder. The bird's head curved toward his heart, and its long, trailing feathers ran down the length of his forearm, cradled by splashes of sea foam, flicks of embers, and startling variegated peonies nesting along the fiery bird's back and talons.

Even in the spit-stealing jab of pain drowning Bobby's senses, the peonies were worth everything.

He'd wanted four—one each for the men in his life and another for the little stubbornly alert newborn who'd made her appearance a month before, but Ichi nixed the arrangement, citing a Japanese dislike for the number and its lingual connection to death. Instead, a tiny white koi dotted with a red smear on its forehead frolicked in the waves below, its tail splashing up a crest of foam as it rode the phoenix's wake.

"Five minute, *anata*." Ichiro's English had fallen apart hours ago, reduced to straight translations from Ichi's Japanese thoughts. "No move."

"I've got to breathe, baby," Bobby grumbled. "And pretty soon, I'm going to have to take a piss again. It's been a few hours."

Lost in sculpting lines and patterns into Bobby's skin, Ichi muttered in both Japanese and Korean to the shop's intern, only to have the pink-haired young man blink at him in confusion. A quick gesture at a vial of black seemed to do the trick, because a second later, Ichiro's table was refilled with little plastic pots of ink, and he'd gone back to work, humming along with the music playing over the speakers.

His arm felt like it was on fire, and Ichiro's five minutes turned to ten. Just as Bobby was about to tap the chair and surrender to a pain overload, the door opened, and Cole strolled in with two carry-totes of neon blue Slurpees.

"God, I love you. Tell me one of those is mine. And if it is, just pour it over my arm. I think I'm on fire." Bobby thankfully reached for one of the slushies as Cole passed them around. "Don't talk to him. He's almost fucking done."

"It looks awesome," Cole murmured. "Shit, you did it in one go? Dude… fuck, it took me three sessions. And I'm pretty fucking sure I passed out during one. Ichi, you gotta come up for air soon."

"I don't think he even hears us anymore." Bobby nodded toward his engrossed lover. "Pretty sure I'm just a piece of paper to him right now. Shit, God, that fucking hurts. Right there. Dear fucking God."

The constant buzzing suddenly stopped, and Ichi pulled the machine up, rolling his chair back a few inches to study the ink. Reaching for something on his table, his hand struck Cole's thigh, and his eyes narrowed, obviously irritated by the intrusion into his space.

"Blue raspberry," Cole said, jiggling a Slurpee in front of his brother's nose. "You know you want one."

"Move," Ichi growled. "In the way."

Ichiro's eyes were still unfocused, a bit dreamy and under a haze as he reached around Cole to get to his supplies. Shaking a bottle that looked filled with piss, Ichiro seemed to be searching for something else. With the solution worked up into a froth, he snapped off his gloves to dig through a bin, coming up with packages of gauze and long sheets of what looked like what butchers put under steaks in the store.

Turning back around, Ichiro once again bumped into Cole, and his disgruntled snarl deepened. "You are in the way. Go sit down. Put the drink over there."

"Ah, feel the love." As he put the Slurpee on the counter running along the wall, Cole hooked a chair with his foot, then dragged it over to Bobby's side. Sitting down, he sipped at his drink while his brother cleaned Bobby's arm of excess ink and blood speckles. "Shit, dude, looks like you went through *Holi* or something."

"Not far from the truth there, Princess." He hissed when the solution hit him, more from the unexpected shock of cool on his inked-up skin. "Damn, can I just go home and bathe in that? Or better yet, how about if *you* bathe me in that."

"Yeah, I love my balls. I've seen Jae mince a cauliflower into rice, and Ichi's got a thingy with needles in it. Passing on that." Cole smirked. "Thanks, though."

"As if I'd even let you near my cock. With my luck, one of your damned teeth's got C-4 in it or something, and you'd blow my dick to kingdom come the first time you gave me head."

"Are you sure you two are friends? Maybe you've been there before me and no one said?" Ichi looked up. "You argue like you're married."

"Shit, Sunshine," Bobby groaned. "No one could survive being married to him. I'm pretty damned sure Jae's immortal and has to resurrect every morning."

"Kind of like Kenny." Cole met Bobby's confused stare with a heavy sigh. "Never mind. Sheesh. I suppose we should be glad you know how to piss indoors and can use a fucking light switch."

The antiseptic smell left a tingle in Bobby's nose, and he fought a sneeze. He still had a pink mark on his arm where Ichi'd lightly slapped him because he'd been fidgeting. The cleaning process seemed to take nearly as long as the tattoo, and Bobby was about to wrench the gauze from his lover's hands when Ichiro finally rolled his chair back and tossed the soiled bandages into the trash.

"There. Done." Ichi grabbed his Slurpee and took a long draw on its straw. "Go look."

"Well, kind of too late to take it back. Not like it's a shirt that doesn't fit or…." Someone stole his breath, because as Bobby turned to look in the mirror, he couldn't find any air in his chest.

Ichiro'd told him to wear an old tank top, and he'd chosen instead to grab a shirt from Cole's business he'd already ruined changing a tire for one of the older ladies in the building. He'd cut the sleeves off and ran in it. It bore coffee stains and an odd rust circle. He wasn't sure where he'd picked it up, but it was comfortable, and he never had to care about what happened to it.

Which was good, because now it looked like Pollock sneezed on it.

The splatters were nothing. The music rolling out of the speakers faded away into a silence so deep Bobby could hear himself breathing in time with Ichiro's soft, whispering sighs. Gone was the buzzing, the stinging, and even the frustration of sitting too long while being so close to Ichiro without being able to touch him.

The torture was worth it, because his life poured down his arm and spilled up over his shoulder, a sunset of feathers, power, and delicate strength.

"Shit… Ichi…." He *still* couldn't breathe.

As hard as he tried, his mind seemed too preoccupied with little details emerging from the tattoo. Speckles of turquoise accented delicate green frills along the bird's tail, and as he turned to the light, the finger-length koi playing in the waves glistened and danced as he moved, its scales edged in a silvery ink to break up the white.

"Oh, babe," Bobby finally whispered. The startling burst of peonies flowed around the phoenix, breaking up the roll of waves beneath the bird, and a hint of lavender and pink left a tint of dusk in the clouds surrounding its wings. "Christ, Ichiro—"

"Let me take a picture. One now and then one later when it's done peeling." Ichiro put his Slurpee down, then got up.

Bobby spent a minute admiring the ink as Cole rolled about on Ichiro's chair, laughing when Bobby brushed up against a wall corner and hissed from a wave of pain.

"No teasing him. It hurts. I'd say you can get drunk now, but you might want to wait until the endorphins wear off, or you'll crash hard."

"Probably fall on your face or something embarrassing," Cole agreed, swiveling in a full circle. "Go take your picture, Ichi, and then we can go meet Jae down at Piggie for dinner. Bobby's got to be starving."

"Shut up, Princess. Let me have this," Bobby teased. He stood still as Ichiro's camera whirred and clicked. "You going to let me see what you've got there, Ichi?"

He snagged Ichi by the waist, drawing him in. Turning his lover around, Bobby ignored Ichi's protests, then tucked the inker into the curve of his embrace, pressing his chest against Ichiro's back.

"Very unprofessional," Ichiro grumbled. "I'm the boss, you know. Kissing in front of the staff."

"Yeah, whatever. Show me the pictures so we can go grill up some meat and ogle pretty Korean boys as they bend over to adjust the flame." He ignored Ichi's derisive snort and rested his chin on Ichi's shoulder, peering down into the camera's screen. Even slightly swollen, the tattoo was glorious—and aching—but Bobby didn't want to let his lover go. "Babe, wow... seeing all of it together. Just... wow. No words."

"Thanks for letting me give it to you," Ichiro whispered, a flush of shyness licking at his words. "For trusting me to do... that."

"No one else in the world I trust more," Bobby said as he kissed Ichiro's neck.

"Even Cole?" He eyed Bobby through his unruly black hair.

"Hell, especially him." He laughed as Cole told him to go fuck himself. "But yeah, thank you for giving me this. Shit, it's so much... you, babe. It's perfect. This is perfect... or okay, almost perfect."

"What do you see?" Frowning, Ichiro turned around in Bobby's arms, craning his neck to take a better look at the tattoo. "What's wrong? I didn't think I missed anything."

"The ink's fine, babe. Gorgeous even." Bobby bent his head slightly, until their temples touched and a wash of shadows warmed the air between their pressed-together faces. He pulled out the shimmering gold ring he'd had burning a hole in his jeans pocket since he'd gotten dressed that morning while watching Ichiro shave off a faint dust of hair from his upper lip. "I'm just going to ask you to give me a little bit more. I want you to give me all of you. So, Ichiro Tokugawa, I'm kind of asking you if you'll marry me and give me everything you've got."

RHYS FORD admits to sharing the house with three cats of varying degrees of black fur and a ginger cairn terrorist. Rhys is also enslaved to the upkeep of a 1979 Pontiac Firebird, a Toshiba laptop, and an overworked red coffee maker.

Rhys can be found at the following locations:
Blog: www.rhysford.com
Facebook: https://www.facebook.com/rhys.ford.author
Twitter: https://twitter.com/Rhys_Ford

Don't miss how the story started!

Dirty Kiss

Cole McGinnis Mysteries

By Rhys Ford

Cole Kenjiro McGinnis, ex-cop and PI, is trying to get over the shooting death of his lover when a supposedly routine investigation lands in his lap. Investigating the apparent suicide of a prominent Korean businessman's son proves to be anything but ordinary, especially when it introduces Cole to the dead man's handsome cousin, Kim Jae-Min.

Jae-Min's cousin had a dirty little secret, the kind that Cole has been familiar with all his life and that Jae-Min is still hiding from his family. The investigation leads Cole from tasteful mansions to seedy lover's trysts to Dirty Kiss, the place where the rich and discreet go to indulge in desires their traditional-minded families would rather know nothing about.

It also leads Cole McGinnis into Jae-Min's arms, and that could be a problem. Jae-Min's cousin's death is looking less and less like a suicide, and Jae-Min is looking more and more like a target. Cole has already lost one lover to violence—he's not about to lose Jae-Min too.

Don't miss the rest of the series!

Dirty Secret

Cole McGinnis Mysteries

By Rhys Ford

Loving Kim Jae-Min isn't always easy: Jae is gun-shy about being openly homosexual. Ex-cop turned private investigator Cole McGinnis doesn't know any other way to be. Still, he understands where Jae is coming from. Traditional Korean men aren't gay—at least not usually where people can see them.

But Cole can't spend too much time unraveling his boyfriend's issues. He has a job to do. When a singer named Scarlet asks him to help find Park Dae-Hoon, a gay Korean man who disappeared nearly two decades ago, Cole finds himself submerged in the tangled world of rich Korean families, where obligation and politics mean sacrificing happiness to preserve corporate empires. Soon the bodies start piling up without rhyme or reason. With every step Cole takes toward locating Park Dae-Hoon, another person meets their demise—and someone Cole loves could be next on the murderer's list.

http://www.dreamspinnerpress.com

Don't miss the rest of the series!

Dirty Laundry

Cole McGinnis Mysteries

By Rhys Ford

For ex-cop turned private investigator Cole McGinnis, each day brings a new challenge. Too bad most of them involve pain and death. Claudia, his office manager and surrogate mother, is still recovering from a gunshot, and Cole's closeted boyfriend, Kim Jae-Min, suddenly finds his teenaged sister dumped in his lap. Meanwhile, Cole has his own sibling problems—most notably, a mysterious half brother from Japan whom his older brother, Mike, is determined they welcome with open arms.

As if his own personal dramas weren't enough, Cole is approached by Madame Sun, a fortune-teller whose clients have been dying at an alarming rate. Convinced someone is after her customers, she wants the matter investigated, but the police think she's imagining things. Hoping to put Sun's mind at ease, Cole takes the case and finds himself plunged into a Gordian knot of lies and betrayal where no one is who they are supposed to be and Death seems to be the only card in Madame Sun's deck.

http://www.dreamspinnerpress.com

Don't miss the rest of the series!

Dirty Deeds

Cole McGinnis Mysteries

By Rhys Ford

COLE McGINNIS MYSTERY ROMANCE: FOUR

RHYS FORD

DIRTY DEEDS

Sheila Pinelli needed to be taken out.

Former cop turned private investigator Cole McGinnis never considered committing murder. But six months ago, when Jae-Min's blood filled his hands and death came knocking at his lover's door, killing Sheila Pinelli became a definite possibility.

While Sheila lurks in some hidden corner of Los Angeles, Jae and Cole share a bed, a home, and most of all, happiness. They'd survived Jae's traditional Korean family disowning him and plan on building a new life—preferably one without the threat of Sheila's return hanging over them.

Thanks to the Santa Monica police mistakenly releasing Sheila following a loitering arrest, Cole finally gets a lead on Sheila's whereabouts. That is, until the trail goes crazy and he's thrown into a tangle of drugs, exotic women, and more death. Regardless of the case going sideways, Cole is determined to find the woman he once loved as a sister and get her out of their lives once and for all."

http://www.dreamspinnerpress.com

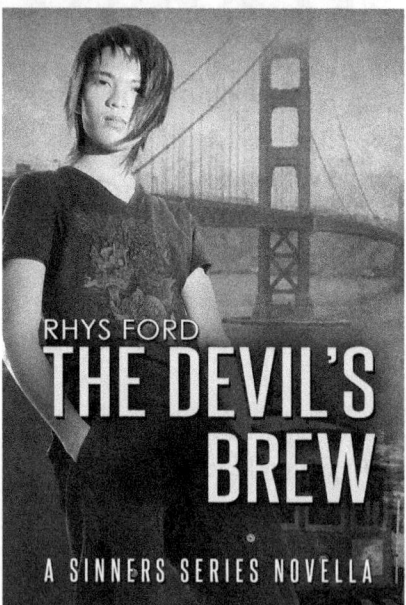

Clockwork Tangerine
RHYS FORD

DETROIT kiss
RHYS FORD
A MAC GERAILT / NAVARRO NOVELLA
PREVIOUSLY PUBLISHED IN CREATURE FEATURE 2

HELLSINGER: BOOK ONE

FISH AND GHOSTS
RHYS FORD

HELLSINGER: BOOK TWO

DUCK DUCK GHOST
RHYS FORD

http://www.dreamspinnerpress.com

www.ingramcontent.com/pod-product-compliance
Lightning Source LLC
Chambersburg PA
CBHW051658260626
47170CB00004B/1559